Jam and Jeopardy

by

Doris Davidson

To Vi
Best Wishes
Doris Davidson

BIRLINN

First published in 2006 by
Birlinn Limited
West Newington House
10 Newington Road
Edinburgh
EH9 1QS

www.birlinn.co.uk

ISBN10: 1 84158 465 7
ISBN13: 978 1 84158 465 2

British Library Cataloguing-in-Publication Data
A catalogue record for this book is available from the
British Library

Typeset by Hewer Text UK Ltd, Edinburgh
Printed and bound by Antony Rowe, Chippenham

Chapter One

Saturday 12th November

Flora Baker pulled her well-worn three-quarter-length Persian lamb coat closer round her ample form – a waste of time, really, since she'd been steadily growing out of it ever since it was bought. 'Oh God, Ronald,' she muttered, through teeth that chattered from the cold, 'I'm absolutely freezing. Why don't you get the heater repaired?'

Her husband scowled. 'I've told you over and over again. I can't afford it.'

'Why don't you buy a newer car, then? You could pay it up by instalments. Easy terms. The never-never, you know.'

'I still couldn't afford it, however easy the terms were. Now shut up. You're like a dripping tap once you start.'

'Ach, Ronald, you're always going on about being on the breadline when all you need to do is tap your old auntie. She's rolling in it and she gave Stephen something last year. Why shouldn't you get something, as well?'

'For pity's sake, Flora, I've enough to worry about at the minute with watching out for black ice on the road, so shut up, will you?'

Sniffing, his wife lapsed into offended silence. She hated coming to see Janet Souter anyway, and her husband falling out with her didn't help matters. If it wasn't for the fact that the old besom had no other relatives except Ronald and his cousin Stephen, she would opt out altogether. But if they got on Janet's wrong side, they might be disinherited and end up with absolutely nothing.

'You've turned up at long last, have you?' Janet Souter's voice was heavily sarcastic. 'I'd given up hope of seeing you today.'

Ronald Baker smiled placatingly. 'We're not that late.'

'I've had my afternoon cup of tea, anyway, so you're too late for that.'

'We were held up by a flock of sheep on the road.'

'You've always some excuse ready, I'll say that for you, but I know what's going on.'

Flora tried to smooth the old woman's ruffled feathers. 'Have you been doing anything interesting this week, Aunt Janet?'

'What do *you* care?' Janet glared at them, but couldn't resist telling them. Talking about herself was her favourite pastime. 'I went to see the youngest Munro girl's wedding on Wednesday. I wasn't invited, of course, so I stood outside the kirk with Grace Skinner and Violet Grant to watch them all going in.'

'They're the two sisters from next door, aren't they?' Flora made a show of being interested.

'You know that perfectly well. Anyway, who should

2

turn up among the guests, as bold as brass in a fur tippet, but Mabel Wakeford.'

'She's next door on the other side,' Flora explained to Ronald, who wasn't in the least interested.

'She thinks she's a cut above the rest of us, because her late husband was a major in the Coldstream Guards, but, as I said to Grace Skinner, Mabel has nothing to be so uppity about. She was only a nurse when she met the Major and, in any case, she was born illegitimate. There was a great scandal at the time, of course. Mary Dewar, Mabel's mother, was the minister's daughter, and she never did get married.'

This was too much for Ronald, who felt obliged to say something. 'You shouldn't go raking all that muck up now, Aunt Janet. It must have been fifty years ago, at least, judging by what I've seen of Mrs Wakeford.'

The thin, frail figure turned on him abruptly. 'I know when it was! I'm not in my dotage yet, even if some people would like to think I was. I'm eighty-seven years old, but my memory's as clear as a bell. It was sixty-one years ago, though Mabel tries to make out she's not much over fifty, with her dyed hair.'

Her nephew wished that he had kept his mouth shut, and tried to change the subject. 'My firm's going through a bit of a sticky patch at the minute, but I could wangle a big contract with a consortium in Leeds if I'd some capital to lay out on materials first.' It was a wasted effort.

'There was Mabel going into the kirk wearing a fur tippet, so I said, "People don't wear tippets to weddings".'

'Who did you say that to?' Ronald's grammar deserted him, and he shrank from the inevitable answer.

'To her, Mabel, of course. Who did you think I said it to? A fur tippet! Pure swank, that's what it was, and it was a mangey looking thing into the bargain.'

A deep sigh escaped from her nephew before he tried again. 'Ten thousand would see me through, and it would just be for a short time, because the Leeds company usually makes a quick settlement.'

The relentless, whining voice went on, undeterred. 'And that young Mrs White down the Lane, May Falconer she was, her husband's away working overseas somewhere and she's carrying on with Sydney Pettigrew's youngest son. A lad of eighteen and she's about about forty, disgusting, I call it. I saw him running up the Lane from her house at five o'clock one morning, when I rose to make myself a cup of tea.'

'Aunt Janet . . .'

'I met him down the High Street later on that same day, and told him what a fool he was making of himself.' Her triumphant look faded when she saw the expressions on the faces of her listeners. 'What are you gaping at? Somebody's got to do it.'

'Oh my God!' Ronald muttered.

'He gave me the height of cheek, though. Youngsters are getting more and more ill-mannered, and that man in the ironmonger's was a bit nippy with me as well when I went in there.'

'What did you say to him, to upset him?'

'Nothing. I went in to get my usual stuff to kill the rats in the garden, so I told him about May White and young Pettigrew, and he said it was a pity some folk couldn't mind their own business. I didn't know who he was meaning, exactly, but I didn't like the tone of his voice. I won't have to go back there for a long time, anyway . . .'

Although the little room was jam-packed with furniture, it was almost as cold as the weather outside, but Janet didn't seem to feel it, Flora noticed. Not much wonder, really, she mused, for she had on umpteen layers of underclothes as well as a felted woollen twinset, with a shawl on top of that. And her legs were encased in hand-knitted stockings, so there was hardly an inch of her bare to the draughts.

She realised with a jolt that the monologue was still going on. 'Anyway, Davie Livingstone said he used arsenic to kill *his* rats, and he brought a wee bagful up to me that night. He used to use it when he worked in the crystal factory. That was before he retired, of course.'

'Arsenic?' Flora screwed up her face. 'It's illegal to have arsenic, I think, and it's very dangerous stuff. You'd better be careful with it, and watch where you keep it, because even if it just gets into a cut on your finger, it can kill you.'

The small, beady eyes regarded her balefully. 'That should please Ronald, then. He'd get all the money he's needing if I died suddenly, but there's no chance of that. I put it at the back of my shed.

Flora glanced at Ronald for help out of this situation, but he was staring thoughtfully into space, so she searched wildly for something to say. At last, she found inspiration. 'We were making the arrangements for our Christmas party at the Guild this week.'

As she'd hoped, her husband's aunt launched into a detailed account of the recent activities of the Tollerton Women's Guild, and kept it up until Ronald rose to his feet.

'We'll have to be going. I said I'd phone George Low at six with an estimate, and I've still to finish it.'

'Oh? . . . Yes . . . well . . . OK.' It had taken a full ten seconds for Flora to catch on, but she stood up thankfully. 'We'll see you next Saturday, Aunt Janet.'

'If you can manage to come a bit earlier you'll get a cup of tea.'

'Don't bother to come to the door with us, it's too cold outside.' Flora struggled into her Persian lamb, while her husband made for the door.

'And Ronald . . .' There was a malicious twist to the old woman's mouth as she called him back. 'You'll see the bag of arsenic if you look in the shed window when you're passing.'

'So what?' He frowned as he turned on his heel and walked quickly through the passage into the kitchen, with his wife trotting behind him. Both were conscious that the old dragon was still watching them.

They always used the back door, having parked their car in the Lane, where it wouldn't cause any obstruction. At some point in Tollerton's past, a far-sighted council had provided this area for the use of the occupants of the three cottages, but none of the present owners possessed a vehicle of any kind.

'Sometimes I feel like killing her.' Flora had to let her seat belt slide back and ease it out more gently before she could click it into position.

Ronald nodded. 'Me too.' He looked pensive suddenly, and turned the key in the ignition of the aged Audi, but even the smooth purr of the engine didn't give him the usual satisfaction. 'The old bitch gets on my wick with all her moaning.'

Manoeuvring a U-turn, he reflected, sadly, that his Aunt Janet was about the only topic of conversation on which he and his wife were in complete agreement these days.

'You'd think she could have lent you a measly thousand, she'd never miss it.' Flora shifted the webbing more comfortably round her 46-DD bosom. 'Of course, you didn't ask her straight out, did you? I sometimes think you're scared of her.'

Her husband didn't argue. He had turned his full attention on the road ahead. Ashgrove Lane was a devil to get out of, an absolutely blind corner where it met the High Street.

Once safely on the straight, he snapped, 'I'm not scared of her, but she keeps going on about the twenty thousand she lent Stephen when his shop was going down the hill. She charges him a helluva lot of interest on it, as well.'

Flora shrugged impatiently. 'So she keeps telling us, and laughing because Barbara gets mad about it. Your cousin's

7

wife's as common as dirt, but give her her due, she's the only one of us who can speak back to Janet. I think Stephen hoped Janet would kick the bucket after she lent them that money, so he wouldn't have to pay it back.'

'Huh! Fat chance of that! She's got it all written down, and she marks off what they give her every month.'

'It's not through a solicitor, though, is it? If she died, nobody'd know about it except us, so it would be our word against theirs. And they don't realise we know, I shouldn't think.'

'Stop worrying about it, Flora. We can sort it all out when the time comes, but, as far as I can see, they'll have paid it all back before the old bitch decides to pop off.'

'She could easily have given you something, though.' His wife harped back to her original line of thought. 'It's not fair, making more of Stephen.'

'She's always been the same, singing his praises to make me jealous. And she's so bloody sadistic, I wouldn't put it past her to be praising me to Stephen to cause trouble between us. She's a born troublemaker.' Ronald paused, his eyes taking on a calculating look. 'She gave me a hell of a brainwave today, though.'

Chapter Two

Stephen and Barbara Drummond arrived at Honeysuckle Cottages a little later than usual the following day and Janet Souter's greeting was almost a repeat of what she had said to her other nephew and his wife.

'So you've managed to come at last, have you? I'd given you up altogether.'

'Sorry, Aunt Janet.' Stephen was about to make an excuse, but the old woman tossed her head and pulled her woollen cape more tightly round her shoulders.

'Nobody considers me. It's always self, self, self. Ronald and Flora are exactly the same.'

Barbara looked down at her hands, with their covering of cheap rings, and braced herself to endure another unpleasant afternoon. She was proved correct. Aunt Janet was at her most obnoxious, and waded in straight away.

'That Mrs Valentine, the minister's wife, came round on Friday afternoon collecting things for the Sale of Work, but the chiropodist from Thornkirk was here at the time, so I told her it wasn't convenient and she'd have to come back later. She was quite annoyed, and it was raining, so,

9

of course, she didn't appear again. A fine sort of wife for a minister, I must say.'

'Did you *have* anything for the Sale of Work?' Barbara asked idly, not really caring one way or the other.

'Oh yes.' The old woman laughed gleefully. 'I'd made a cherry cake, and I was going to give her what was left of the raspberry jam I made in the summer, but she didn't have anything. The sale was yesterday, so I'll just keep the three jars for myself.'

Her childishness annoyed Stephen, who had other things on his mind. 'Aunt Janet, here's ten pounds towards the money we owe you. It's all I can manage this month, I'm afraid.'

The white head spun round. 'Ten pounds? Chickenfeed! That's not even paying off the interest. You've a poor head for business, Stephen, that's what's wrong with you. Well, it's your lookout, for you'll be paying me back for years to come.'

'Will I go and put the kettle on for a cup of tea, Aunt Janet?' Barbara was trying to avoid further lectures.

'Tea? Oh no, I had my flycup before you came, and it'll soon be my suppertime.'

This was no time to fall out with her – not when they owed her so much money and she might demand instant repayment – so Barbara swallowed the tart retort that sprang to her lips. With a great effort, she smiled instead. 'We're sorry about being late, but Stephen didn't get home for lunch till after two, the shop was so busy.' She regretted the last few words as soon as she uttered them.

The old woman tutted with disapproval. 'If women can't buy what they need through the week, it's their own fault. You shouldn't trade on a Sunday, Stephen, it says so in the Bible.'

Where in the Bible did it say that, Barbara wondered, and a smile crossed her face at an imagined eleventh commandment: THOU SHALT NOT OPEN A GROCER'S SHOP ON THE SABBATH DAY, NEITHER SHALT THOU SELL POTATOES, NOR ONIONS, NOR CIGARETTES. These were the items most requested by Stephen's customers, who were not particularly good at forward planning. Her amusement was cut short.

'It's maybe funny to you, Barbara, but if everybody flouted the teachings of the Good Book the world would be in an even worse state than it is now, and that's saying something.'

The Drummonds were saved from further philosophic gems by the peal of the front doorbell, and when Janet went to answer it, Barbara turned impatiently to Stephen.

'She's getting on my bloody tits!'

'Barbara!' His wife's choice of words often upset him.

'She gets worse every damned week, and I can't stand much more of it.'

'You'll have to think up a convincing excuse so we can leave.'

'We could say we've got guests coming for dinner at seven.' Barbara reflected, not for the first time, that her husband needed a good kick up the rear end to make him show some initiative.

11

A rather vicious smile played across the old woman's face when she returned to the room. 'That was Violet Grant from Number Three. Grace Skinner's sister, you know.'

'They're the two widows, aren't they?' Barbara asked.

'Violet's the older one. She was asking if I'd seen their dog, seems he's disappeared. Maybe he's eaten some of the arsenic I laid in the garden yesterday morning. Davie Livingstone gave me some to kill the rats. I've told them umpteen times I wouldn't be responsible for what happened if I caught their mongrel in my garden again. I can't stand dogs.'

'Nor people,' Barbara muttered under her breath.

'I sent her away with something to think about, anyway.'

Stephen cleared his throat nervously. 'I'm sorry, Aunt Janet, but we'll have to be going. We've some friends coming for dinner at seven and Barbara's still a lot to prepare.'

'You always consider other people, never me. I'm only the old aunt with all the money.'

'Now, that's not fair!' Barbara couldn't stop herself from saying it, and the other woman wasn't to know that the dinner was a trumped-up excuse. 'Tonight was the only night they could come.'

Janet Souter screwed up her mouth. 'Huh! Arriving late and leaving early. You'll soon not bother to come at all. I'd better keep an eye on that arsenic in my shed, in case you try to finish me off.'

12

Stephen gave a nervous laugh, and tried to soothe her hurt feelings. 'No, Aunt Janet. We love coming to see you, and we'll be back next Sunday.'

'Come at a decent time, then.' She was only slightly mollified, and they could hear her muttering to herself as they went out. 'Dinner, if you please. Supper's not good enough for them.'

As their old Escort rattled out of Ashgrove Lane on to the High Street, Stephen started humming.

'Why the sudden good humour?' his wife asked, suspiciously. 'You're usually just as cheesed off as me when we've been to see the old bitch.'

Even the last word failed to irritate him at that moment. 'I've found the answer to everything.' He smiled smugly.

'What d'you mean? Really, Stephen, you can be so annoying at times.'

'I've thought of the perfect solution to all our troubles, and that's all I'm saying.'

Janet kept standing at her back door, smirking to herself as she recalled the seeds of temptation she had sewn in the minds of her nephews.

'You're looking pleased with yourself.'

Startled by the voice, she looked up to see Mabel Wakeford regarding her inquisitively.

'It's just something I said to the . . .' She broke off, then went on, 'I may as well tell you. I've given Ronald and

13

Stephen something to chew over. I told them about the arsenic . . .'

'Oh, Janet, are you trying to see if they'll use it? Do you think that was wise? You told me they were both short of funds, and they might . . .' Mabel, too, broke off but hastened to add, 'No, no, your nephews would never think of anything like that. They wouldn't want to hurt you in any way.'

Janet gave a most unladylike snort. 'You think not? Well, let me tell you that the thought has crossed both their minds, I can vouch for that. And I hope they do try. The thing is, they'll both be disappointed. I have a trick or two up my sleeve, you see.'

She turned away abruptly but was chuckling as she closed her back door behind her. Stephen and Ronald were surely mad enough at her now to do what she hoped they would do. She had told them both about the arsenic, and where she kept it, so now she'd just have to wait till next weekend.

She trusted that one of them would make an attempt to poison her. They were both such nincompoops, but surely at least one of them would have the nerve. If one of them did try, though, she intended leaving him all her money. It would prove that he had some willpower of his own, some drive, some spunk. If neither of them had a go, she'd instruct Martin Spencer to make out a new will leaving her entire estate to some charity. That would show them what she thought of them.

She was under no illusions about why they came to see

her every weekend. They were making sure of their inheritance, and family loyalty and affection didn't come into it.

Barbara was a common trollop, really, but she was the only one of the four who ever showed any spirit, and that's why the Drummonds had been given the twenty thousand pounds a few months ago. Barbara would occasionally answer back, or have an argument with her, and Janet loved verbal sparring. She couldn't stand Flora, though. A big fat elephant with the personality of a mouse, she should have been Stephen's wife – like to like.

Janet Souter had never been very fond of her nephews, even when they were children, although she hadn't seen so much of them then. Their mothers, her two younger sisters, Alice and Marjory, had married well, and moved away to Aberdeen. Both had been made widows quite young, but were left quite comfortably off. They had sent their sons to good schools, and even financed them when they set up in their own businesses.

Her sisters had died more than a decade ago, within a year of each other. Neither of the boys had much between their ears – Stephen had failed all his exams – and they couldn't handle their affairs properly. They were desperate to get their hands on her money, especially Ronald. Well, she was giving them a chance to prove their merit.

She rose from the wooden armchair, and threaded her way through the furniture that cluttered up her small living room. The passage was cold, so she hoisted her shawl round her shoulders as she went into the icy kitchen to put the kettle on.

She sat on her stepstool to wait for it to boil, and began to plan the trap she was going to set for her two nephews. It would have to be well thought out.

Chapter Three

Although it was already ten o'clock in the morning, and the temperature had risen little, the bushes and trees still wore a thin coat of icing, and the part of the main road that Mrs Wakeford could see from her window had the shiny surface of an ice rink. She had wondered if her neighbour would tackle her usual Friday morning shopping trip, but Janet Souter seldom admitted defeat. Almost never, in fact.

Having spent most of the night planning her own urgent mission, Mabel now changed her old slippers for a heavy pair of shoes, and slipped on her winter coat. Then, after closing her back door behind her as quietly as she could, she went over the low fence that separated the two gardens. This flouting of a long-standing unwritten rule made her feel so guilty that she almost turned back, but she overcame her conscience and made for the shed first. Janet Souter had gone too far in raking up scandals, especially one from over sixty years ago. And if she wasn't stopped, she could uncover a much more damning incident of not quite so long ago – an incident that had been kept successfully hidden from the whole village. Knowing Miss Nosey Parker Souter, though, she had probably worked it out.

Mabel was trembling with apprehension, anger and fear of being caught when she entered her own home again about thirty minutes later. It had taken longer than she thought, but it had had to be done, otherwise her life wouldn't be worth living.

The butcher's shop door banged loudly as Janet Souter came out, smiling grimly to herself. She'd shown that John Robertson that he couldn't make a fool of her! Two pounds fifteen for that little bit of steak. He was another one who believed she was in her dotage, but the piece of mutton would do her nicely for two days, and it only cost one pound thirty.

'Morning, Miss Souter.' The man approaching was beaming at her, but she was in no mood for pleasantries and turned a sour face towards him.

'Good day, Mr Pettigrew. I hope Douglas is keeping well, after his all-night sessions?'

Sydney Pettigrew, the chemist, a large, well-built man with a receding hairline, had reached his own shop now, and she was gratified by the change in his expression as he stood holding the door handle. 'What do you mean "all-night sessions"?'

'Don't tell me you didn't know your son sometimes stays out all night?'

Her sarcastic sneer annoyed him, and he spoke more

sharply than normal. 'He sometimes sleeps at his pal's house. You know what youngsters are like these days.'

Her top lip curled even more. 'You don't know yours, then, for it's Gilbert White's wife who keeps him out, not his pal.'

His brows came down. 'What? Oh, I think you're mistaken, Miss Souter.'

'No, no, I'm not mistaken. I've seen him creeping up the Lane past my house at five o'clock in the morning. A fine carry on, and her a married woman.'

The man looked as if he wanted to say something, but decided against it, and contented himself by murmuring, 'I'll put a stop to it. It won't happen again.'

The old woman smirked broadly when he went inside his shop. That was one in the eye for young Master Pettigrew, she thought. When she'd confronted him last week, he'd told her to mind her own business and threatened to sort her out. Well, he was the one who was going to be sorted out. His father would see to that.

When she reached Ashgrove Lane, she walked up the garden to her back door; it was quicker than going round the front. Stopping to admire her lilac tree, she wondered why Violet and Grace had not removed the body of their dog, but probably they were too scared to come into her garden. This was Guild night, though, when they knew she would be out, so they would more than likely grab the chance sometime this evening.

'I warned them often enough about their mongrel

19

digging holes in my garden,' she muttered. 'It serves them right that he got what was coming to him.'

Her back door was unlocked, because the key was too big to carry in her pocket. She was too forgetful to hang it on a hook inside her coal bunker like she used to, so she didn't bother. She supposed it would really be safer not to leave it unlocked all the time – after all, the front door had a yale lock with just a small key – but she'd always been in the habit of going out by the back. Except on Fridays, when she went to the Guild with Mabel Wakeford. Old habits die hard. Still, there had never been any burglaries in Tollerton, very few crimes of any kind. The two bobbies here had it very easy.

She laid her shopping bag on the draining board, and took a flat plate out of the cupboard. Then she unwrapped the piece of mutton, laid it on the plate and placed her mesh, domed meat cover over it. She didn't have a refrigerator, silly modern contraptions, but the weather was so cold that the mutton would keep all right till she cooked it tomorrow. She couldn't do it tonight, because this was Guild night.

It was a pity she wouldn't be able to have her usual steak pie on Sunday, but, on the other hand, she wouldn't have to make any pastry. She never did much in the afternoons, except her tapestry, but she found herself dozing more than stitching nowadays, one of the penalties of old age.

When she finished putting away her groceries, a bag of flour was still left sitting out. She mustn't forget about it – it was the whole crux of the matter, her very lifeline – but she'd have her snack lunch before she carried out the most important task of the day.

At seven-thirty in the evening in Number Three Honeysuckle Cottages, Violet Grant and Grace Skinner, two widowed sisters, were still heartbroken about the disappearance of their Skye terrier. They were positive that he had been poisoned, but getting him back had had to wait until Friday, the only night that Janet Souter went out. They were too afraid of her to chance going into her garden at a time when she could see them. It had taken much willpower for them to leave their darling pet so long in enemy territory, but deliverance was close at hand.

They were both dressed in old grey tweed skirts and dark grey jumpers, but Violet wore a matted green cardigan on top, while Grace had on a black jacket, originally part of a suit, but now rather the worse for wear.

They weren't exactly on the bread line, but they had to be very careful with the widows' pensions they received from the state, and the small pensions allotted to them by their late husbands' employers. What little money they had in the bank was purely for emergencies, and couldn't be touched in case they needed it in their old age.

'She even suggested Benjie might have eaten some of the arsenic she laid in her garden to kill the rats. Oh, Grace, what'll we do if he has?' Violet, two years older, depended on her sister for every little thing. 'We'll have to go round and look. He could be lying in agony . . .'

Grace Skinner had been extremely upset when the distressed Violet had reported her conversation with their

21

neighbour last week, but had realised that they would have to wait until Friday to search for their beloved pet, that being the only night that Miss Souter went out. She issued a warning before they set forth on their mission. 'We'll have to be careful that nobody else sees us trespassing in her garden.'

'Suppose *she* sees us herself?' Violet asked, fearfully.

'We'll make sure she's out. If there's no light at the back, it'll be safe.'

The sisters now donned flat stout shoes, slipped on threadbare tweed coats and, it being pitch dark by that time, Grace took their large torch with her. After making sure that the coast was clear, they helped each other over the small fence. The rear of the house was in absolute darkness, so Grace swept the light in several large arcs, starting from a different position each time. It revealed nothing, and after a few moments the petrified Violet was all for giving up their quest.

'Benjie hasn't eaten any of that arsenic after all, thank goodness. He'll come back eventually, when he gets tired of his freedom. Let's go home now . . . please.'

Grace gave a low moan. 'Wait. Look.'

As the beam of light lit up the pathetic form of the small dog, the sisters clutched at each other. 'That horrible, wicked woman! Poor, poor Benjie.' Tears coursed down Violet's face. 'I wish she was dead, too. What harm had Benjie done her?'

Grace gripped her lips tightly together, and, taking off her coat, she bent down and enfolded the dead animal

22

tenderly within its tweed depths. When she straightened up, holding the precious bundle, she said, 'We'll get our revenge, Violet, I swear!'

Although she was only fifty-seven years old to her sister's fifty-nine, Grace had always taken the initiative. She had looked after Violet when they were growing up, and also later, when Kenneth Grant died, leaving a childless widow quite unable to cope.

When their grief spent itself, Violet asked, 'What did you mean about getting revenge?'

Grace stuck her chin out fiercely. 'I don't know yet, but I'll think of something.'

Only ten minutes later, she leapt to her feet in great excitement. 'How could I have forgotten? I'll use her own arsenic to pay her back.'

'Oh no! You can't possibly do that, Grace. It would be . . .' her voice trailed away to a whisper. 'It would be . . . murder.'

Grace's vengeful expression didn't change. 'What she did was murder, too. Don't forget that, Violet. An eye for an eye, a tooth for a tooth.'

'Don't quote the bible at me. It doesn't mean . . .'

'It means what I want it to mean – pay-back in kind. Now, just wait there – I won't be long.'

Chapter Four

Thursday 24th November

It was so cold that Willie Arthur pulled his red ski hat right down over his ears before he took two newspapers out of his bag and folded one of them very carefully. If he crumpled the old dragon's *Courier*, he'd be for it, and she'd go complaining to Miss Wheeler again.

Whistling, he shoved a copy roughly through the letter box of the first cottage, then stopped, puzzled, when he came to Miss Souter's door. Her pint of milk was still sitting on her step. She was usually up at the crack of dawn – before dawn, in the winter – often waiting to grab her paper before he folded it. She must be ill.

He looked furtively through her bedroom window and saw that her bed had been made, and that everything seemed to be in order, so he walked past her door to the living room window, but there was no sign of her there, either. She must be at the back, in her kitchen or the bathroom, both of which had been built on to the original house.

If she was up, she couldn't be ill. She must have just forgotten to take her milk in. Her memory would be

24

slipping a bit at her age. He pushed the *Courier* under the flap and turned back. He was finished with Honeysuckle Cottages for the time being, because Number Three just took the *Evening Citizen*.

He jumped down the steps and lifted his bicycle from the grassy bank, wishing that these three cottages had their front doors to the Lane like the houses at the foot. This was a funny set-up, with no front gardens, just a narrow path along the buildings, and a barbed-wire fence separating them from a field. It was their long back gardens which ran on to the Lane, and they were the last three houses in the village, or the first three, depending which way you were travelling.

When he turned left into Ashgrove Lane off the High Street, he glanced at the rear of the cottages and saw that smoke was spiralling from the chimneys at each end, but not from Miss Souter's. His unease returned, making him wonder if he should go and look in her kitchen window to make sure she was all right, but he was running late already, and the old woman would go spare if she caught him snooping round her back door.

He carried on to the terraced houses at the bottom of the hill, where he had only one *Courier* to deliver, because the other five took the *Evening Citizen*. Walking up the first path, he could see old Mrs Gray smiling to him from her window and, as he acknowledged her, he thought what a difference there was between the two oldest women in Tollerton. Miss Souter, though she nipped around the village like a two-year-old, was nasty and

25

cantankerous, but Mrs Gray, just as old, if not older, and crippled so much with arthritis that she couldn't get out at all, was always friendly and cheery.

He shoved his last paper through the letter box, and saluted to Mrs Gray again before he ran down the path and jumped on his cycle. He puffed laboriously up the hill, then, once he was on the level again, he pedalled like mad down the High Street to leave his newspaper bag at Miss Wheeler's shop – grocer-cum-baker-cum-newsagent-cum-post office – before going to school.

'See you at half past four,' the postmistress remarked, from behind the grille.

Willie was on his way out when he remembered. 'Miss Wheeler, old Miss Souter's milk hadn't been taken in when I delivered her paper, and her fire wasn't lit.'

His employer, tall and angular, looked at him pityingly. 'She's a very old lady, Willie. She's been having a lie-in.'

The fourteen-year-old shook his head. 'I don't think so. I looked in her bedroom window and her bed had been made, but there was no sign of her. Nor in the living room, because I looked in there as well.'

'She'd have been in the bathroom having a wash, I suppose. That one can look after herself.'

'OK, if you say so.' Willie had passed on the problem, so he went off to school with a clear mind, and without further thought for Janet Souter.

Emma Wheeler did think about her, but only for a short time. Old Miss Souter was always ready to complain about the least little thing and didn't deserve anybody's concern.

A customer came in for two postal orders and stamps, followed closely by a senior citizen collecting his pension, followed even more closely by a long queue of housewives needing newly baked loaves, so it was well after half past ten before Miss Wheeler's conscience pricked her.

'What do you think, Phyllis?' she asked the young girl who served at the bakery counter. 'Should I tell the police about Miss Souter, so they can go to find out if there is anything wrong with her?'

Phyllis Barclay was seventeen years old, and had been working for Miss Wheeler for nearly a year. She was a pretty little thing with long blonde hair, but she was rather shy and retiring. She considered the question carefully. She'd been on the sharp end of Janet Souter's tongue more than once, and was completely terrified of her, but she didn't like to think of the old woman lying ill on her own. Thank goodness it wasn't her place to make the decision.

'I don't know, Miss Wheeler,' she said at last. 'Whatever you think's best.'

The woman pursed her thin lips. Miss Souter would be livid if the policeman went up there and there was nothing wrong with her, and she'd blame the postmistress for interfering in what was none of her business. It would be better to play safe and do nothing. 'If Derek Paul comes in today,' she said, to salve her conscience, 'I'll have a word with him, but I think I'll leave things as they are meantime.' She picked up her pencil and started doing some calculations on a piece of paper.

Phyllis could sympathise with her employer's reluctance to act on Willie Arthur's information. Miss Souter was not a person you would knowingly offend.

At half past four, the boy went back to collect the evening papers, and ducked down behind the counter for his bag. 'Did you do anything about what I told you in the morning?'

Emma Wheeler looked slightly guilty as she pushed forward a bundle of *Evening Citizens*. 'No, Willie. I did mean to speak to Derek Paul if he came in, but he must have been for his *Courier* before you told me, though I didn't notice.'

'Oh well, I suppose she's OK.' The boy shoved the papers into his bag and slung it over his shoulder.

He forgot all about the matter until he was nearing the end of his round, but when he approached Honeysuckle Cottages and saw that there was still no smoke issuing from the middle chimney, he felt most apprehensive.

He took the steps in one leap, and ran along the path. The milk bottle was still sitting at Miss Souter's door, and he wondered what he should do. Luckily, the door of Number One opened, and Mrs Wakeford came out. She was a pleasant, friendly woman, who often gave the boy a newly baked biscuit or a piece of sponge cake, and he decided to ask her advice.

She spoke before he could find the right words. 'Willie, would you please post this letter for me when you get back to the shop? Here's 40p and you can keep the change from the stamp.'

28

'Mrs Wakeford,' the boy said hastily, before she went inside again. 'I'll put a stamp on for you, of course, but there's something . . . Miss Souter's fire hasn't been on all day, and her milk's still at her door.'

'Oh, my goodness!' The woman looked flustered. 'Have you rung her bell to see if she's there?'

'No,' he admitted. 'But there was no sign of her in the morning, either, and she's usually up before I deliver the papers.'

'You should have told me in the morning, Willie. She must have been taken ill. You wait there and I'll go and phone the police station.'

He wondered why she wasn't going to phone the doctor if she thought the old woman was ill, but it was nothing to do with him. He slipped along to Number Three to deliver the *Citizen* and put his finger on the bell of the middle house on his way back, but nothing stirred. Miss Souter was definitely incapable of answering the door.

At last, Mrs Wakeford reappeared. 'Constable Paul's going to ask Sergeant Black to come up as soon as he comes back on duty, which shouldn't be very long, but he told me to phone Doctor Randall as well.'

'I'd better finish my round, Mrs Wakeford. I've just five for the foot of the Lane, then I'll be back.' Willie thought she looked as if she needed somebody to be with her, and he didn't want to miss any of the excitement when the sergeant came.

When he ran off, Mabel Wakeford stood wringing her

hands for a few seconds, before she went inside to have a small glass of the brandy she kept purely for medicinal purposes. If ever she needed it, now was the time.

Willie returned in less than ten minutes, just before the police sergeant and the doctor, whose cars arrived one after the other. They parked in the Lane, to save congestion on the High Street, and walked quickly along to the steps where Mrs Wakeford and her stalwart, rather excited, protector were waiting.

Sergeant Black took charge immediately. 'Something wrong with Miss Souter, eh? Doctor, you'd better give me a hand to break down her door.'

'No, no.' The woman clutched at his sleeve. 'There's no need to break in, her back door's never locked. You can come through my house, to save you going all the way round by the road. You'll just have to go over the fence.'

'Right you are, Mrs Wakeford.' John Black was slightly puzzled. If she knew that Miss Souter's back door wasn't locked, why hadn't she gone in herself to see what had happened to her neighbour? Still, the old woman had a reputation for quarrelling with everybody, so they may not have been on very good terms.

Mabel watched him striding over the low fence which separated the gardens, and waited for him to try the handle of Janet Souter's back door. Her legs were shaking, and her heart was beating twenty to the dozen.

'It *is* open,' the sergeant said. 'I'd be obliged if you didn't come in, though, Mrs Wakeford, nor you, Willie. Just the doctor and myself, in case there's anything . . .'

James Randall smiled apologetically to her, then followed John Black into Miss Souter's kitchen. Almost immediately, the sergeant's head popped round the door again.

'She's lying on the kitchen floor, I'm afraid. I think she's dead, but the doctor's examining her now. I'd suggest that you both go inside to wait, because I'll have to take statements from you, you understand, and it's cold out there.'

Willie noticed that his companion seemed to be rooted to the spot, and took hold of her elbow. 'Come on, Mrs Wakeford, I'll make you a cup of tea when we get inside.'

She went with him, as docile as a baby, and collapsed inelegantly into an armchair by her fireside. 'She's been murdered,' she whispered.

The boy's mouth and eyes sprung wide open. 'M . . . murdered?' This would be something to brag about to his pals, if it were true – that he'd been there at the finding of a murdered woman. Slowly, his features returned to normal. 'How d'you know she's been murdered?'

'I just know.'

It struck him that she might be suffering from shock, and hot, sweet tea was the remedy for that, as he'd learned at the first-aid class he'd attended after school a few months ago.

He went through to the kitchen, and felt quite important as he filled the kettle and ignited the gas with the torch that hung at the side of the cooker. He even began to whistle while he looked in the cupboard for cups, but he stopped the tuneless noise when he remembered what had happened next door. Murder! He might get his photograph in the papers. 'Boy alerts police to murder of woman', the headline would say.

When he returned to the living room with a loaded tray, he found that Mrs Wakeford was still sprawled in the same position as when he'd left her.

'She's been poisoned,' she informed him in a low voice. 'That arsenic she had was too big a temptation . . . and she told everybody about it.'

'That's right,' Willie nodded eagerly. 'I heard some folk saying what she needed was a dose of her own arsenic. But that was only talk,' he added heartily. 'None of them would really have done it.'

'Somebody did.' Mrs Wakeford stirred her tea for the third time, then laid the spoon down on the tray because the boy had not given her a saucer.

'I came straight over,' announced Sergeant Black, appearing from the passage. 'I've left the doctor with Miss . . . the dead woman, for I can't help him with that. Now!' He took out his notebook and held his Biro ready. 'To business! Who was the first person to notice that something might be wrong with Miss Souter?'

'Me.' Willie was practically jumping with excitement. 'I noticed her milk hadn't been taken in when I was delivering her paper in the morning.'

The sergeant looked up, surprised that it had been so long ago, then he bent back to his task. 'What time would that be?'

'Must have been about twenty to nine, for I just had to deliver one at the bottom of the Lane before I went back to the shop to leave my bag. I was in the school playground just before the bell went at five to.'

Black was writing in a methodical, careful manner, and the boy paused, to give him time to catch up.

'I thought she might be ill, 'cos she's usually up long before I get here, so I looked in her bedroom window first. Her bed had been made, but I couldn't see her anywhere, so I had a look in her living room, as well. She wasn't there, either.' Willie was relishing his starring role.

'Did you tell anyone about it at that time?'

'No, you see, I was a bit behind with my round, so I just carried on. But I did notice her fire wasn't on, so I told Miss Wheeler when I went back.'

'Ah!' The sergeant's Biro was moving much more quickly now. 'Do you know if *she* did anything about it?'

'She said she'd tell Derek . . . er . . . Constable Paul, but when I asked her at half past four, she said she hadn't seen him all day. I think she was too scared of Miss Souter to do anything.'

'I see. What time would you say it was when you delivered the evening papers here?'

Willie considered. 'I'd say it was about twenty past five, but you can check Mrs Wakeford's phone call to the police station, because she phoned as soon as I told her about the milk.'

'Thank you, Willie.' John Black turned to the woman,

33

now sitting upright in her seat. 'Have you anything to add to what Willie's told me, Mrs Wakeford?'

'It was her own arsenic that killed her.' The whispered words seemed to be forced out of her.

The Biro hovered for a moment. 'Arsenic? Where on earth did Janet Souter get hold of arsenic?'

'She got it from Davie Livingstone for killing the rats in her garden, and she went round boasting about it. Anybody with a grudge against her could have done it.'

A sense of disquiet made the sergeant feel very much at a loss. 'Ah, yes . . . well . . . but a grudge isn't the usual reason for committing murder. It needs something far stronger than a grudge to drive a person, or persons, to those lengths.' He stared at her intently, and she squirmed under his scrutiny.

'At least, you know now how she died,' she said, on the defensive. 'That should save you time in your investigations.'

'Where did Davie get the arsenic?'

'They used it in the glass factory where he worked before he retired. He took some home for the rats in *his* garden.'

A short silence indicated that the sergeant was rather unsure of what to do next, but his puzzled face suddenly cleared. 'Why are you so positive that it was the arsenic that killed her, Mrs Wakeford? Do you know something about her death?'

She looked more agitated than ever, and bit her lip.

'Come now,' Black persisted. 'You'd better tell me whatever it is you think you know. We'll find it all out eventually.'

Her eyes looked helplessly at him before she burst out, 'I didn't want to have to tell you this, and it's maybe not true, but Janet Souter told me, last Sunday night, that her two nephews were trying to kill her. She said they'd put arsenic in her flour bin and her sugar bin. I know it sounds ridiculous, but that's what she said.' The woman seemed happier now that she'd told him.

The sergeant wasn't happier. This complication was something he could have done without, but he couldn't ignore it. In the middle of phrasing his next question in his mind, he became aware that young Willie Arthur was standing, eyes like saucers, drinking in every word that the woman had uttered.

Clearing his throat, he said, 'Willie, thank you very much for answering my questions so well, but I needn't keep you here any longer. And Mrs Wakeford has just made a statement which must be kept absolutely confidential, so you must never breathe a word of it to anybody. Do you understand?'

'Yes, Sergeant.' Willie's blissful expression revealed his pleasure at sharing a secret with the police.

'And Willie,' John Black added, when the boy turned to go, 'remember, I'm trusting you.'

'Yes, sir. You can depend on me. Scouts' honour.' His tousled head was held high when he went out.

The sergeant turned to the woman, who was sitting on

35

the edge of her chair nervously. 'Now, Mrs Wakeford. Tell me everything you know.'

'If anybody in Tollerton had to end up murdered, I'm glad it was that Miss Souter.'

'Derek! That's not a nice way to speak of the dead.'

'She wasn't a very nice person, Sergeant.'

'Even so!' Police Sergeant John Black drummed his Biro on the counter, and the young constable recognised this sign of deep thought and kept quiet, waiting for the profound utterance which should follow.

Sure enough, in a few minutes, the Sergeant looked up from his contemplation of the blank form in front of him. 'You're right, though, Derek. She wasn't a very nice person,' he declaimed, with all the wisdom of an oracle.

Derek Paul smiled. 'I don't think there's a soul in the village that'll be sorry she's . . .'

'I wouldn't say that. She aye made big contributions to all the kirk appeals.' Black had obviously tried to find at least one saving grace in the character of the dead woman.

Derek snorted. 'My mother said Miss Souter was trying to buy her way into heaven, for she wouldn't get in any other way, but she made such a song and dance about it, it wouldn't work.'

'There's aye some sort of appeal,' the sergeant said, ruefully. 'My hand never seems to be out of my pocket. If it's not Oxfam, or a disaster or Save the Children, it's the Fabric Fund, or the Organ Fund, or some other kind of Fund.'

36

'And she went to the kirk every Sunday.' To the young constable, a non-church-goer, like most of his age group, this was the final proof of a depraved mind.

'If *you* went a bit oftener, lad, you'd have more Christian charity.' Black looked down again. 'I'd better get this report made out. Name of deceased . . . Miss Janet Souter. Address . . . 2 Honeysuckle Cottages, Ashgrove Lane, Tollerton, Grampian Region. Age . . . How old would you say she was? Eighty?'

The young man grimaced cheekily. 'Nearer a hundred, I'd say, by the way she spoke sometimes.'

'Oh no. She wasn't as old as Mrs Gray down the Lane, and *she* told the postie it was her ninetieth birthday last Tuesday. I'll put down eighty, anyway.'

There was silence while the sergeant finished completing the form, then he straightened up. 'I'd better go back to her cottage and have a proper sniff round. I got such a shock when I found her lying there, nothing else registered, and that business with Mrs Wakeford absolutely shattered me.'

'Is this your first murder case, Sergeant?' Derek was rather excited about it, because nothing very interesting ever happened in the area.

John Black frowned. 'We don't know yet if it *is* murder. The doctor was positive it was a heart attack, then Mrs Wakeford said the old lady had been poisoned. Everything would have been plain sailing, if it hadn't been for that.'

'So you've to wait for the result of the post-mortem to find out the exact cause of death?'

'To confirm the doctor's diagnosis, I hope. Where's my hat?'

The sergeant's cheesecutter had a habit of finding new places of concealment, but the constable located it under a pile of official communications and held it out.

Black grabbed it ungraciously. 'You know where I'll be if anybody needs me?'

'Yes, Sergeant.' Derek Paul was quite happy to be left in sole charge of the police station. Tollerton was no hotbed of crime, and he'd have peace to finish the *Courier* crossword he'd started that morning. He'd only three clues to solve, so it shouldn't take him long, though they were a bit tricky.

Outside, John Black placed his hat on his head carefully. Not at an angle, like some of those fancy TV bobbies wore theirs, but square on and well down, as befitted a sergeant with his length of service. He wondered, for a moment, about taking the car. It wasn't too cold for November, and a brisk walk would do him good, for all the distance he had to go. The bright moonlight swung the balance, so he left his car keys in his pocket and started up the High Street.

'Good evening, Sergeant.'

'Oh, hello, Mrs Gill. I didn't notice you.' He tipped his hat and would have kept on walking, but the woman stood up, smiling knowingly.

'You were busy thinking about the murder, I suppose. I could hardly believe it when they told me old Janet Souter had been poisoned. She was asking for trouble, of course, keeping that arsenic in her shed.'

'Oh?' He pricked up his ears, hoping for some relevant information. 'Who told you about that?'

Mrs Gill laughed. 'She told me herself, last week. She was telling everybody she met. I think it made her feel important, or something, but it backfired on her for she must have put the idea into somebody's head.'

'Excuse me, Mrs Gill, but I have to be getting on.' Black felt quite annoyed, not so much by the unfruitful hindrance, but by the extra doubt the woman had raised in his mind.

James Randall had been quite definite that the old lady had died as a result of myocardial infarction, as he'd called it at first: plain heart-failure, to the layman. Then Mrs Wakeford had upset the applecart with her little contribution, and a second assumption of murder by poisoning made it two too many for the sergeant's peace of mind.

He strode purposefully along, and was passing the chip shop when the postman came out carrying a fat bundle wrapped in white paper and sending out a very appetising aroma.

'Off to carry on your investigations?' Ned French was smiling in the same knowing way as Mrs Gill had been. 'Have you found out yet how the murderer gave the old woman the arsenic?'

'I suppose Miss Souter told *you* about the arsenic, as well?' The sergeant's voice was tinged with sarcasm.

'Yes, she told me, and she even took me out to her shed to show me where she kept it.' The postman's smile disappeared, and he added, defensively, 'But I'm not your man.'

'Hell, no, Ned. I never thought you were.'

John Black carried on into Ashgrove Lane, and opened the dead woman's back gate. He walked up the garden and went into the shed, which stood halfway between the gate and the house. On the shelf, sitting there for all to see, was a plastic bag maybe a quarter full of a white substance. This would be the arsenic that everyone but the police seemed to have heard about before, but it would have to be tested to make sure.

He left it where it was – Miss Souter may not have been poisoned at all – and pulled the door shut, then turned the big key protruding from the lock and slipped it in his pocket. No sense in leaving the stuff easily available for any other prospective killer who wanted to dispose of some-body.

He let himself into the cottage and walked through the small kitchen, across the passage to the not-much-larger living room, where he sat down heavily on the two-seater settee. Removing his hat, he laid it on the trolley beside him, and smoothed down his thinning grey hair.

He should really be searching for clues . . . No, he shouldn't. If it *was* murder, he shouldn't touch anything, and, anyway, the place was absolutely crammed with furniture so he wouldn't know where to start.

In what had once been a bed recess, there stood an old oak sideboard and an ancient Welsh dresser. Low cabinets flanked the tiled fireplace, one holding a large geranium and the other a bulky wireless. There was no sign of a television set, so Miss Souter hadn't moved with the times, and she wasn't missing much, Black reflected, with the drivel that passed as entertainment nowadays.

In front of the cabinets were two Cintique chairs, and four upright chairs were arranged round the gate-legged table under the window, but he presumed she used the trolley for eating on when she was on her own.

Curiosity made him look behind him, and his eyebrows rose at the sight of the massive bookcase, the books, all shapes and sizes, stuck in higgledy-piggledy. Janet Souter obviously had a wide taste in reading. Ethel M. Dell and Barbara Cartland rubbed shoulders with Agatha Christie and Ngaio Marsh. Leather-bound Shakespeares sat side by side with dog-eared Kiplings, Irwin Shaw with Catherine Cookson. A few surprises!

It occurred to him as he faced the fireside again that, with the settee he was sitting on, and the trolley, the old lady must have had a hell of a job hoovering! If she had such a thing. But he hadn't come here to test her cleanliness, so he tried to channel his thoughts more constructively.

Whatever the result of the autopsy, he'd have to do something about the statement made by Mrs Wakeford after the body had been found. At first, he'd believed that the poor lady had cracked up with shock, but Mrs Gill and Ned French had given him cause to think again.

It was quite upsetting, really: everything had seemed so straightforward.

The sergeant opened his eyes – he had not been asleep, but could often recall events more clearly if there was nothing to distract him – and stared, unseeingly, at the blackness of Miss Souter's fireplace. It was several minutes before it registered with him that the cinders hadn't been cleared out or reset. His brain came to life instantly.

This meant that the old woman must have died last night, before she went to bed at all, since her bedclothes were undisturbed. He became more uneasy about what Mrs Wakeford had told him earlier that evening, even though the doctor had stated categorically that it couldn't have been a violent death.

'There are none of the symptoms of poisoning evident.' James Randall had been astonished when he learned what Mrs Wakeford had said. 'It's come to a pretty pass when a doctor's word is doubted.'

'I'm not doubting you.' Black felt confused. If he believed Mrs Wakeford, he was bound to be doubting Randall.

'That's what it sounded like.' The doctor had packed his bag angrily. 'Anyway, the post-mortem'll prove me right. Janet Souter did not die from the effects of arsenic poisoning. It was a coronary, pure and simple.'

'I'll have to tell them about the arsenic, though.'

'Tell them what you bloody well like. It makes no difference.'

42

Remembering the contretemps, John Black sighed. He'd never come up against anything like this, for as long as he'd been in the Force, and he'd only a couple of months to go. The mortuary-cold atmosphere in the room suddenly penetrated his bones, and he picked up his hat and stood up.

But . . . if it *wasn't* heart failure, he could perhaps solve the murder single-handed and retire in a blaze of glory. A great weight lifted from his troubled mind as he made his way to the back door.

It should be simple enough to find out what had happened. It would just be a matter of proving which of Miss Souter's two nephews had actually done the job.

Locking the door securely, he wished that he knew what had gone on in this cottage to make the old woman suspect that they were trying to kill her.

John Black leaned back with a sigh. 'Well, Derek, that's the problem passed on. The Thornkirk lot'll be here as soon as they can.'

'It's a shame you had to call them in,' the young constable remarked. 'I'm sure we could have managed on our own, even if it was murder.'

The sergeant's mouth screwed up. 'Maybe . . . maybe not.'

He had thought about it all the way back from Honeysuckle Cottages, and had come to the conclusion it was more than likely that he'd end up with egg on his face if he

43

tried to cope without help. Murder was the big one, and it needed experience to carry it off.

It was going to be difficult to explain why he'd waited for almost two hours before notifying Thornkirk, but Randall would verify that he'd said the death was from heart failure. And it could be heart failure at that. It was this story of Mrs Wakeford's that was the stumbling block.

He was going to look foolish either way, the sergeant reflected. On the one hand, for not believing the doctor, if he was correct, and on the other, for not reporting a murder immediately, if it was murder after all.

Chapter Five

Friday 25th November

Ronald Baker scowled ferociously at his wife. 'Would you stop going on about it? I told you – there's nothing we can do except wait. She'll have to use the stuff eventually.'

'Are you absolutely sure you . . .' Flora ventured.

'Of course I'm absolutely bloody sure. My brain's not pickled like yours.'

'But that's . . .' She counted on her fingers. Saturday, Sunday, Monday, Tuesday, Wednesday, Thursday . . . and now it's Friday. Seven days, now.'

'So?'

I don't know if I'll be able to stand any longer of it. I'll go round the bend. I'll drop down in a dead faint. I'll . . .'

'For Chrissake, stop babbling on about what *you'd* do. What about me?' Ronald's nerves were stretched to near snapping-point and, if his wife had been sober, his expression of sheer hatred would have effectively silenced her.

Flora registered only surprise at his anger. 'What about

you? You're the one that's needing her money for your precious business. You're the one that thought you were clever enough . . .'

'You'll be very happy to use the money, though, when it comes to me,' Ronald interrupted. 'You'll spend it like water, the same as you've always done with all our cash.' He became heavily sarcastic. 'What you spend it on, God only knows, for you're never stylishly dressed like Barbara, and your hair never looks right, for all your visits to your expensive hair stylist.'

Most of Flora's spare cash *was* spent on buying good-quality, sensible clothes, and on paying out a fortune to her hairdresser every week, but she was cut to the quick by this attack on her and burst into tears. 'You've never wanted for anything, Ronald Baker,' she sobbed. 'You've always had three good meals a day, and you buy expensive suits, and . . .'

'Stop that! I have to dress smartly to arrange business deals with customers.' Ronald threw up his hands. 'I can't have an intelligent discussion with you these days without you turning on the waterworks. It's the same thing, day in, day out.'

Not absolutely sure if she deserved this onslaught, Flora lapsed into offended silence.

Their resentful contemplation of each other was brought to an abrupt end by the jangle of the door bell, and the sight of Flora staggering to her feet made her husband snap. 'I'll go. You're in no fit state.'

He stamped through the hall and flung open the door,

to be taken very much aback when he found two serious-faced, uniformed policemen standing on the step.

'Ronald Baker?'

'Yes, you'd better come in.' As he led them into the living room, his heart was beating madly now that the crucial moment had arrived, and his tongue felt several sizes too big for his mouth. 'What can I do for you?'

The taller of the two constables consulted his notebook. 'You are the nephew of Miss Janet Souter, of 2 Honeysuckle Cottages, Ashgrove Lane, Tollerton?'

'That is correct.' He suddenly realised that he should be showing some surprised concern, and added, 'Nothing's happened to her, I hope?'

'I regret to have to inform you that, at seventeen forty, your aunt was found dead in her home.'

'Oh.' It came out as a sigh, and he hastily tried to call up some suitable emotion. 'That's bad news. Really terrible.' He glanced at Flora, whose pallor could have been attributed to shock at the information, but Ronald's guilty brain feared that the callers might suspect something.

When her mouth opened, he spoke quickly, before she could say anything. 'You'll have to excuse my wife, she was very fond of my old aunt. Can you tell me how it happened?'

'We were given very little information, sir.' The same policeman did the talking. 'We received a telephone message at nineteen thirty – half past seven, sir – that she had been found in the kitchen of her cottage in Tollerton, and asking us to notify you and her other nephew, as her only known relatives. She had been dead since about midnight, we were told.'

'It must have been a heart attack.' Ronald's face now bore an expression of deep sorrow. 'She was looking very tired when we visited her last Saturday. It's only to be expected at her age, of course, she was eighty-seven, but it's so sudden. I'll have to arrange the funeral, I suppose.'

'I'm sorry, sir, but the body won't be released just yet. In all cases of sudden death, an autopsy has to be carried out to ascertain the exact cause.'

Flora moaned. 'Oh God, Ronald. I told you . . .'

'It's all right, my dear.' He dug his fingers into her arm in warning. 'Don't be upset about them having to do an autopsy. Aunt Janet won't know anything about it, you know.' He glanced at the policemen apologetically. 'My wife's highly strung, and this . . .' He shrugged his shoulders, expressively.

'Most people don't like the idea, sir. If there's nothing else, we'd better be on our way to notify the other nephew.'

'Stephen? Oh, yes, of course. Before you go, Constable, I suppose it's all right if we go to her house tomorrow, to sort out her things, and so forth?'

'I'm sorry, sir, but no one will be allowed in meantime. It's the usual formality until the cause of death is established, but it should only be for a few days.'

'I see. Thank you, and I'll see you out.'

When the door closed behind them, Flora rose to her feet with an effort and went over to the table. She was standing looking in puzzled amazement from the empty decanter to her empty glass, when Ronald returned.

'The brandy's finished again.'

'Haven't you had enough, woman? You finished what we had yesterday, and I only bought one bottle of brandy today, so you must have drunk all that as well.' But he couldn't stay angry for long, not with the exciting anticipation of imminent wealth surging through him. 'That's it. She's gone at last, and we'll soon get our hands on all that lovely money.'

'Yes, and no more trips to see dear old Auntie.' She laughed, but her fuddled brain was aware that things weren't as plain sailing as they seemed. 'There's something, Ronald . . . it's not . . .' It came to her sickeningly. 'It's this autopsy. I don't like the idea of that.'

'Listen, Flora.' Ronald spoke patiently, as if to a child. 'It's just a formality, like sealing up her house.'

'Yes, all right, if you say so.' The empty brandy glass was deposited on the table, and she tottered over to her chair.

'We'd better go over to see what Stephen and Barbara are saying about it. We'll have to agree on funeral arrangements, and all that, but we'll wait till they've had time to get over the shock.'

Flora nodded her head, lay back and closed her eyes.

'You were a great help, I must say.' Barbara Drummond glared at her husband. 'Those two bobbies must have thought you were a complete halfwit.'

'I couldn't help it. It came as a shock, knowing she was actually dead.' Stephen wiped his brow with his hand.

'It shouldn't have, seeing it's what you've been hoping for. Honestly, Stephen. I thought you were going to pass out when they said she'd been found lying dead in her kitchen. What did you expect? That she'd die neatly in her bed?'

'No, no, but it was still a shock.'

'You left me to do all the talking. It's a good thing I can keep my head in a crisis.' Barbara's sneering tone changed suddenly. 'It's just a matter of routine, this autopsy and the sealing up of the house. Only for a day or two, they said, then we'll get in there and find the will before we contact her solicitor . . . For heaven's sake, man, cheer up a bit. It's all over now, and you should be happy about it. At least you managed to do something for yourself and didn't leave it all to me.'

He gave a wan smile in return, but looked startled when the doorbell rang again, and made no move to answer it. Barbara screwed up her mouth before she went to find out who was calling, and was not altogether surprised to see Ronald and Flora.

'Come in,' she said, and stood aside to let them pass. She noticed that Flora's gait was rather unsteady, and guessed that she'd been at the brandy, probably celebrating the old aunt's demise. If there had been any liquor in her own house, she'd have been celebrating too.

'What a shock about Aunt Janet.' Ronald's eyes had

searched for a bottle of some kind before he remembered that Stephen hardly ever had any whisky in the house.

'Yes, isn't it awful?' Stephen nodded his head several times. 'I could hardly take it in when the police told us.'

'All's well that ends well,' observed Flora cheerfully, then became flustered as she realised that she shouldn't be saying anything like that at a time like this.

Ronald frowned. 'Take no notice of Flora. She's been tippling, I'm afraid.'

Lucky bitch, thought Barbara. The Bakers were rolling in it already, and now they'd be sharing the old bat's money as well, when they didn't really need it. She assumed a suitably sad expression. 'It's horrible to think she died there on her own.'

'We'll have to hope she didn't suffer,' Ronald said, equally sadly. 'Now, Stephen, do you want to arrange the funeral?'

'You'd better do it, I couldn't face having to speak to any undertakers. But won't we have to wait till the police release the body?'

'We can have it all planned out anyway, and we'll have to look through her papers for . . .'

'They said nobody would be allowed in yet.'

'I meant as soon as we can.'

Barbara butted in. 'I'd think her solicitor would have her will, so he'll be attending to that side of things.'

'I suppose so.' Ronald looked thoughtful. 'You'll have to tell him about the twenty thousand you got from her, Stephen, so everything can be fairly divided.'

'Who told you about that?' Barbara barked.

'Janet told us herself, so you'll have to come clean with Martin Spencer.' Ronald gave a low laugh.

'You greedy devil!' Barbara burst out. 'You don't really need her money. You've got plenty already.'

'That's not the point.' It was better not to mention his pressing need for capital, Ronald reflected. 'Fair's fair.'

'He's right, Barbara,' Stephen said, quietly. 'I'll tell him about that loan, Ronald, so you won't be done out of anything.'

'Well, I like that!' Barbara stopped at Stephen's glare.

'There's no sense quarrelling about it,' he said. 'The old woman has just died of a heart attack, and we're at each other's throats already.'

'She didn't die of a heart attack.' Flora's voice rang out loud and clear.

Her husband gripped her arm. 'Never mind what she's saying. I told you, she's drunk. Come on, Flora, it's time to go.'

He shepherded her towards the door, turning as they reached it to say, 'I'll contact the undertaker in George Street in the morning, Stephen. I've heard he's quite good, and quite reasonable. I'd better choose a fairly decent coffin, though, seeing she's our last relative. We'll leave the actual date open, but I suppose she'd want to be buried beside her father and mother?'

Stephen shrugged. 'Whatever you think.'

'No problem about expense, anyway. There'll be plenty

to give her a decent send-off. Cheerio, and I'll let you know the arrangements.'

'Hang on.' Barbara held up her hand. 'Flora, what did you mean when you said she didn't die of a heart attack?'

'Did I say that?' Flora considered for a moment, then her hand flew to her mouth, and she glanced at her husband. 'I'm sorry, Ronald, I didn't mean to . . .'

'Don't say anything else, you're absolutely pissed.' He pushed her through the door. 'She's speaking rubbish, Barbara.' He followed his wife out and closed the door.

'That's dashed funny. How could she know it wasn't a heart attack? It floored me that they knew about the twenty thousand, but that . . . and you let them walk all over you.' Barbara spat it out.

Stephen sighed. 'The workings of Flora Baker's mind, and yours, too, for that matter, have always been a closed book to me, and I've had to knuckle down to Ronald all my life. Now, don't start any more arguments with me, Barbara. I've had enough of them – and your nagging.'

The astonishment on his wife's face made him feel quite proud of the way he had stood up to her, and he realised, in a flash, that things had turned out very well for him after all. Once he received his aunt's money, he meant to be master in his own house, and Barbara may as well start getting used to it now.

After having spent half the night with police from Thornkirk General Enquiry Department, Sergeant Black was feeling rather ragged. They'd searched Janet Souter's cottage thoroughly, but had found nothing suspicious, apart from the bag of arsenic in her shed. They'd pounced on that, happily assuming that this had been used to murder the old woman, although Doctor Randall had been outraged at his word being doubted.

'I know heart failure when I see it,' he'd said indignantly, when he was called back to the cottage. 'She didn't die from the effects of poisoning, and that's definite.'

'Did she have a history of heart trouble, Doctor?' Sergeant Watt of Thornkirk had looked at him questioningly.

'No, she hadn't, but it often happens like that. Nothing at all, then poof! A massive coronary. I've seen it before. Death by poisoning's different altogether.'

Watt had smiled sarcastically. 'If I'd a pound for every time a doctor's been proved wrong, I could have retired a wealthy man long ago.'

James Randall had turned puce and picked up his bag. 'I'm going home. I've got to get up early in the morning. I've my living patients to consider.' Then he'd slammed out of the house and left Sergeant Watt looking uneasily at John Black.

The Grampian men had recorded everything they found, and had made a list of all the foodstuffs in the cottage before packing them in boxes and sending them off to Aberdeen to be tested for contamination, along with the little plastic bag from the shed. The public analyst would be delighted with all the extra work, the local sergeant had thought, wickedly, when he left them just after three in the morning.

Now it was half past six in the evening, and he was standing at his own front desk, half asleep, and thanking his lucky stars that the buck had been passed to somebody else.

He looked up as Sergeant Watt walked in. 'Found anything?'

'Not a damned thing!' The Thornkirk sergeant sounded disgruntled. 'You know, I'd have been quite happy to have found some proof that the old woman had been murdered so I could hand the whole thing over to Regional Headquarters. There's something definitely fishy about this case.'

'That's what I thought.' Black looked pleased.

'It's this story of Mrs . . . Wakeford's that puzzles me. I can hardly believe that any woman in her right mind would do what she says the dead woman did. But maybe the old biddy wasn't in her right mind?'

'She never gave any indication that she wasn't, but I'm beginning to wonder about it myself.'

'Or maybe it's Mrs Wakeford that's got delusions?' Watt sat down on the bench when Derek Paul handed him a mug of tea.

'No, I think Mrs Wakeford's telling the truth.' John Black stepped back to let the constable deposit another mug on the counter in front of him. 'What happens now?'

'There's really nothing we can do until we have the result of the post-mortem, but I left word for them to ring straight through to here. They're taking a heck of a long time, though.' Watt took a sip of tea, and willed the telephone to ring. 'Maybe he *has* found something.'

It was only two minutes later that the telephone made them all jump up expectantly. 'Tollerton Police. Sergeant Black speaking.' He held out the receiver.

Sergeant Watt stood up. 'Watt here . . . No traces? . . . What's that?' He listened for a few minutes. 'Oh, so it's definitely murder? Thanks.' He laid the phone down. 'Well, so that's it!'

John Black waited, rather impatiently, for him to explain, but Watt sat down and took another gulp of tea first.

'That was the pathologist. Apparently, the doctor at Thornkirk found no traces of arsenic in the body, but he did find the mark of a hypodermic needle on the back of the dead woman's neck. So he sent her off to Aberdeen, with the details of the discovery of the body, etcetera, etcetera.'

'So it wasn't the arsenic?' Black made a face. 'Was our doctor right, then? Was it heart-failure?' Randall would be cock-a-hoop if it was.

'No, it wasn't heart failure either. The Aberdeen pathologist discovered that she was full of insulin, injected into her system through her neck.

'I didn't know that insulin could kill.'

'He says it can, if it's introduced into the system of a person not suffering from diabetes.'

'Well, well!' John Black was impressed. 'There's never

56

been a murder in Tollerton before, as long as I've been here.'

'There's always a first time. But that's it taken off our hands now. It goes to Grampian CID, and the procurator fiscal has already been notifed. He has to receive reports of all murder investigations in his region.'

He straightened his tie and put on his hat. 'I'll go and call off my boys at Honeysuckle Cottages. It's up to the Homicide boys from Aberdeen now, though I don't expect you'll see them till tomorrow. I wish them luck, they're going to need it. Mind you, I think Mrs Wakeford's probably right. Not about her being poisoned with arsenic, but about the nephews being the ones who disposed of the old woman. So long.'

Sergeant Black was left with only his young constable with whom to discuss this extraordinary new development. 'Fancy her being killed with insulin. That's a new one on me.'

Derek Paul nodded sympathetically. 'You're always learning. Who could have done it, though? It must have been somebody with medical knowledge, and access to insulin and a needle, but there's only Doctor Randall in the village, and you surely don't think he did it?'

'Thank God we don't have to figure it out, Derek. That's what the CID are paid for. The trouble is, they'll likely be real whizzkids, setting the whole place's teeth on edge with their efficiency.'

The constable had been thinking. 'There's old Mary

Lawson, of course, the district nurse. Health visitor, she's called now.'

'Eh?' John Black's mind had to be jerked back from the horrifying prospect of the CID men upsetting his villagers. 'What are you on about now?'

'The health visitor from Thornkirk, Mary Lawson. She'd know about hypodermic needles and insulin.'

'Oh, aye,' the sergeant sneered. 'She's just the one to kill an old woman around midnight. Mary Lawson's an old woman herself, nearly retiring age, if not past it. Have some sense, Derek, for God's sake.'

'I was only trying to think of somebody in the medical line. There's nobody else, is there?'

'Oh, shut up,' Black said, testily. 'And get on with typing that report.'

Chapter Six

When the street door opened, twenty-four-year-old Derek Paul looked up impatiently from the *Courier* crossword and wondered idly who the two strangers were.

One of them looked like a rugby player gone slightly to seed. At least six feet four, with broad shoulders and a broken nose. His shirt collar was creased, and the old tweed jacket and corduroy trousers wouldn't have looked out of place on a scarecrow. His grizzled hair was cropped quite short, and, although curly, would have been all the better for a good brushing. On the other hand, maybe a good brushing would've had no effect. Some people's hair was like that.

Derek shifted his sights to the other man. Younger and not quite so tall, he was immaculately dressed in a navy suit, pale-blue shirt and striped tie. His reddish-fair hair was well cut, not too long, not too short, and the constable wondered how much he paid his hairdresser. It certainly wasn't a barber's cut. A proper business gent, this one.

Derek hoped that they were only after directions, but civility cost nothing after all. 'Yes? Can I help you?'

59

The older man, perhaps around forty, could even be nearer fifty, stepped right up to the counter and fixed the constable with dark-brown eyes, severe under their bushy eyebrows. 'I hope you can.' The voice was gruff and carried on, 'I'm Detective Chief Inspector McGillivray of Grampian CID, and this is Detective Sergeant Moore.'

Before the second sentence was half finished, Derek Paul had straightened up, almost to attention, and was looking at the two men with respect. 'Oh, I'm sorry, Chief Inspector. I didn't realise who you were. We didn't expect you here quite so early.'

'Obviously,' McGillivray said, dryly.

'You're booked in at the Starline Hotel, sir, a few doors up the High Street.'

'Thank you, Constable. Give my sergeant a hand with our bags, and I'll hold the fort here.'

'Yes, sir.'

McGillivray leaned against the counter and extracted a flattened pack of cigarettes from his jacket pocket. This shouldn't take long, he reflected, as he flicked a battered lighter. An eighty-something-year-old woman, in a little place like Tollerton? No hardened criminals could be involved, so it would be a piece of cake to break the guilty person's alibi. Just a matter of asking the right questions at the right time.

He took a crumpled envelope out of his breast pocket. The superintendent had handed it to him that morning before they left. They'd been three hours on the road – with only one stop for a quick snack – and hadn't had time to look at it yet, but he knew that it contained the known details of the murder. He ran his forefinger under the flap, and had just finished reading the report when the other two returned.

'What's your sergeant's name, Constable?'

'Black, sir.'

'Is he anywhere about?'

'He's waiting for you up at the murdered woman's cottage in Ashgrove Lane, sir. Oh,' Derek reached under the counter. 'Here are the details of Miss Souter's nephews and their wives, as far as we have been able to ascertain from Mrs Wakeford, who lives next door.'

'Thanks. Did you know the woman yourself?'

'Miss Souter, sir? Oh yes, everybody knew her, and nobody liked her very much. She was a regular besom, sir.'

'What was the state of her finances, would you say? Was she well off?'

'Absolutely loaded, sir, but she wasn't a free spender. She knew the right side of a penny, sir.'

Callum McGillivray smiled. 'Most people with money do, lad. That's why they *have* money. And money makes more money – the more you have, the more you get. Not fair, eh? Well, if you tell us how to get there, we'll be on our way to . . . Ashgrove Lane, wasn't it?'

'Yes, sir. Your car's facing in the right direction, so it's just straight up the High Street and third turning on the right. You can't go wrong, sir. If you go any farther, you'll be out of the village altogether. There're three houses at this end of the Lane, that's Honeysuckle Cottages, and

Miss Souter's is the middle one. If you leave your car in the parking place in the Lane, you'll be going in by her back door.'

'Thank you. That seems straightforward enough. Your directions are very clear. There's just one thing, Constable . . . um?' The inspector's voice rose, in interrogation.

'Constable Paul, sir.'

'Well, Constable Paul, when someone walks into a police station and finds the person left in charge lolling all over the front desk, it doesn't give a very good impression. Smarten yourself up, lad, otherwise you'll never get anywhere in the Force.' McGillivray turned and walked to the door.

'Yes, sir, I'm sorry, sir.' Derek Paul wondered if that would be the last he'd hear about his indiscretion, or if the inspector would report it to Sergeant Black. The sarge would give him hell if he found out. Anyway, that chief inspector was one to talk about people not being smart. He looked like something out of a ragbag himself, and that hadn't stopped him from getting where he was.

The young man sighed at the injustices of life, and started on the crossword again.

When the green Vauxhall drew away from the kerb, DS David Moore said, 'This shouldn't be a long job, sir. Rich old ladies are usually knocked off by their relatives.'

'Quite. And this one was loaded, according to the PC,

but things are not always what they seem, Moore. There might be more to this than meets the eye.'

'There's the police car,' Moore remarked in a few minutes, indicating right and waiting until an oncoming car had passed. 'The middle cottage, I think.' He turned the steering wheel and entered Ashgrove Lane.

They had almost reached Janet Souter's back door, when it opened and the local sergeant came out. 'Detective Chief Inspector McGillivray?'

The inspector nodded. 'And this is Detective Sergeant Moore, who'll be helping with the investigation. I gather there's been a bit of a problem?'

John Black caught the almost imperceptible cautioning look in McGillivray's eyes, and said, 'Yes, sir. When I questioned Mrs Wakeford, next door, she told me a most peculiar story, and that, along with one or two other things being said in the village, is the cause of the trouble. It's going to be a most complicated case, as far as I can make out, much more difficult than was anticipated at first, sir.'

'Where exactly was the body found, and who found it?'

Sergeant Black did not need to consult his notebook, the facts were printed indelibly on his mind. 'Miss Souter was found lying dead on her kitchen floor, just there.' He pointed to the spot as they went in.

The two detectives looked at the chalk mark on the floor. 'She didn't have much choice about where to fall,' Moore observed. 'There was just room for the body, and no more.'

The inspector surveyed the tiny room. From the back door, working clockwise, there was a deep porcelain sink under the window, a wooden draining board over a cupboard, then a set of wooden drawers. A folding table, covered with Fablon-type plastic, and a step-stool took up the short wall, and, on the wall opposite the sink, a wide kitchen cabinet reached almost to the low roof. The door leading into the passage was on the other short wall, and a narrower kitchen cabinet took him to the back door again.

The body had been lying on the strip of matting which covered the vacant floor area. As Moore had said, it was the only place there had been room for it to fall.

McGillivray's attention returned to Sergeant Black, who continued with his report. 'Doctor James Randall and myself were the only persons present at the discovery of the body.'

'What brought you up here in the first place?'

In his eagerness to tell the facts, Black forgot to be official. 'It was Willie Arthur, the paperboy. When he'd been here, about twenty to nine in the morning, he'd noticed the old woman's milk at her door, which worried him a bit because she's an early riser. But he didn't really start to panic till he came back on his evening round, about ten past five.'

'He informed the police then, did he?'

'No, he told Mrs Wakeford next door, so she phoned the station, and then the doctor. Randall said it was heart failure, and that she'd died somewhere between midnight and two o'clock.'

McGillivray interrupted. 'It was found later, however, that her death was not due to natural causes, after all?'

'That's correct, sir, but the weird thing about the case was the information received from Mrs Wakeford, just after we found the old lady lying on her kitchen floor. I think it would be best, sir, if you talked to her before you go any farther. If you follow me, I'll show you the way.'

'Lead on, Macduff.'

David Moore thought that the inspector was being rather too breezy given the circumstances, but supposed that murder, to him, was only another part of his job. McGillivray had been in the CID for quite a number of years, while to him, Moore, this was his first case of murder and, as such, would be something of an ordeal.

As they went over the fence, the inspector asked, 'Had anything been stolen, or disturbed?'

'Not that we could find out, sir.' Black knocked loudly on the door, which was opened immediately by Mrs Wakeford.

She appeared very nervous, but led the three men into her living room, though not before McGillivray hit his head on the low door frame. Black introduced the detectives and told her to sit down and feel at ease. She sat gingerly on the edge of a chair, and waited for the inspector to speak.

'Sergeant Black tells me that you have a statement to make, Mrs Wakeford. Just take your time, and give me as many details as you can.' McGillivray glanced towards

Moore, and was pleased to see him ready, notebook and pen in his hands.

The woman did not seem willing to talk, looking beseechingly from one man to the other, until Black said, 'Perhaps you would feel more at ease over a cup of tea?'

'What? Oh, yes I would. Will I go and make a pot?' She glanced at McGillivray uncertainly.

'Why not? I'm sure we could all do with a cuppa.' He sat down on the settee, motioning to the other two to follow suit, while Mabel Wakeford disappeared through to the kitchen.

Black remained standing, but leaned forward and whispered confidentially, 'You'd think she was the guilty party, she looks so damned scared, but she doesn't want to tell her story, you see, because it involves, incriminates, somebody else.'

'I see.' McGillivray never condemned anyone before he had sifted through all the evidence he could unearth.

David Moore had been sure of the woman's guilt at first sight of her terrified face, but he now decided that it was too early to make snap judgements, and that she was far too much of a lady to be a possible killer.

Mrs Wakeford carried in a tray. 'Do you all take milk and sugar, gentlemen?' She seemed to have recovered her composure a little.

'No tea for me, Mrs Wakeford,' Sergeant Black lifted his hat from the sideboard. 'I'll have to be getting back, but I'll leave you in the inspector's capable hands. Tell him everything you told me, and anything else that comes to mind.'

'I'll do my best, Sergeant Black.'

'That's right.' He opened the door and went out.

Mrs Wakeford filled three cups and added the sugar and milk as indicated by the two detectives. 'Would you care for a biscuit, or a scone, or something?'

She hovered over them until they smilingly refused before she took her own seat. 'It's Earl Grey,' she confided. 'I always use it. It's much better than teabags.'

David Moore nodded intelligently, hoping that he wouldn't disgrace himself by dropping the delicate rose-patterned cup and saucer, which appeared to be part of an old and valuable set.

The inspector looked round approvingly as he stirred his tea. The furniture and furnishings were of fine quality, and in very good taste. The place wasn't overburdened with ornaments, either, just a few fine pieces here and there.

His turned to the woman sitting opposite him. Quite slim, with blue-rinsed hair beautifully coiffed, she wore a neat twinset with a single strand of pearls round her neck. Her well-cut tweed skirt and well-crafted suede shoes made him put her down as having a substantial income from some source or other, and her age would probably be between fifty-five and sixty.

He caught her timorous eyes and smiled. 'This is much more friendly, better than being all stiff and formal, don't you think? Shall we begin now, Mrs Wakeford?'

'Yes, if you like.' She relaxed a little, then asked, timidly, 'Will what I say be taken down in writing?'

'Some, but don't think about it. It's only to help us make up a picture of what has happened – a background, as you might say.' Taking a mouthful of tea, he was pleased to find that it was a good strong brew. Some old dears made tea so weak it needed crutches to come out of the pot.

Mrs Wakeford took a dainty sip of hers, black with no sugar, then sat forward. 'Janet Souter has been my neighbour for nearly thirty-five years,' she began. 'Ever since she came back to Tollerton from Edinburgh, and bought her cottage, though we were never very friendly. I mean . . .' she looked confused. 'We were on quite good terms, but we didn't pop in and out of each other's houses all the time, if you know what I mean?'

She paused to take another sip of tea, blotted her lips with a lace-edged handkerchief and looked across at McGillivray, who smiled encouragingly.

'Very occasionally, she came in and had a cup of tea with me, or I went and had one with her, but usually only when she wanted to tell me, or ask me, something. And we went to the Women's Guild meetings together every Friday night in the winters, because it seemed more sensible than each going on our own. She would tell me about her nephews sometimes, complaining about them mostly, because she didn't think very much of them.'

'Why was that?'

'She said they couldn't run their businesses properly, and that their wives weren't much help.'

'She didn't think much of their wives either, then?'

'Not much. She called Flora, Ronald's wife, a great fat pudding.' Mrs Wakeford gave a little smile. 'She did tell me once, though, that Stephen's wife, Barbara, had more sense than the rest of them put together.'

'She liked Barbara, did she?'

'I wouldn't go as far as say she liked her. She didn't like anybody, really, but she admired Barbara's spirit. Stephen's a bit of a stick-in-the-mud, apparently, and his wife prodded him and kept him up to scratch as much as she could. He always looked harassed and worried any time I saw him, not like her. Brassy blonde, cheap showy clothes, mutton dressed like lamb. And she tottered about on her high heels with a cigarette hanging out of her mouth, most of the time.'

Mabel paused, checking to see if the inspector was interested in this, and was pleased to see him listening carefully.

'She wasn't the type of woman I'd have expected Janet Souter to tolerate, even, but it seemed there was something in Barbara that appealed to her. Maybe it was because Barbara was the boss, and ordered Stephen around all the time – henpecked him, in fact.'

McGillivray was on the point of asking her to give him their names and addresses, when he remembered that the young constable had handed him a sheet of paper with all the details of the nephews and their wives, so he contented himself by prompting, 'And what about the other nephew, Ronald, wasn't it?'

'Ronald? He'd a bit more sense than his cousin, as far as I know, and was master in his own house. He always looked the proper businessman, with his navy suit – rather the style of your sergeant, there, but maybe a fraction taller.'

David Moore looked up and smiled to her in return for the perhaps unintended compliment on his appearance.

'He's not as tall as you, though, I don't think, Inspector.' Saying this, Mrs Wakeford permitted herself a little smile, too, recalling how McGillivray had hit his head on her doorway when he first came in.

He understood what was amusing her, and thought ruefully that low-roofed cottages were hell when you were six feet four.

The woman continued with her descriptions of her neighbour's relatives. 'Ronald's wife, Flora, was different altogether. She was never what you'd call elegantly dressed, though her clothes looked very expensive. She was rather stout, and, with being so short, she was really quite dumpy. She let Ronald have his own way over everything, and never argued with him. Mind you, I'm only going by what Janet Souter told me. I didn't know them myself, except to see them coming and going.'

She stopped speaking when McGillivray stood up to help himself to a second cup of tea. 'May I?' he asked, holding up the teapot.

'Oh yes, I'm sorry,' she twittered. 'I forgot to ask you. Go ahead, Inspector. There is plenty.'

Before she was finished, he was laying down the teapot again. 'The two nephews and their wives came quite regularly to visit her, I presume?' He added two spoons of sugar to his cup before resuming his seat.

She nodded. 'Yes, Ronald and Flora came every Saturday afternoon, and Stephen and Barbara came on Sundays.' She was talking much more freely than she had done at first, and even seemed to be enjoying it. 'Not this past Saturday but the Saturday before, Janet told me that Ronald was furious because she wouldn't lend him the money he'd asked for. I know she was charging Stephen a high interest on what she'd lent him, because she told me that weeks ago.'

'I gather from the way you're speaking, that she took great pleasure in all this?'

'She was a dreadful woman, with a cruel streak in her. Oh!' Mrs Wakeford's hand flew up to her mouth. 'I shouldn't be saying that, should I, when she's just been poisoned?'

The inspector looked sympathetic. 'You can't change your opinion of a person because she's dead.'

'No, I suppose that would be hypocritical. I must admit that I never liked her very much. In fact, there were times when I positively hated her, to be perfectly honest, and I think most people in the village felt the same way. I was more or less accustomed to her, of course, and she *was* somebody to talk to, but . . . well, I was shocked at what

71

she told me next.' Mabel moved uncomfortably in her chair.

At last she was coming to the nitty-gritty, McGillivray thought, and smiled to make her feel more at ease.

She hesitated then said, in a low voice, 'She said she'd made a point of telling Ronald and Stephen about the arsenic she'd got.'

Swallowing nervously, she went on. 'As I told you, I was shocked at that, and I warned her she'd been stupid . . . she could be putting ideas into their heads, but she just *laughed*.'

Again, Mrs Wakeford paused, as if unwilling to say more. 'Then she said she *hoped* they'd try to poison her.'

David Moore looked up from his note-taking with interest, but the inspector signalled to him with his eyes and he bent over industriously again.

'I was worried about it for a while, but I came to the conclusion she must have gone out of her mind and was speaking a lot of nonsense. But after Stephen and his wife left on the next Sunday – this past Sunday, the twentieth – she came in and said her nephews *had* tried to poison her. Both her flour and sugar bins had been tampered with.'

The two CID men glanced at each other, then McGillivray asked, 'How did she find that out? Did she say?'

Mabel shook her head in doubt. 'I don't know if she was telling the truth, or if it was something she'd dreamt, or even made up to make me feel sorry for her.'

'Let me judge for myself, Mrs Wakeford. What did she say?'

'She said she'd put a crumb of toast on both bins, and the one on the flour had gone after Ronald had been on Saturday. She'd put on another one and the two crumbs had disappeared after Stephen left on the Sunday. She said that both men had made an excuse to be on their own in her kitchen.'

She took a shivery breath and leaned back as if glad that she had got it all off her chest.

'Well, I'll be damned!' McGillivray wasn't often surprised by any information he received, but he'd never heard anything like this before. 'I'm sorry, Mrs Wakeford. It just slipped out.'

'It's quite all right, Inspector.'

'She was a devious one, wasn't she, if she actually laid traps for her nephews?'

'It seems like it, and she laughed about them doing it, and said they were going to be disappointed. She didn't tell me why. But she did say she was looking forward to seeing their faces the next weekend, this weekend of course, when they discovered that she was still alive.'

The inspector was silent for a moment, going over what he had just been told, then he leaned forward. 'Just a minute, Mrs Wakeford. If Miss Souter said she knew about it, and didn't use the stuff, how do you think she died?'

She clutched at her pearls, and hesitated briefly. 'I think she must have used some of it by mistake, before she threw it out, or whatever she meant to do with it. Her mind must

73

have been going mustn't it, it she was laying traps for people? It's too awful to think about, really, but she kept on about them having tried to poison her. She even said she was going to give them some home-baked cakes the next time they came down, so that she could watch their faces. Of course, she didn't live to carry that out, but she was glorying in the idea. A wicked, wicked woman, Inspector.'

'With a twisted mind, it seems.' McGillivray ran his fingers through his short hair, each curl springing back into its original position.

'But remember, Inspector,' Mabel went on hastily, 'she may have been imagining it all, or making it up out of spite. I told you she was a nasty person, and I just can't think that either Ronald or Stephen would have done anything like that. They looked such quiet men. And yet . . .'

'And yet?' McGillivray waited expectantly.

'And yet, she's dead, isn't she?' She buried her face in her hands.

'Yes, she's dead, Mrs Wakeford, but don't upset yourself. We'll find out who murdered her. Now, is there anything else you haven't told us?'

'No, that's everything. Sergeant Black knew on Thursday that I was holding something back, and he made me tell him.'

'You couldn't have kept that to yourself, anyway. It would have preyed on your mind, and you'd have had no peace.'

'It's just that . . . I didn't want to cast suspicion on Ronald and Stephen, when her story was maybe a pack of lies to land them in trouble.'

McGillivray smiled, and rose to his feet. 'We'll get to the truth, don't you fret. If they're innocent, they've nothing to fear. We may have to speak to you again, Mrs Wakeford, but we'll leave you meantime. Will you be all right?'

'Yes, of course. I've got over the initial shock of her actually being poisoned. I'm quite strong, really.'

'Good. We'll see ourselves out, and thank you for talking to us so frankly.'

They left by the back door, and were walking down the garden towards the Lane, when Sergeant Black came out of Number Three. 'Hop over the fence,' he instructed. 'I've just told the two ladies here that you'd be calling. I think you should see them.'

He went over one fence, while McGillivray and Moore cleared the other one, and they met at Janet Souter's door.

'What d'you think so far?' John Black asked.

The inspector turned to his sergeant. 'Let's hear you.'

'Well, Mrs Wakeford seems to be sure about it being the arsenic,' Moore began, pleased at having been consulted. 'So it looks fairly certain that one of the nephews must have succeeded in killing the old lady. But which one?'

McGillivray looked amused. 'Don't believe everything you hear, lad. That story takes a lot of swallowing.'

John Black scowled. 'Mrs Wakeford wouldn't lie, sir. She's a pillar of the church, and works a lot for charity.' He

75

was obviously incensed at the idea of her veracity being doubted.

'They're often the worst kind,' McGillivray observed dryly. 'But I didn't say I thought *she* was telling fibs. It's the dead woman's story I find hard to credit. Now, fill me in about these other ladies.'

When Mrs Skinner took them in, McGillivray recognised, immediately, the signs of fear in Mrs Grant, so he gave her a reassuring smile. 'I'm trying to fill in some background. What type of woman Miss Souter was, that kind of thing.'

It was Grace who answered, quietly and deliberately. 'She was difficult, disagreeable, quarrelsome, and constantly complained about the least little thing. Now she's gone, my sister and I will have peace to live our lives without her interference.'

Before he bent his head to the task of note-taking, David Moore noticed that Violet Grant was breathing rapidly, and had her eyes fixed apprehensively on her sister as if she were afraid of what she was going to say and was willing her to tread more carefully. If they hadn't been such genteel ladies, he could have believed that they had something to hide, but it was likely pure nervousness on Mrs Grant's part.

The inspector was admiring the forthrightness of the tall, thin woman sitting in front of him. Most females, when faced with a situation like this, wouldn't have admitted so readily to bad feelings about a murdered person, but this one exuded an air of confidence, a will of iron.

'What sort of things did she complain about, Mrs Skinner? We must make a picture of Miss Souter's personality, you see, to help us to find a reason for her murder.'

'Yes, of course. I quite understand.' Grace smiled. 'They were trivial things, usually, just enough to niggle us. About our dog digging in her garden, for instance.'

McGillivray gave no indication that he'd seen Mrs Grant's extreme agitation at this point. Her face had blanched and her hands were clutching at her skirt. 'Does your dog often go into her garden, Mrs Skinner?'

'I'm sure she put out bones and things to entice him in the first place, then she started throwing stones at him, or even kicking him if she was near enough, so he hadn't been going there so much.'

Callum McGillivray shifted the focus of his penetrating gaze to Violet, whose cheeks suddenly flooded with colour. 'What breed of dog is he, Mrs Grant?'

'He was a Skye terrier . . . mostly,' she whispered, and her eyes filled with tears. She fumbled for her handkerchief and wiped them away.

Her interrogator persisted, his training forcing him to pursue the important part of her answer. 'Was? Your dog is no longer with you, I take it?'

Grace Skinner shot a warning glance at her sister, and spoke quickly, before Violet could reply. 'Benjie died last week, I'm sorry to say.'

'What was the cause of his death, ma'am?' The inspector heard Mrs Grant draw in her breath sharply.

'He contracted some kind of canine disease,' Grace said, evasively.

Moore was surprised that McGillivray probed no further, seemingly satisfied with her answer, and Violet visibly relaxed at his next question.

'What other complaints did Miss Souter make?'

'She was offensive about my daughter's caravan sitting in the Lane for a few days.' Grace looked indignant even at the memory. 'She said it obscured her view – yet they were only here for two weeks every year.'

'Not a very sound reason, then?'

'Not really. It was just another excuse to find fault. Then she complained about my sister playing the piano on a Sunday, said it spoiled her afternoon nap.'

'I only played sacred songs, or something quiet,' Violet volunteered, unexpectedly. She seemed less afraid now, and watched, with pride, as McGillivray looked with admiration at the old mahogany upright, lovingly polished to a high sheen.

'I can't remember everything,' Grace continued, 'for they were all rather trifling, but she was growing worse and we couldn't have stood much more of it.'

'I see.' He placed his finger tips together, as if in prayer, and considered for a moment before he went on. 'Did she ever speak to you about her nephews?'

'She didn't speak much to us at all, except to complain about something, and she didn't discuss her nephews or their wives, but we saw them coming and going every weekend.' She shook her head as an unwelcome thought struck her. 'You're not thinking that one of them used the arsenic on her?'

'It would seem the obvious conclusion to make.'

Violet gasped and jumped to her feet. 'Would you like a cup of tea, Inspector?'

'No, thank you.' McGillivray smiled politely. 'Mrs Wakeford very kindly made tea for us when we were in there. Please sit down, Mrs Grant.'

Grace had clearly welcomed the diversion her sister had caused. She'd been rather shaken by the interview after all, and the respite gave her the chance to reassemble her nerves. 'Was there anything else, Inspector?' Her voice was steady.

'No, I don't think so, for the present.' McGillivray stood up, then added, 'Did Miss Souter ever tell you that somebody was trying to poison her?'

Grace looked startled. 'Did she say that?'

A small sigh disturbed them, as Violet Grant slowly slid off her chair in a faint.

When Sergeant Black arrived back at the police station, he saw James Randall coming out of his surgery, on the other side of the High Street. 'Good morning, Doctor,' he called. 'Have you a minute? We've had the result of the autopsy.'

Randall frowned, but walked over. 'You sound pleased about it. Don't tell me it was a suspicious death after all?'

'Not just suspicious, Doctor, murder!' Black tried not to look too triumphant that the other man had been proved wrong. 'The first examination showed a needle mark in the back of her neck, so they sent the body to Aberdeen. The pathologist found that she'd been injected with insulin.'

'Insulin? But she wasn't a diabetic . . . Oh, of course. That's why it killed her. By God! That was a crafty move on somebody's part. It gives exactly the same symptoms as a heart attack. Years ago it wouldn't have been detected at all, but they've new methods of spotting things now. As far as I was concerned, she gave every appearance of having suffered a coronary.'

'Yes, sir.' Black wore an expression which plainly said, 'Pull the other one!' and Doctor Randall was stung into saying, 'If you don't believe me, ask the pathologist.'

'It's not me you'll have to convince, it's the Grampian CID men. They're questioning the ladies at Honeysuckle Cottages at the moment but I'm sure they'll want to see you too.'

'Fine by me, I'll go up there as soon as I've made my first call.' James Randall walked angrily over to his car. Almost fifteen minutes later, he'd arrived at the top of Ashgrove Lane, and was sitting trying to make his mind up which of the two cottages to try, when two men came out of Number Three and made to go into the middle house.

He stepped out on to the road and called out, 'Good morning. I'm Doctor Randall.'

The older, and scruffier, of the two hurried down the path. 'Ah, I'm Detective Chief Inspector McGillivray, Grampian Region CID. I was wanting a word with you.'

'So I believe. I was speaking to Sergeant Black, and . . .'

McGillivray turned round and shouted to David Moore. 'Carry on in there yourself, Sergeant. I won't be long.' He waited until the young man disappeared inside before he turned back.

'Black tells me Miss Souter was killed by insulin being injected into her system?' Randall was still smarting at the sergeant's manner.

'A clever dodge, wasn't it, Doctor? Unfortunately for the killer, it can be detected in a post-mortem these days, otherwise it would have passed for a heart attack.'

Randall laughed ruefully. 'I wish you'd tell Black that. His opinion of me hit rock bottom, because I'd sworn the old lady died naturally.'

'Did you know her very well?'

'Not really. She was one of that disappearing breed of women, strong as an ox, who never need the services of a doctor. I could safely say that I haven't seen her more than five times in the twenty-three years I've been here, and three of those were when she fell on the ice and broke her ankle. The last time I saw her was . . . oh . . . must be seven years ago.'

'Was that for anything serious?'

Randall laughed. 'I called on her to tell her that, because she'd reached eighty, I'd be looking in from time to time to see that she was keeping well. She informed me, in no uncertain terms, not to bother, and that she'd send for me if she needed me.'

'She'd never given you any cause to be angry with her?'

The doctor laughed even louder. 'Are you trying to tell me I'm a suspect? She was a damned awkward patient at the time of her broken ankle, but doctors come up against her kind all the time. Not that there are many round here, I'm glad to say. This is the only practice I've ever had since I qualified, and I'm very happy here, even if I wasn't too sure when I first came. Small village, large farming hinterland and all that, but they're a friendly lot, and I was never treated like an outsider.'

'Have you picked up any gossip, or rumours, that might point to a possible killer? Someone she'd done the dirty on, or anything like that?'

'Nothing, I'm afraid. I don't really listen to any of the local tittle-tattle, being a bachelor.'

'Ho, hum! Oh well, I'd better let you get back to your healing. Sorry to have held you up, Doctor'

Randall saluted. 'That's OK. You've got your job to do, the same as I have. Call on me any time, if you need me.' He ducked into his car and reversed into Mabel Wakeford's gateway.

'Friendly sort of fellow, that doctor,' McGillivray remarked, when he joined his sergeant in Janet Souter's cottage.

Chapter Seven

Slumped on the bed, Callum McGillivray dislodged his left shoe with his right foot and let it drop to the floor, then repeated the process with his other shoe.

'That's better,' he sighed, wiggling his toes in relief. 'New shoes play merry hell with my tootsies.' He heaved his muscular body up a bit, and doubled the pillow to make a pad for his back. 'We haven't got much, have we?'

Sitting on the upright chair, which was the only other place in the hotel bedroom he could park himself, David Moore pulled his notebook out of his pocket. 'It's funny, though, nobody we've spoken to so far had a good word to say about Janet Souter.'

He flipped back some pages. 'According to what they told us, she went out of her way to put people's backs up.'

'Mmm . . . hmmm.' The inspector had fished out his cigarettes, and was trying to coax some life into his lighter. When a tiny flame did appear, he touched it lightly with the cigarette between his lips and puffed madly until it ignited.

'Old women often turn nasty and disagreeable, but she

83

sounds a right besom. Mrs Wakeford never mentioned any actual trouble between herself and the dead woman, but Mrs Skinner couldn't wait to tell us things she'd done to annoy them. Would she be smart enough to put up a bluff, would you say?'

'You mean she was deliberately trying to put us off the track by running down the victim like that?' Moore pondered briefly, then shook his head. 'You can't suspect Mrs Skinner. She was just being honest about all the trouble they'd had with Janet Souter.'

'You think so?' McGillivray rubbed his stubby forefinger across his chin, then screwed up his eyes against the smoke from his cigarette. 'And the other one, Mrs Grant, was as jittery as a virgin on her first night. Her faint couldn't have been better timed.'

'Oh no, sir, it wasn't put on. She's a very nervous lady, and the questioning had been too much for her.'

'Oh aye?' The inspector sounded sceptical as he drew an envelope out of his pocket. 'We'd better have a look at the bumf that constable gave me.' He opened the typewritten sheet and began to read aloud.

'Miss Janet Souter's nephews. One, Ronald Baker, fifty-five, of 36 Newton Avenue, Thornkirk. Small engineering business. Wife, Flora. Two, Stephen Drummond, fifty-one, of 147 Kingswood Drive, Thornkirk. Grocery shop. Wife, Barbara. Dead woman's estate left equally between Ronald Baker and Stephen Drummond, confirmed by her solicitor, Martin Spencer, business address, 21 George Square, Thornkirk.'

He lifted his head. 'That seems straightforward enough. Ronald and Stephen have an obvious reason for getting rid of the old aunt – probably got fed up waiting till she popped off under her own steam. We'll let them sweat till tomorrow, I think. A little bit of suspense sometimes works wonders.'

Laying the paper on the bed beside him, he looked at his watch. 'Twenty to twelve. Just time for you to nose round the local shops, before lunch at one. That's one thing about a small village, everything's within spitting distance, and the shopkeepers might have picked up bits of gossip from their customers. And, if you've time, Moore, see if you can track down that boy who delivered the papers. He might have remembered something that struck him as being out of the ordinary.'

'Yes, sir.' David Moore stood up and pushed his chair back under the small table.

'I'll stay here, to give my feet a rest, and write out a few notes on what I think we've got already. See you later.' The inspector lay back, with his hands behind his head.

The young sergeant reflected ruefully that his feet would also be glad of a rest, after hunting round the murdered woman's cottage and garden for a couple of hours. Thank goodness the shops were only a few doors away from the hotel, and all quite close together, as McGillivray had said. The ironmonger was first, so he looked at the name above the door and went in, trying to look a bit more alert than he felt.

'Mr Hood? I'm Sergeant Moore, Grampian CID, and

I'd like to ask you a few questions about Miss Janet Souter, of Honeysuckle Cottages.'

'Certainly, Sergeant. I heard she'd died.' Robert Hood straightened his grey nylon overall round his podgy body and tried, by drawing himself up to his full five feet five, to look important. 'I didn't know her all that well, she only bought odds and ends occasionally, and the last time I saw her was two or three weeks ago when she came in for rat poison. She was troubled with rats in her garden – has been for years.'

'She'd bought rat poison before, had she?'

'Quite regularly, but the rats kept on appearing. There's an old warehouse, you see, near the railway line at the foot of Ashgrove Lane, that's where they breed, I think, and the old woman often forgot to put the lid back on her dustbin when she was putting out rubbish, so that would have attracted them. But she didn't buy the rat poison that day. Davie Livingstone happened to be here at the same time, and he told her he'd give her some arsenic.'

Moore looked, he hoped, suitably surprised. 'Oh?'

The ironmonger grinned. 'Don't tell me you hadn't heard about the arsenic?'

'Well, yes, I had.' The sergeant looked sheepish. 'But how did this man come to have arsenic? It's not a thing you keep handy in case you need it.'

'Davie worked in the glass factory before he retired, and they use arsenic for making glass. Anyway, he was bothered with rats himself for a while, and he'd made a point of taking a small amount home with him every week for months before he stopped working. He told Miss Souter it was quicker and better than rat poison, and he said he'd take some up to her. He sometimes did a bit of gardening for her, the rough stuff, you know.'

'But, Mr Hood . . .'

The man raised one hand from the counter and held it up. 'Before you say it, I know it's against the law to have arsenic, but I thought, if it made Davie happy, what the hell? He'd have known exactly how dangerous it was.'

'It was more dangerous for a woman of Miss Souter's age to be tampering with it . . . Would he have been on good enough terms with her?'

Robert Hood spluttered. 'Nobody was on good terms with her, and you're surely not suspecting him of an ulterior motive? Davie Livingstone wouldn't hurt a fly . . . Just rats,' he added.

The sergeant considered for a moment. 'Do you think Miss Souter could have taken the arsenic accidentally, forgotten to wash her hands, or something like that?'

'Oh, no. She wasn't senile, and Davie warned her to wash her hands thoroughly. She wouldn't have been careless with it, I'm sure. She's definitely been murdered.'

The sergeant pursed his lips. 'Can you think of any person who might have wanted to kill her?'

'I know she wasn't well liked, but . . . murder! That needs to be a very special kind of hate.'

'Yes. Was there anyone . . . have you heard any rumours?'

Robert Hood shook his head. 'She was always rubbing

somebody up the wrong way, and I've heard lots of people moaning about her, but there's been nothing all that bad for a long time.'

'Oh well. Thank you for giving me your time, Mr Hood, and if anything comes to your mind, let me know. Just contact the police station.'

'I'll certainly keep thinking, but I don't believe I'll be able to help.'

The butcher, John Robertson, tall and well built, rolled his eyes dramatically when Moore asked him how well he'd known Janet Souter. 'A headcase, that woman, a real headcase. Came in here at least once a week, occasionally twice, and was never satisfied with anything. Stringy beef, fatty sausages, too dear. You know the kind of thing. Not bloody happy unless she was upsetting somebody.'

His ruddy face suddenly lit up. 'I'll give you an example. Just a week ago yesterday, she gave me a mouthful in front of all my customers about the price of the steak. She ended up buying mutton instead, because it was cheaper, yet she's bought steak every Friday for years.' He laughed. 'That's the kind of woman she was, Sergeant, and I say good riddance to bad rubbish. I wish I'd thought of doing away with her myself.'

David Moore wasn't surprised at what the man had told him. It was just the sort of behaviour that he'd have expected from the dead woman, judging by all the opinions of her, so far. 'You're telling me that she was a nasty person, Mr Robertson, but would you know of anybody who might have wanted to kill her?'

The butcher laughed grimly. 'The whole village has felt like killing her at one time or another, I'm sure.'

The detective remained serious. 'That's not quite the same as carrying it out, though.'

'No, that's true. Poisoning's a dirty game; it has to be well thought out, not a spur-of-the-moment sort of crime. If she'd been hit on the head with a blunt instrument, or stabbed with her own kitchen knife, or strangled, or something physical like that, I'd have said quite a few people could have been capable, but not poison.'

Scratching his head, he went on, 'It leaves a bad taste in your mouth, poison.' He let out a loud guffaw, and slapped the counter with his large hand in appreciation of his own accidental wit. 'Never mind me, Sergeant, I didn't mean that the way it sounded, but it's true, whatever way you look at it, isn't it?'

David Moore smiled. 'Thank you, Mr Robertson, you've been very helpful.' He walked out of the shop, leaving the butcher still chuckling to himself, but reflecting that murder wasn't really anything to laugh about.

His call at the bank manager's house drew a blank, because the man didn't know Miss Souter except to see her, and from what he had heard from others.

'She didn't deal with us here. Apparently, she was afraid people would get to know her affairs, though I'm sure I would never have passed on any information about her if she had used our facilities.'

'No, of course not,' Moore felt obliged to agree.

The hairdresser was very busy, but took time to say that

Janet Souter had gone there once a month, and had never been pleased with what had been done.

'If there had been another hairdresser in the place, she'd have gone to them and complained, the same as she did here.'

'Have any of your customers spoken about her murder? I'd have thought that would be a subject they'd love to get their teeth into.'

'Some of them have mentioned it.' The young woman glanced at her watch. 'But they're all sure it was one of her nephews that did it. Now, I'm sorry, but I have to get on.'

Moore had thought he'd pick up some gossip in the hairdressing salon in the High Street, but no such luck. He crossed disconsolately to the other side of the street, where there were only two shops, a chemist and a general store.

In the first, the chemist, a tall, balding man, looked up, smiling until the sergeant stated his business. Then his air of bonhomie disappeared. 'Miss Souter *was* a customer, but not one I was ever very friendly with, I'm afraid. Her health was always good, so she never bought medications of any kind, only small items of toiletries, and she never failed to complain about the prices. She was disagreeable and unpleasant, and I, for one, am not sorry she's dead.'

He looked at Moore and smiled grimly. 'I expect that shocks you, but you'll probably get the same reaction from all the other shopkeepers. She wasn't very popular with any of us.'

'So I've gathered.' Moore returned his smile, ruefully. 'Have you any theory about who killed her?'

'Anyone, I suppose. We all knew she had some arsenic, but it's most likely to have been one of her nephews, isn't it? None of us was going to gain anything by doing away with her.'

The shop next door was a general store, with a notice up outside informing the world that it was also a post office. The bell tinkled when David Moore went in, and three pairs of eyes turned to look at him. He wished that he'd remembered to check the name outside, but moved over to the post office grille.

'Er, good morning. I'm sorry to bother you, but I'm Detective Sergeant Moore from Grampian Police, and we're investigating the murder of Miss Souter of Honeysuckle Cottages. I hope you don't mind answering some questions, Miss . . . er . . . ?'

The thin, sour-faced postmistress gave a slight condescending smile. 'It's Miss Wheeler, and Sergeant Black of the local police has already asked me what I know. I don't think there's anything further I can tell you.'

'Perhaps you could tell me what sort of person she was, and that kind of thing.' The woman's manner had made him feel at a disadvantage, so he pulled out his notebook to give his visit an air of serious officialdom.

'Oh, that's different.' Miss Wheeler was obviously pleased to be asked this. 'I've known her for twenty-two and a half years, ever since I came here to take over this shop.'

'Were you friendly with her?'

'Not so much friendly, she wasn't that kind of person. It's a shame to speak ill of the dead, but really, Sergeant, I don't believe she had any friends in Tollerton at all. She was a most unlikeable woman.'

'That's right.' The interruption came from the customer standing at the other counter.

'Excuse me, Mrs Pritchard, but the sergeant is talking to me.' Miss Wheeler's voice, cold and reproving, showed that she objected to the spotlight being diverted from her.

David Moore hastened to pour oil on the troubled waters. 'If you care to wait a moment, Mrs Pritchard, I'll have a word with you when I've finished with Miss Wheeler.' The woman appeared to be fractionally appeased, but continued to glare at the postmistress.

'As I was saying,' that lady went on triumphantly, 'Janet Souter took a delight in making things unpleasant for other people. She is – was – one of the oldest inhabitants, and thought she owned the place. Nobody has a good word to say for her, not even the minister's wife, and she's a perfect lady, but the old woman didn't behave very nicely to her, either.'

'The minister's wife?'

'Mrs Valentine. She came here with her husband about four or five years ago. A very nice couple, and he's a real gem. Face and physique like a film star, and all the girls go wild about him, but he doesn't let it go to his head. He's a far better man than our last minister.'

'His wife, though,' Moore prompted. 'You said . . .'

'Oh, yes. Janet Souter snubbed her several times that I know about, over Sales of Work and various other fund-raising events, but Mrs Valentine never said anything against her, though we all knew there was no love lost between them.' Emma Wheeler shot a quick glance at Mrs Pritchard, as if daring her to argue.

'Do you know of anyone else who might have had a real grudge against the old lady, enough to . . .'

'To murder her, d'you mean? It is murder, then. We thought it was, seeing all the different police going around. It's not much help to you, Sergeant, but we've all felt like murdering her at times. That's not the same as actually doing it, of course, is it?'

'No, no, of course not.' David Moore was fast becoming acutely aware of how difficult the case was going to be. 'In your own dealings with her, did you ever have occasion to be really angry with her?'

'Lots of times, but nothing so bad as make me turn homicidal and poison her.'

'Thank you, Miss Wheeler, for being so honest with me.' As Moore turned round, he noticed that the young assistant behind the counter was regarding him with a scared, wide-eyed, open-mouthed expression, and decided that he may as well have a word with her afterwards too. She looked to be about sixteen or seventeen, and sometimes youngsters innocently re-vealed more information than the older, more wordly wise.

But the customer, a woman nearing fifty, was waiting

rather impatiently. 'Now, Mrs Pritchard, have you anything further to tell me?' He gave her his full attention, although he presumed that she merely wanted to add her tuppence worth about being shabbily treated by the murdered woman.

'Well, it's not that I knew Miss Souter very well, but I do know she caused an almighty row between Sydney Pettigrew, the chemist, and his youngest son.'

This was more like it, and Moore held his pen ready.

'It was over May White. Her husband, Gilbert, works with an oil company in Abbie Dabbie, or something like that, so he only gets home once or twice a year.'

Emma Wheeler sniffed at this, but made no comment, so Mrs Pritchard carried on. 'Well, May had been encouraging young Douglas Pettigrew to come to her house. It had been going on for months, and all of us down at that end of Ashgrove Lane knew about it, but it was none of our business. Douglas is about eighteen, and she must be about forty or so, though she looks in her early thirties. It wouldn't have happened in my day, but you young folk today have a different outlook on life from us older ones, haven't you?'

She looked at the sergeant, and winked. 'It's a permissive society nowadays, but the old witch – that's what we called Janet Souter – found out about it. I think she saw him sneaking home early one morning, and put two and two together and made four, you know. She told Sydney what his son was up to, and, of course, she painted as black a picture as she could.'

David Moore paused in his note-taking as Mrs Pritchard stopped for breath. This was exactly what he was after, scandal of some kind. 'So Douglas Pettigrew, and his father, would both have had cause to hate Miss Souter?'

The woman screwed up her face. 'Hate's maybe too strong a word, though, more dislike. Anyway, Sydney forbade Douglas ever to see May again, and went and had a row with the Falconers – that's her parents – as well, saying it was all May's fault for encouraging his son.'

'It *was* all May's fault,' the young girl burst out. 'She was always asking him down there, with all sorts of excuses. Douglas told me himself.'

'Phyllis Barclay!' Emma Wheeler felt obliged to reprimand her assistant. 'You don't know anything about it.'

The girl looked indignant. 'Oh, yes, I do. He was going with me till she started with him.'

The two older women raised their eyebrows at this. It was obviously news to them.

'He told me he didn't want to go in the first place, but she pleaded with him to mend a fuse for her. He said he felt sorry for her, being on her own so much, and not having a man about the place to do things for her, so he gave in. He only meant to go the once, but she persuaded him to go back, to fix a washer, and stupid little jobs like that, and he ended up going two or three times a week. He said he couldn't help himself, for she made him feel important.' She swallowed to keep from crying.

95

David Moore made a few notes and left the conversation to develop by itself. Much more was being revealed than under his official questioning, so it was best to let the three women continue under their own steam.

Miss Wheeler was saying, 'You never told me you'd been going out with Douglas Pettigrew, Phyllis.'

'It wasn't anybody's business.' The girl was defiant. 'I told him it would all be over between us if he didn't stop seeing her, and he just laughed. He said May knew how to whet a man's appetite.' There were tears now in the lovely blue eyes.

'Well, I never!' Miss Wheeler's face registered all the shock which might be expected in an elderly maiden lady.

'But he carried on with her, didn't he?' Mrs Pritchard was eager to hear more of the liaison.

'Yes, he did, till Miss Souter told his father, and I don't really know what happened then.' Phyllis Barclay stopped, quite surprised at herself for telling these people so much. 'But I do know Douglas would never have poisoned the old lady,' she added, almost in a whisper.

There was a lengthy silence, during which her story was digested by the other three occupants of the store, until the door opened and a tall, gangling youth entered.

'Hi!' he said, to everyone in general. 'I just came to tell you I'll be a bit late coming for the *Citizens*, Miss Wheeler. I'm playing football this afternoon.' He let his eyes wander round, then, sensing an atmosphere.

The sergeant realised that this must be the paperboy he had been told to question, and assumed his most official voice as he stepped forward. 'You are William Arthur? I'm Detective Sergeant Moore of Grampian Police.'

He was amused to see the boy's cockiness deflate a little, but Willie couldn't help much. He'd noticed that Miss Souter's milk was sitting at her door in the morning, and had told Miss Wheeler when he went back to the shop. Moore looked at the postmistress with his eyebrows raised.

'I didn't do anything about it.' She hurried to defend herself. 'You see, I was worried about what would happen if I sent the police up and nothing was wrong. She'd have been absolutely furious, and she'd likely have come stamping down here to give me what for.'

He could understand the poor woman's dilemma, so he turned to the paperboy again.

'I didn't know what to do, either,' admitted Willie. 'Miss Souter was an old . . . but she was always on the go. I suspected something must be wrong with her, so I told Mrs Wakeford at teatime when I saw the milk still at the door. I didn't realise she'd been poisoned, though.'

'Who told you she'd been poisoned, Willie?' Moore wondered how this had got out. He was sure that John Black would never have divulged any such information, not to the paperboy, at any rate.

'It's . . .' The boy caught himself, remembering his promise to the local sergeant, then went on hastily. 'It's all over the village, and somebody was bound to do her in some day, the way she went on.'

'Willie!' Miss Wheeler cautioned the boy, although she had hinted at much the same thing herself.

'Did you notice anything unusual when you were there in the morning, Willie? Anything different, that a stranger might not have seen? Something that might give us a clue to finding out who killed her?'

The fourteen-year-old pondered for a moment, then said, 'No, but I've never looked in her window before, so I wouldn't have known anything was unusual, would I? Miss Wheeler said she was going to tell the copper . . . Constable Paul, but she didn't see him. But Mrs Wakeford phoned the police station as soon as I told her about it in the afternoon.'

He looked slightly downcast as he added, 'Sergeant Black wouldn't let me and Mrs Wakeford into Miss Souter's house, though.'

Moore pushed in the top of his Biro, and clipped it into his breast pocket, then slid his notebook down behind it. 'Thank you all very much for your cooperation.'

'That's all right, Sergeant. Call again any time.' Miss Wheeler took command again as he walked out of the shop.

He glanced through the window when he walked past, and saw them, as he'd expected, deep in speculation as to who could be responsible for the murder. He was annoyed, but not altogether surprised, to find the inspector still lying on his bed when he returned to the Starline. McGillivray looked up, and Moore was sure that he'd been asleep.

'Did you uncover any skeletons in any of the village cupboards, lad?'

'Not really, sir. The only interesting thing that came out was a bit of scandal concerning a young married woman who lives at the foot of Ashgrove Lane.' The sergeant sat down wearily and unbuttoned his jacket.

'Oh yes?' McGillivray perked up. 'There's nothing better than scandal for making feelings run high and tempers snap in the heat of the moment.'

Moore recounted the stories Mrs Pritchard and Phyllis Barclay had told him, while his superior listened attentively with his head on one side.

'So. This young lad . . .'

'Douglas Pettigrew, the chemist's son.'

'This Douglas Pettigrew would've been pretty mad at the old woman for sabotaging his love nest; and the married Jezebel would likely have been none too pleased about it either, but hardly angry enough to make her kill, eh, Moore?'

'Probably not. She's likely just been amusing herself with the boy to pass the time, nothing very passionate.'

The inspector swung his legs round. ' "Hell hath no fury . . ." '

'She wasn't scorned, sir. Maybe thwarted.'

'We'll have to keep her in mind, just the same . . . and the boy.' McGillivray sat on the edge of the bed, thinking, until the sergeant cleared his throat. He looked up. 'Did anything else turn up, Moore?'

'Nothing exciting. The murdered woman wasn't well

liked, but I don't think any of the people I spoke to disliked her enough to poison her. The ironmonger said she'd got the arsenic from a Davie Livingstone to kill rats, and he'd told her it was dangerous, so she wouldn't have been careless with it.'

McGillivray rubbed his stubbly chin. 'Maybe, but she was eighty-seven, after all, and her memory wouldn't have been so good. She could have contaminated her own food, if she'd forgotten to wash her hands, or left some of it on her clothes. What d'you think?' His eyes were twinkling, and Moore wondered what he was up to.

His stomach was crying out for food, but he had to take the time to correct the Inspector. 'No, sir, it couldn't have been that. Mr Hood said she wasn't senile, and would have been very careful because this other man had warned her it was deadly stuff.'

McGillivray pulled his shoes towards him. 'Is that a fact? Moore, you'll just have time to give yourself a wash before lunch.'

The sergeant stood up thankfully, then paused with his hand on the door knob. 'It just occurred to me, sir, the chemist said he'd never had any real trouble with Miss Souter, but she was the one who told him about his son and this Mrs White. Would there be any significance in him not mentioning that?'

'There might be.' The inspector winced as his tender feet came in contact with the new leather. 'If he was guilty, he wouldn't want you to know that he'd a reason for

100

getting rid of her. On the other hand, if he was innocent, he could have considered that it had nothing to do with the case, and that it was nobody's business but his family's. Get moving, Sergeant. My belly thinks my throat's been cut.'

Chapter Eight

Walking alongside him down Ashgrove Lane, David Moore wondered what the DCI had been up to while he'd been calling on the shopkeepers. McGillivray wasn't a bad old boy, really, quite pleasant to work with, and this being their second assignment together, the young man was learning to respect his superior's thorough methods of detection, unorthodox as they appeared to be at times.

Ashgrove Lane was quite long, with hedges and fields on both sides once they left Honeysuckle Cottages behind. The old railway station could be seen some little distance away to the right, with the abandoned warehouse – the source of the rats, according to the ironmonger – on the near side of it.

The cluster of buildings they came to were much nearer the road, and more modern, than those at the top, but lacked the quaint character of the low old-fashioned cottages.

'Which one would be the love nest, I wonder?' McGillivray mused, screwing up his eyes to read the nameplates.

102

'Ah, here it is.' He opened the second gate and walked up the short path.

His press on the bell was answered by a young woman who could have passed, at first glance, for being under thirty, but was probably a good few years older than that. Her face was free of any make-up except for the deep red gash of her mouth. The DCI thought that she possibly felt naked without her lipstick.

'Mrs Gilbert White?'

'In the flesh,' was the light-hearted reply.

'May we come in?'

A flash of alarm showed in the green eyes for a fraction of a second. 'But who . . . ?'

'I'm sorry, I should have introduced myself. Detective Chief Inspector McGillivray, Grampian CID, and this is Detective Sergeant Moore.'

Showing them into her living room, she asked anxiously, 'There's nothing wrong, is there? Gilbert hasn't been in an accident, or anything?'

McGillivray hastened to reassure her. 'No, no, Mrs White. I apologise if I frightened you. We're investigating the murder of Miss Janet Souter of Honeysuckle Cottages.'

'Yes, I heard about that. It was about time somebody bumped the old bitch off.'

'May we sit down?' The inspector was already lowering himself into an armchair by the electric fire.

'Sure, why not? Make yourselves at home. Would you like a drink?'

'No, thank you. Not when we're on duty.'

She fluttered her long eyelashes. 'Oh, come on. A little drop won't hurt you.'

Moore glanced at McGillivray hopefully, although he expected to hear another firm refusal, and was deeply thankful when the inspector said, 'A very small one, then, and I really mean small.'

'You too, Sergeant?'

'Yes, please.'

'Coming right up.' May White switched off her stereo and went across the room to the cocktail cabinet against the rear wall. Her catlike movements were accentuated by the fact that her legs were encased in tight black satin trousers, and her scarlet T-shirt outlined her shape in perfect detail. The two men watched with great admiration while she poured out three generous measures of whisky.

When she turned to ask, 'Lemonade, soda or water?' the inspector had to drag his mind away from the pleasant contemplation of her figure. 'Just a splash of soda, please.'

When she sat down, opposite McGillivray, she held her glass up. 'Good luck in your quest, gentlemen. I don't think I'll be able to help you, mind, but fire away.'

'We've been led to believe that Miss Souter was instrumental in bringing your . . . association with Douglas Pettigrew to an abrupt end,' he began.

May giggled. 'Association? That's putting it mildly. We'd a real hot affair going till she put her oar in and told his dad. Now he's not allowed to come here any more.' She took a small sip of the spirits, held it in her mouth for a second, then swallowed.

'So we could gather that you had good reason to dislike her?'

'Enough to murder her? Oh no. I despised Douglas for just knuckling down and not defying his father, so he's not worth a damn to me now. I like my men to be men.' Her eyes teased.

'You weren't heartbroken by his desertion, then?'

'I was bloody annoyed, but my heart doesn't break so easily. There's plenty of other fish in the sea.' She leaned back in her chair and stuck her stockinged feet out towards the fire. 'He was only a boy, but he amused me for a while. Gil's away such a lot, he can't expect me to be faithful to him.'

McGillivray persisted. 'The boy himself, though. He was apparently very angry with Miss Souter. Would he have been hot-headed enough to kill her?'

Her laughter was derisive. 'Hell no. I'd a helluva job getting him where I wanted him.' She leaned over and lifted a packet of cigarettes from a coffee table. 'Smoke?'

'Not just now, thanks.' McGillivray waited until she flicked the table lighter and inhaled deeply. 'Maybe the boy was deeply in love with you. Love makes people do strange things.'

'Oh, I know, but not Doug. I think you're barking up the wrong tree there. A lot of people in Tollerton hated the old sod, for she was always interfering and causing trouble.'

'Can you think of anyone in particular?'

'There's the two old dears next to her, for a start, the sisters. She made their lives an absolute hell. She even poisoned their dog. Oh!' May looked regretful. 'I don't think they'd have killed her, though. They're very gentle ladies. Mrs Grant's under her sister's thumb, of course, but I can't picture even Mrs Skinner poisoning anybody.'

'No? Maybe you're right.' McGillivray considered for a moment, filing away the information about the poisoned dog. 'Can you think of anyone else?'

'What about the nephews? I'd imagine they'll come into her money, and it's often the nearest and dearest who kill the rich old lady, isn't it?'

The inspector smiled. 'In some cases, yes. We'll be going to see them tomorrow. There's no one else?'

May shook her head. 'Most of the old biddies round here think I'm a proper tart, but I wouldn't cast suspicion on any of them out of spite. No, I'm afraid I can't help you.'

McGillivray drained his glass and laid it down, then he rose to his feet. 'It was worth a try, but, by the look of things, we'll be interviewing people till Kingdom come.'

'Is there nothing else I can do for you?' She looked at him invitingly from under her sweeping lashes.

'No, Mrs White. I'm sorry to have troubled you.'

'It was no trouble, believe me. I'm always glad of male company.' She winked at David Moore when she showed them out, making him blush to the roots of his reddish fair hair.

He followed the inspector up the Lane until the older man slowed down enough to let him catch up.

'Phew!' Callum McGillivray let out a long sigh. 'I think we're lucky to have got out with our trousers on. She's a proper man-eater, that one.'

Moore groaned. 'I'll say! But I don't think she'd anything to do with Janet Souter's murder.'

'Probably not, but she's got nerve enough.'

When they neared the cottages, McGillivray said, 'Why didn't Mrs Skinner tell us the truth about their dog's death, I wonder? Could she have something to hide, for all her seeming honesty? I think we'll pay them another visit, on the pretext of finding out more about young Pettigrew and Madam White. I trust Mrs Grant's recovered from her fainting spell. It was most peculiar, happening at the precise moment I mentioned that the dead woman thought somebody was trying to poison her.'

Moore passed no comment. He was rather disappointed that the inspector had such a suspicious mind.

When Mrs Skinner took them in, her sister was sewing, but as soon as she saw the callers, Violet jumped up in alarm, letting her embroidery slip from her fingers onto the floor.

'Sit down, Violet!' Grace almost barked it out. 'What's the matter with you?' She turned to the two men. 'My sister's always timid with strangers. She has a very nervous disposition.'

McGillivray smiled. 'No need to be scared, Mrs Grant. I just want to discuss a little matter with you both, that's all.'

He pulled a chair round and sat down, leaving his sergeant to watch the reactions of the two women; one poised and seemingly perfectly at ease, but the other biting her lip and casting pleading glances at her sister.

The inspector assumed his most apologetic manner and leaned forward to speak confidentially to them. 'You see, ladies, in all murder investigations facts come to light which, although serious to the persons concerned, have no bearing on the crime in hand. Do you understand what I mean?'

'Of course.' Grace Skinner nodded her head graciously.

'Yes,' whispered her sister, one hand clasping and unclasping at the worn upholstery of her chair.

'It has come to light that Miss Souter uncovered a clandestine love affair between Douglas Pettigrew, the chemist's son, and a Mrs Gilbert White.'

'Oh that!' Grace laughed. 'Everybody knew about it except the Pettigrews. It'll peter out in a few weeks.'

'Oh yes, May's affairs usually do,' put in Violet, her anxiety gone now that the reason for the visit had proved to be nothing to do with them.

'That's as may be,' McGillivray said. 'But Miss Souter took it upon herself to inform the boy's father, and caused much ill feeling between them.'

'That old busybody!' exclaimed Grace. 'I'll never understand why she couldn't keep her nose out of other people's business.'

'Maybe she thought it was her duty,' Violet ventured.

'Duty my foot! She was an interfering old . . . I'm sorry,

Inspector, but bitch is the only word to describe her, and I'm not given to profanity.' Grace looked incensed.

'Quite.' McGillivray let a smile play across his craggy countenance. 'We have also been informed that she'd approached the young man himself, earlier.'

'Oh, yes, I remember now.' Violet looked quite animated. 'I was passing along the street at the time and he told her to mind her own b— business, and he said the word right out. Then he threatened her. 'I'll get you yet, you old . . . Violet couldn't bring herself to repeat the word.'

'You never told me,' her sister accused.

'I forgot about it, till the inspector reminded me.' Violet looked contrite. 'It was the day you got that letter from Marilyn, telling you Terry'd got promotion, and you were so full of it, the other thing went right out of my head.'

The inspector carried on. 'So young Pettigrew had reason to be furious with her before she told his father, and this second interference may have kindled a strong enough feeling for him to . . .' He stopped short as Mrs Grant bounded to her feet again.

'But *Douglas* didn't poison her!'

'Violet!' Grace's curt reprimand made her sister colour and become confused.

'Oh, Grace, I never said . . . I didn't mean . . .' She clapped her hand over her mouth, and her eyes were staring.

The silence which fell could have been cut with a knife,

but, in a few seconds, and much to Moore's surprise, McGillivray stood up. 'Thank you for your help, ladies.'

When the two detectives arrived at the police station, John Black took them into the small, back room which he'd allocated as an incident room. 'Have you found any leads yet, sir?'

'A few things have cropped up.' McGillivray pulled out his cigarettes, tried his lighter unsuccessfully several times, then accepted the box of matches the sergeant handed him. 'Did you know about the row between the chemist and his son, caused by the dead woman?'

Black smiled. 'It caused a row between the Pettigrews and the Falconers as well. That's May's father and mother, and now the two families don't speak to each other. Sydney blamed May for leading Douglas on, and Bob Falconer said it was Douglas's fault.'

'Whichever, Miss Souter had thrown a spanner in the works by telling his father, and the lad had been told to stop seeing the married lady. Would he be unstable enough to commit murder because of that?'

John Black thought, then frowned. 'No, not Douglas. He's quite a nice boy really, and I think May turned his head with her attentions. Her carryings on are well known and it would just have been another conquest to her, so she wouldn't have had any reason to kill Miss Souter, either. No, Inspector, I'm pretty sure you can count both of them out.'

McGillivray sighed. 'I don't know. A youth in the

throes of his first sexual experience might just . . . Perhaps not, in this case. Unfortunately, Moore didn't turn up anything else promising. Just a whole lot of nastiness on the part of Miss Souter, but fairly trivial, eh Moore?'

The young sergeant was glad to be consulted. 'Yes sir, and I don't think any of the shopkeepers would have killed her for complaining about their prices or their service. And they all mentioned the arsenic quite freely, so there must be someone else who had reason to poison the old lady that we haven't come in contact with yet.'

The inspector winked to John Black. 'I think it's time we put him wise, isn't it?'

As Black nodded, grinning from ear to ear, Moore asked, 'Have you been keeping something from me?'

McGillivray adopted his praying hands position and laughed. 'Janet Souter didn't die as a result of arsenic poisoning, lad.'

'Didn't what? What did she die of, then?' The young man's face was full of righteous indignation.

'A large dose of insulin had been injected into her bloodstream.' McGillivray leaned back smugly.

'God! You're a crafty bugger! . . . sir.' Moore's voice had risen angrily, but he checked himself. 'How long have you known?'

Callum McGillivray and John Black were laughing hilariously at Moore's outburst, and it was a minute before an answer came.

'It was in the report the Super gave me this morning before we left Aberdeen.' The inspector wiped his eyes.

111

'I'd a gander at it when you and the PC were taking the bags to the Starline.'

'Why didn't you tell me before? God, I feel a proper pillock, questioning all those folk without knowing the truth myself.'

'I'm sorry, lad, but I wanted you to listen to their stories about the arsenic first, without anything else cluttering up your brain. It's definitely part of the picture – no smoke without fire – and we'll have to get to the bottom of that before we'll get at the truth. They've all assumed it was the arsenic, but only the murderer knows what really killed her.'

Black picked up the telephone at the first small tinkle. 'Tollerton Police . . . Yes, he's here.' He passed the receiver over to McGillivray.

'Yes? . . . Good! Let's have it.' The inspector listened intently for a few moments, then said, 'Thanks.'

As he laid the instrument back on its cradle, he looked at John Black. 'That was the report from the public analyst at HQ, on the items of food they've been testing.'

Moore's resentment evaporated, and he turned round to learn what the results were.

'Everything's quite clear. And he said he'd made a double check on the flour and the sugar because he'd been told that was where the stuff probably was.'

The local sergeant raised his brows. 'So the nephews hadn't put arsenic in her bins after all?'

'If Janet Souter's story was true, she must have disposed of the contaminated goods. Of course, Mrs Wakeford may have invented the whole thing herself, because the bag from the shed, supposedly containing the arsenic, held only ordinary self-raising flour. God, what an involved business this is turning out to be.' McGillivray scratched his chin.

'Sir,' David Moore began, 'if the old woman was expecting her nephews to try to poison her, maybe she hid the arsenic and laid out the flour for them to use. The arsenic has maybe nothing to do with the case?'

McGillivray snorted. 'It has nothing to do with her death, but it sure as eggs is eggs has something to do with the case. I'd think that whoever actually killed her started the story about the nephews, etcetera, to throw suspicion off himself, or herself, and the only person to speak about that was Mrs Wakeford, who says she got it from the victim herself.'

Sergeant Black looked worried. 'You can't possibly suspect Mrs Wakeford. She's a proper, genteel lady, in the true sense.' He stood up and pushed in his chair.

'We'll stop on for a while, Sergeant. I'd like to go over what we've got already.'

'Yes sir. This room's at your disposal whenever you need it.' Black's voice was rather cold. 'I have to get back to my own duties.'

'Of course. Moore and I'll manage fine. Thanks.'

Ignoring the near slam of the door, McGillivray turned to his sergeant. 'I think I'll make a list of suspects. It helps my old brainbox when I see things written down in black and white. See if you can find some paper, lad.'

David Moore started opening the drawers in the desk, and was successful at his second attempt. 'There you are, sir.' He took out several sheets of paper and laid them down.

'I've been thinking. If the old lady had filled a plastic bag with flour, and the nephews had used that, thinking it was the poison, it would explain why there was only flour in her flour bin, but . . .' McGillivray screwed up his face, puzzling over it, 'in that case, there should have been flour in her sugar bin. At least, according to what Mrs Wakeford told us about the crumbs of toast.'

'Mind you,' he said, after a while, 'if the ironmonger hadn't vouched that this Davie Livingstone did give her some arsenic, I'd have thought it was pure fabrication on somebody's part. But she told all and sundry about it, so it must be true enough. But if she'd hidden the real stuff, where is it now?'

He stood up. 'I think I'll get the bobby to turn her shed inside out, to see if he can unearth it. I don't like the idea of arsenic lying handy.' He went to issue his instructions, and returned almost immediately.

'Now, let's see what we've got, so far.' Pulling his pen out of his pocket, he drew a sheet of paper towards him, and jotted down his headings. 'Sus . . . pects and Mot . . . ives.' He lifted his head again, beaming. 'All ready to begin.'

'We haven't many suspects yet, have we?'

The inspector tapped his nose with his pen. 'Never say die, lad. We could surprise ourselves with what we come up with. Number One. Mabel Wakeford. Too vehement in her denials of any friction with the deceased. Extremely flustered. Was first to mention arsenic and practically accused nephews before it was even found out that the old woman had been murdered. The question is, why? And what reason would she have had to kill Janet Souter? Circumstantial evidence, but unknown motive.'

'I don't think she could have had anything to do with the murder, Inspector, and you offended Sergeant Black by suggesting it. But things look bad for her, I must admit.' Moore added the last few words reluctantly.

'Number Two,' McGillivray continued. 'Grace Skinner. Seemed altogether too sure of herself, and omitted to mention their dog had been poisoned, presumably by deceased. Why? She was quick enough to tell us other things Janet Souter had done to annoy them – little things, she kept emphasising. Now, I'm positive their dog's death would not have been a little thing to them, so – so that might be her motive for the murder.' He scribbled down a few more words, ending up with a question mark.

David Moore shook his head, but said nothing.

'Number Three. Violet Grant. Scared out of her wits, and knows something she's not telling.'

'She would have told you, if her sister hadn't stopped her. And she might have cracked if you'd carried on questioning.'

McGillivray clicked his tongue. 'No, I wanted them to feel safe for a little while longer. When the pressure's off, people sometimes get careless and come out with more than they mean to. Whatever it was that Mrs Grant wanted to say, it was probably just conjecture on her part.'

'I suppose so, but she was positive Douglas Pettigrew didn't kill Miss Souter. How could she have known anything about that?'

'It's been what she wanted to think, no doubt, knowing the boy quite well, but, if there's more to it than that, we'll sniff it out eventually.'

The young sergeant twisted his mouth. 'And her motive would be the same as her sister's – the dog?'

Nodding his head, the inspector continued with his list. 'Number Four. Mrs May White. That young woman may be forward, flighty, and a nymphomaniac, but I don't think she's a killer. She didn't seem all that upset about the end of her affair with young Pettigrew. Still, one never knows.'

Moore laughed. 'I've heard you saying, sir, never discount any suspect until they're proven innocent.'

'Right, lad. We'll make a proper detective of you yet. On with the motley. Number Five. Young Douglas Pettigrew himself. We'll need to have a chat with him soon. On the face of it, he's the most likely one so far, with his passion having been knocked on the head – or wherever.' McGillivray grinned impishly. 'And his father's a chemist.'

'So he could easily have got hold of a hypodermic syringe and insulin.' Moore looked enthusiastic.

'Good lad. You're on the ball. Number Six. Ronald Baker, the nephew. I did a bit of telephoning while you were out before lunch. His engineering firm's on the verge of bankruptcy and he's in urgent need of a few thousand to buy equipment for a contract he hopes to land.'

Moore's eyes lit up. 'He had a motive, then. He'll likely get all the money he needs now his aunt's dead.'

'Yes, I checked on that, too. Her estate is divided equally between the two nephews, and Martin Spencer, the old lady's solicitor, told me that a considerable amount is involved. He couldn't say exactly how much, but he's going to find out as soon as possible.'

'Did he give you any idea of how much it would be?'

'When I pressed him, he said it would probably run into five or even six figures.'

'Wow!' The sergeant was impressed. 'And murders have been committed for a lot less than that.'

'True, but it doesn't automatically follow that Ronald Baker's a murderer because he's in desperate need of capital.'

'No, sir, of course not, but he looks promising.'

McGillivray smiled sadly. 'Number Seven. Stephen Drummond, the other nephew. His grocery shop is in none too healthy a state either, so he's every bit as promising.'

'Oh.' Moore sounded crestfallen.

'He was in worse straits some time ago, but he'd produced £20,000 from somewhere, and cleared himself. He said he inherited it from an old uncle in Canada, but there's no trace of them having any other relatives. The Thornkirk police checked up on that. And Ronald Baker didn't receive any money at the time, which would seem odd.'

A puzzled look appeared on the young sergeant's face. 'But if Stephen Drummond got all that money, and put his shop back on its feet, he wouldn't need to kill his aunt for more, surely?'

The inspector nodded approvingly. 'Unless she was the one who'd given him the two thousand, and was demanding repayment.'

Moore's face cleared. 'That could be it. She could have been badgering him for it, so he killed her.'

McGillivray smiled at his eagerness. 'All supposition, of course, but we'll try to get to the bottom of the mysterious benefactor when we go to Thornkirk tomorrow.'

A light tap on the door made him turn his sheet of suspects face down on the table. 'Come in.'

A youth, about six feet tall, with fair hair standing out in spikes, positioned himself just inside the door. He fiddled with the zip of his leather jacket for a moment, then said, 'Excuse me, Chief Inspector? I'm Douglas Pettigrew.'

No flicker of the surprise he felt showed on McGillivray's face. 'Ah, shut the door, lad, and sit down.'

'No thanks. I heard you'd been asking folk about Miss Souter, so you've likely been told what I said to her the other week.' He looked uncomfortably from one to the other, and, when no response came, he carried on nervously. 'She was a bloody evil woman, and I hated her guts. She found out about May and me . . . Mrs White, I mean.'

'The one who lives down the Lane,' McGillivray said lightly.

'Yes, and I'd been a proper fool over her, she was married and everything, but I thought she'd taken a fancy to me and I fell in love with her. Besotted with her, would be more like it.'

He swallowed, and became so agitated that the inspector took pity on him and said, kindly, 'I think you should sit down, lad, and tell us all about it.'

Douglas took the vacant chair and ran his hand over his hair. 'It's been a total mess. I thought she was serious, but I know now she was only having a bit of fun. At the time, I thought it was great. This experienced woman, and she didn't laugh at me for being . . . So I started staying all night. I went home about five in the morning, and if my Mum noticed my bed hadn't been slept in, I told her I'd been sleeping at my pal's.

'Mum and Dad didn't suspect anything, till that old . . . till Miss Souter told them. She'd seen me going home one morning, and she collared me in the High Street and sneered about May. I was so mad at what she said . . .'

'You told her to mind her own bloody business,' McGillivray finished for him, with a twinkle in his eye.

'You know? I suppose a lot of folk heard me.'

'You also said you'd "get her".' Moore had been looking back his notes to Violet Grant's recollection of the incident.

The boy looked perplexed. 'Get her? No, I told her I'd sort her out, but that was just . . . I wasn't really going to do anything to her, I just wanted to stop her interfering.'

'You didn't plan to finish her off altogether?' The Inspector watched Douglas's face whiten.

'No, honestly. I know it looks bad for me, and I knew about the arsenic, everybody did, but I wouldn't have poisoned her.'

'Not even after she told your father about your nocturnal assignations?'

'No, Inspector.' His eyes met McGillivray's squarely. 'Dad was raging, of course, and told me to stay away from May's house or he'd give me a leathering. Some hopes he had of that. I could have stopped him with one hand tied behind my back. I would have defied him, I meant to, but my mum had a long talk with me later on and made me see I'd been making a proper fool of myself. She said I wasn't the first with May, and I wouldn't be the last.'

McGillivray smiled. 'A sensible woman, your mum. So you got over your infatuation?'

'I was hurt at the time, but I calmed down. I never poisoned Miss Souter. To tell the truth, I began to feel sorry for her. A lonely old maid, getting her kicks from annoying other people.'

'Yes, she did seem to have a way of putting people's backs up.' Callum McGillivray leant his elbows on the table and pursed his lips. In a few seconds, he straightened up. 'Thank you for coming to see me, Mr Pettigrew, and for explaining your situation. Have you any ideas as to who might have killed her?'

Douglas had risen to his feet and looked startled by the question. 'N . . . no. I hadn't even thought about it.'

'No matter. Thank you again.'

When the door closed behind the boy, the inspector turned his sheet of paper over and picked up his pen. 'Back to business, and back to Number Five. Douglas Pettigrew. Denies poisoning victim, but had motive and possible opportunity at any time.'

'Don't you believe him, sir?' The sergeant reddened at the look he received. 'No, of course. Never discount a suspect till he can prove his innocence.'

McGillivray smiled grimly. 'Never forget that, lad. He said he hadn't poisoned her, but as you and I both know now, the old woman wasn't poisoned. He had motive, opportunity, and easy access to insulin and a needle, as you said yourself.'

'So did lots of other people, I'd imagine. You don't honestly think he did it, do you, sir? After all, he came here of his own free will.'

'He could've been ferreting about to see what we'd found out.' The inspector folded his list and placed it in his breast pocket. 'You thought we hadn't many suspects, but there's seven names on my sheet already, and that's six too many.'

David Moore spent the next hour typing a detailed report of all that had transpired since their arrival in Tollerton that morning, while McGillivray made a few telephone calls checking on Stephen Drummond's mysterious windfall, with no success. Then he sat so deep in thought it appeared that he had fallen asleep, but he sat up alertly when the noise of the typewriter stopped.

121

'You know, Moore, if that arsenic hadn't been dragged into it, I'd have gone about this investigation in a different way. I'd have concentrated on finding somebody with easy access to insulin, and enough medical savvy to know the stuff would kill her. Not many people would know that.'

'No, sir. Is there anybody who would fit the bill?'

'The doctor, the chemist and his son are the only three who spring to mind, and I can't think Randall had any cause to do it. The other two – well, Sydney Pettigrew surely wouldn't turn killer because an old woman knew his son was carrying on with a married woman? Douglas, now, is a different matter. His animal instincts were aroused anyway, by May, and, I suppose, in an emotional state like that, he could easily be carried away by the desire to take revenge on Miss Souter for telling his father. But surely not in such a devious way?'

David Moore sat up suddenly. 'Sir, why don't we start asking people if they're diabetic? We'd find out who had insulin, then we could find out if they'd any kind of motive, and tie the case up that way?'

'Because,' McGillivray said, heavily, 'I don't want other people to know about the insulin. As long as we keep making it look as if our enquiries are purely about the arsenic, the murderer's going to think he's got away with it.'

The sergeant couldn't quite understand how that would help, but he nodded intelligently.

The inspector smiled and explained. 'A cornered killer,

or a killer who fears his little trick's been discovered, often turns nasty and kills again. I want to avoid that, if I can. And sometimes a killer tries to make another person look guilty. I'd have said, originally, that the first person who mentioned the arsenic, and tried to point a finger elsewhere, was the person we were after.'

'But that was Mrs Wakeford.'

'Exactly. And the dead woman's nephews would have been the obvious suspects, anyway, even if she hadn't implicated them. God, Moore, my brain's going round and round in ever decreasing circles, like the Hoojah bird, and you know what happened to it.'

The young sergeant chuckled.'It flew up its own . . .'

'Right! Now, if you've finished that report, we'll have time to snatch forty winks before dinner.'

As they stood up to leave, the door burst open and Derek Paul charged in. 'I found it, Inspector.' He held up a smallish plastic bag containing a white, powdery substance.

McGillivray's head had jerked up angrily at the intrusion, but now he beamed with delight. 'Good lad. Where was it?'

'Well, there was a pile of logs in one corner, and I decided I'd better shift them in case the arsenic was underneath somewhere. I was going to pile them into the old barrow that was sitting upside down in another corner, and when I lifted it up, there was the bag. I'm sure it's the arsenic, sir.'

'Yes, it probably is. Thanks, Constable, you've solved one problem anyway, and it didn't take you long.'

Full of pride, Derek Paul left the room and the inspector frowned suddenly. 'Why the bloody hell didn't the Thornkirk lot find this? They were supposed to have searched thoroughly.'

'Sergeant Black handed them what he said was the arsenic,' Moore reminded him. 'It was the analyst's report that showed it to be flour.' He thought it best not to say anything about their own unfruitful search. They had gone through the house and the garden like a dose of salts and hadn't gone into the shed either.

McGillivray's brows lifted. 'It must have been the old she-devil herself, right enough. That's why she was so positive her nephews would be disappointed.'

'She must have had a mind like a corkscrew,' remarked Moore. 'What a thing to do.'

'Somebody else's mind must have been even more twisted, though.' McGillivray lifted the plastic bag off the table. 'I'd better get this sent to Thornkirk to make sure it really is the arsenic, but I'm ready to bet a month's salary that it is. Then we'll maybe get peace to go back to the Starline and catch up on that forty winks before dinner.'

He looked at his watch. 'Damn. Twenty winks is nearer the mark now.'

Chapter Nine

At eight forty Callum McGillivray looked out, with disgust, from the Starline's dining-room window at the sleety rain teeming down outside.

'Bang goes my constitutional,' he remarked, sadly.

'What are we going to do, sir?' David Moore could hardly conceal his relief at not having to walk anywhere in that weather. It would be bad enough going by car.

The inspector rubbed his chin thoughtfully. 'I'd better give Black a ring, in case anything's cropped up since we left.'

He was gone for less than five minutes. 'He says he's picked up a little bit of scandal, but he thinks it could wait till morning, so it can't be anything of earth-shattering importance. I was thinking, though, what would you say to popping into the bar for a while?'

'I'd say that was a good idea, sir.'

'Right! Lead, on Macduff.'

'The name's Moore, sir.'

McGillivray pretended to cuff his sergeant's ear as they made their way through Reception. 'Lead on, Moore? That doesn't have the same impact, does it?'

The young man grinned. 'Sounds better to me.'

The lounge was crowded, so they had to stand up at the bar, which quite pleased the inspector, who knew from past experience that much gossip was exchanged over a pint in small communities. Unfortunately, the conversation centred on the Thornkirk football team, which had been winning all its games that season, and had beaten a Second Division club that very afternoon.

At last, one cheery red-faced man turned round, beer mug in hand, and stared at them accusingly. 'You're the 'tecs here about old Janet Souter's murder.'

'Guilty.' McGillivray smiled broadly, although he was rather disappointed that they'd been recognised, because the men might close ranks now and tell them nothing. On the other hand, some people found it exhilarating to talk about a murder if they weren't actually involved.

'A dirty business, murder,' another man commented.

The inspector nodded. 'It is. Did you know the dead woman at all?' He knew they would expect him to ask.

'Oh, aye.' The first man laughed. 'I'm Ned French, the postie. She was a right old battleaxe, and no mistake, though I never really fell foul of her. She was glad to get letters, likely.

McGillivray turned to the other man. 'Did you know her?'

'Nobody could help knowing her, she made sure o' that, but I delivered her milk. Bill Smith's the name, and many's the ear-bashing I got for being late wi' her pinta.'

'Did you see her every day?'

'Every blessed day, but not on the morning of the day she was found dead. I thought she was having a long lie, maybe feeling her age a bit, so I just carried on. I wish I'd looked in her window now, though. If I'd seen her lying ill in her bedroom I could have got the doctor up. She might still have been alive, and they could have taken her to hospital to have her stomach pumped out, or whatever it is they do for poison nowadays. I feel kind o' guilty for not making sure she was well enough, for she wasn't, was she?'

'You weren't to know,' McGillivray said. 'That's life.'

The postman laughed. 'Not in her case it wasn't.'

'That's not funny, Ned,' snapped the milkman.

'You know fine nobody's sorry she's gone.' Ned French did, however, have the grace to look a little ashamed.

David Moore, who had been keeping one eye open for movement in the seating area, nudged his superior. 'There's a vacant corner now, sir.'

The inspector smiled apologetically to the two men. 'Excuse us, we're going to have a sit-down. My feet are just about killing me. What'll you have? This one's on me.'

Having paid for two pints, he followed Moore to the cushioned bench along the wall and, as he'd expected, the conversation at the bar continued to revolve round the murder. Now he'd maybe find out something.

'I know Janet Souter was an old pest,' the milkman was saying, 'but she shouldna've been bumped off. Nobody deserves that . . . especially poison.'

'She asked for it, Bill.'

'What d'you mean?'

127

Ned French assumed an expression of great wisdom. 'Well, broadcasting about that arsenic she got and putting the idea in somebody's head. Only a damn fool would do that.'

'She was far fae bein' a fool, though; she'd a' her back teeth in, that lady. The idea musta been in his head afore,' the milkman reflected. 'The arsenic was just a means to an end.'

'It must've been one of her nephews. She was worth a good bit, and they likely got sick of waiting for her to kick the bucket.' The postman took a long draught and finished his beer. Licking his lips, he pushed the empty glass towards the barman. 'Same again, Joe. What about you, Bill? Right, a pint for Bill, an' all.'

When the barman laid the brimming glasses down in front of them, Ned clamped his hands round his. 'Makes you think, poison. Maybe Joe here's doctored our beer. Eh, Joe?'

The barman looked outraged. 'For God's sake, Ned, don't act the goat. It's not funny, like Bill said. It could have been anybody. We all knew she'd got arsenic from Davie Livingstone. Could've been you, even. You were at her door often enough wi' letters, you could easily have done it. Or Bill there, when he was delivering her milk.'

'Oh, aye, we're real criminals, Bill and me.' Ned French threw back his head, roaring with laughter. 'There's lots o' folk I'd like to get rid of – the wife, for a start. What about you, Bill?'

The milkman laid down his tankard, looking serious. 'I dinna ken, Ned. It's OK laughing about it, but somebody must've done it.'

'That's right, Bill.' The barman looked solemn. 'Me and Dolly was just speaking about it at teatime. Somebody must've wanted the old woman out of the way desperate, afore he went an' poisoned her. Her nephews, now, they ken't they'd get her money eventually. She was nearly eighty-seven, Dolly says, and she'd have died naturally in a year or two, so there wouldna've been any need for them to do it.'

'Not unless they were needing the cash in a hurry,' the postman agreed.

'They both had their own businesses, I remember her telling me once,' Bill Smith put in. 'So they must've been well enough off, you'd think.'

The two drinkers mulled this over while Joe served another customer farther along the bar. When he returned, he took up his story again.

'As my Dolly was sayin', what about young Douglas Pettigrew? He threatened to sort her out for telling his father about him and May Falconer.'

The postman shook his head. 'No, that was afore she tell't his father. She'd said something nasty to Douglas about May, and that's why he lost his head. Mind you, that lad's got a wicked temper.'

Ned French paused to take a drink, and Callum McGillivray nudged his sergeant. Moore obediently cocked his ears and paid avid attention to the men's conversation.

'You were saying, Ned, about young Pettigrew's temper,' the barman prompted.

'Oh aye. It was a few weeks back, but I saw him putting his hands round Jim Dunne's throat to strangle him.'

'God Almighty! What for?' Joes eyes nearly popped out.

'It turned out they'd been discussing girls, and Jim had said May Falconer was the one to go to if you wanted a lark and a roll in the sack. Douglas turned white and jumped on him. The other lads had to haul him off, and he was shouting, "I'll kill you for that, Jim Dunne" when they dragged him away.'

'Well, I never heard anything about that.' Joe sounded indignant as he leaned his elbows on the counter. 'He comes in here now and then, but I've never once seen him lose his temper. But it just shows you. He *could* have killed the old woman.'

Ned considered, then frowned. 'Poisoning's nae a young person's style. If she'd been strangled, now, I'd say Douglas could be the killer, he's strong enough.'

'Aye, he's a strong laddie.' The milkman nodded, wisely.

'Aye . . . well . . . but she wasna strangled.' Ned drained his glass again, but gestured that he didn't want a refill. 'I'd better get home, or the wife'll be up to high doh.'

As he walked past the two detectives, the postman sketched an exaggerated salute and said, 'Good hunting, Inspector.'

David Moore opened his mouth to say something, but

closed it quickly when McGillivray kicked his ankle. The conversation at the bar was not yet finished.

'I'd never have thought Douglas Pettigrew had a temper like that,' Bill Smith was saying. 'Would you, Joe?'

'It shook me, but like Ned said, he's nae the poisoning type. That's more a woman's game, if you ask me.'

'May Falconer? She's game for anything. Would you believe, she comes to the door on Fridays in her nightie to pay her milk? And nae like my wife wears, buttoned right up to the chin. Nae much left to the imagination about May's. Just flaunting herself.' Bill laughed softly. 'And she's got plenty to flaunt. If I wasna a respectable married man . . .'

'Chance would be a fine thing.' Joe turned away to serve again, but was back in a few moments to carry on with the fascinating topic.

'All May Falconer's ever been interested in,' he said, confidentially, 'even afore she wed Gilbert White, is men, and boys. They tell me young Willie Arthur had to run for his life one night when he was delivering the papers.'

'Ach, you're pulling my leg,' laughed the milkman. 'But she's a proper man-eater.'

'My very words,' whispered McGillivray, taking a sip of his whisky during the slight pause that followed.

Having given due consideration to the possibility of May White being a poisoner, the barman gave his verdict. 'She never gets serious with any of them, though. She only married Gilbert 'cos he'd a good job that took him away most of the time, but she's not a murderer.' He rinsed out a couple of glasses and picked up the drying towel. 'No, they'll have to look in another direction for the killer.'

Bill took a gulp from his tankard, then frowned. 'I just minded. A few days afore Miss Souter was murdered, that Mrs Grant next door to her – the quiet one – was telling me their dog had been poisoned. She was real cut up about it, and said the old woman had admitted doing it. Sneered about it.'

'Mrs Grant would never have killed her, Bill. She wouldn't say boo to a goose.'

'No, nae her,' the milkman said hastily. 'Her sister. That one's the boss. I wouldna put it past her, and having her dog killed could be reason enough. Some folk get really attached to their dogs.'

'True enough.' Joe mopped up a drop of spilt beer. 'Me and Dolly think the world of our Bully. If somebody poisoned him, Bill, I'd feel like killing them, I know that.'

'There you are then.' Bill Smith finished his beer. 'That's what I mean, but if the 'tecs can't figure that out for themselves, it's nae up to me to tell them. God, look at the time. I'd better be off an' all, or my life'll nae be worth livin'.'

He set his glass down on the counter and went out, nodding to the two men sitting on the corner bench as he passed.

The inspector was about to rise and leave, when he realised that Joe was entering into a discussion with another customer. He motioned to his sergeant to sit still, and settled back himself.

'I couldna help hearin' what you and Bill were saying, Joe, and there's another female involved in this, you ken.' The small fat man had moved along and was leaning across the counter. 'Mrs Wakeford, her that stays in Number One of the Cottages.'

'Good God, Harry! She's a real lady. You surely canna think she'd anything to do with this?'

'I'm only going by what the wife told me a week or so back.' Harry looked hurt. 'Old Janet Souter had been spreading muck about Mrs Wakeford – that she shouldna be so stuck up when her mother was never married. When my Nora heard about it, she went and asked old Mrs Gray, at the foot of the Lane, if it was true. She must be about ninety, but she said it was right enough. Mrs Wakeford *had* been born on the wrong side of the blanket, and her mother had been single till the day she died. She said it was just like Janet Souter to dig that up after over sixty years, and likely it was just Janet Souter an' her that would've remembered about it.'

Joe poured himself a small whisky. 'I never heard about it afore, any road, but Mrs Wakeford surely wouldna have poisoned the old woman just for that?'

Harry smirked. 'But that wasna all. Mrs Gray tell't my Nora another spicy bit. Apparently, Mrs Wakeford had a bairn hersel', long afore she married the Major.'

This rendered Joe speechless, and he waited, with eager eyes, for Harry to continue.

'She'd have been about sixteen or seventeen at the time, and she was sent away for a few months. Her mother put it about that she'd got a job in Aberdeen some place, but a rumour went round that she was expecting. You ken what women are like, they can twist things any way they want. Mair than likely there wasna a grain o' truth in it.'

The barman nodded, never taking his eyes off the other man.

'Wherever she'd been, she came back empty handed, so the rumour petered out and was forgotten.'

'Except by old Mrs Gray.'

'Well, she said she wouldna've minded onything about it, either, if my Nora hadna jogged her memory. But she was sure there had been a bairn, and it musta been adopted, or died even. Now, if that was true, Mrs Wakeford could have got the wind up in case Janet Souter would rake it up next, and had made sure the old woman would never get the chance.' Harry swigged his beer down as if his mouth was parched from all his talking, then placed the empty glass on the counter and looked up hopefully.

Joe slipped him a free drink. 'You get your eyes opened, sometimes, and that's a fact. I'd never have thought that about Mrs Wakeford. I'd have said butter wouldna melt in her mouth, but you never ken, do you? An' what if Janet Souter *had* spewed out to the poor woman that she kent about her murky past? It's just the kinda evil thing that old bitch would've done. That would give Mabel the perfect reason for shutting her up . . .' He stopped, scowling. 'But I canna believe she'd have . . . No, no, we may as well forget that.'

Shaking his head at what Harry had been saying, Joe moved along to serve another customer. 'Yes, sir?'

Harry, realising that the interesting discussion had been terminated, was drawn by a heated argument that had burst into life about the day's football results, and took his pint glass across to where the protagonists were already waving their fists.

McGillivray let out a low whistle. 'My God, Moore, I didn't expect anything like that when I came in. Talk about a bonus. It makes you think, eh? There's a lot more to our Mrs Wakeford than meets the eye.'

'Oh, but sir, I'm absolutely positive she wouldn't have been capable of murder. Anyway, having an illegitimate child is nothing nowadays.'

'I'm inclined to agree with you, lad, but I am in urgent need of some shut-eye. It's going to take me a long time to recover from getting up at three o'clock this morning to make the never-ending journey to this godforsaken part of Bonnie Scotland.'

Moore nodded. 'Aye, I feel a bit under the weather myself. My eyes are stinging with cigarette smoke as well as lack of sleep.'

'Right then, we may as well toddle upstairs, and, since tomorrow's Sunday, I'd say a nine o'clock breakfast would be early enough, eh? Mind you, a twelve o'clock brunch would suit me better, but . . . we must show willing.

Chapter Ten

After breakfast, the two detectives walked along to the police station. The sleet had stopped overnight, but the pavements were still wet, and the wind still howled.

Callum McGillivray turned up his coat collar. 'A lazy wind,' he growled.

David Moore looked puzzled. 'Lazy? What d'you mean?'

'Too lazy to go round you, so it goes right through you.'

Moore groaned.

John Black followed them into the incident room in a mild state of excitement. 'I found out last night that Janet Souter had been sneering to people about Mrs Wakeford being illegitimate. Mrs Macdonald came up to me and told me, so if she knew, it had likely got back to the lady herself. Would that be sufficient reason for her to . . . ?' He looked extremely uncomfortable about saying it, but it was his duty to pass on all information relevant to the case; and he had never been one to shirk his duty.

'I wouldn't think so, Black, but I've been finding things

136

out too.' McGillivray placed his hands together. 'Not only was Mabel Wakeford born on the wrong side of the blanket, she'd been sampling forbidden fruit herself before she was married, and had been left in the family way by all accounts.'

The local sergeant was astounded. 'Oh, no. There's never been a breath of scandal about her before, not as long as I've been here, and that's coming on for twenty-five years. Who told you that?'

'We did a bit of eavesdropping in the hotel bar last night,' the inspector admitted, 'and apparently the information came from a lady at the foot of Ashgrove Lane. She's about ninety, I believe.'

'Ah, yes, old Mrs Gray. She used to be quite a character about the place till she was housebound. Arthritis, I think. And she dug all this up, did she? I wouldn't have thought she was one for that kind of thing.'

Callum McGillivray smiled. 'It was pulled out of her, it seems, by someone harvesting the seeds Janet Souter had sown. Now, *that* secret, if it's true, is something that Mrs Wakeford would have wanted to suppress. But would she have had the ability to procure insulin and a hypodermic needle? That's what we'll have to try to find out.'

Moore butted in. 'And she was the first person to mention the arsenic, remember, and you said that might have been done to confuse the issue.'

The inspector nodded absent-mindedly. He was savouring the thought of giving John Black another surprise. 'We picked up another titbit, though. Did you know that Douglas Pettigrew almost strangled somebody on the street a while back?'

Black looked suitably shaken. 'No, I hadn't heard that. But why on earth would he want to strangle anybody?'

'He'd been having an argument with another youth, over Mrs Gilbert White.'

'And of course you knew that she's our local seductress. Well, your sojourn in the bar certainly paid dividends.'

'It was quite profitable, and it shows that the young man in question would be capable of losing his temper to such an extent as to render him murderous. We also know he could have obtained a syringe and insulin from his father's shop.'

'That's true,' Black said sadly. 'You'd better have another word with him, Inspector.'

'I fully intend to. In fact. I think I should see him before I do anything else. Does he live near here?'

'Across the street, above the chemist's.'

'Where else?' McGillivray groaned.

'He works in the garage at the end of the High Street every second Sunday, though. He takes turns with the time-served mechanic.' Black screwed up his face in thought. 'I think this is his week on. Yes, he wasn't there last Sunday when I went in for petrol.'

'That's at the other end of the street from Honeysuckle Cottages, I presume? Right, Moore, we'll stretch our legs and walk along there first, then we'll come back and pick up the car to go to Thornkirk to see the two nephews.'

The owner of the garage was obliging enough to let

them use his small office to talk to his young apprentice, who came in looking rather apprehensive.

'Mr Dow says you want to see me?'

'That's right. There's a little matter we'd like to clear up.' The inspector turned to his sergeant. 'Moore, read out what you wrote in your notes last night.'

David Moore had recorded, after they'd gone upstairs, as much as he'd remembered of the conversations they'd overheard in the lounge bar, and while he read out the few lines pertaining to the quarrel, the eighteen-year-old's face grew redder and redder as his lack of control was recalled to him.

'Now then, Mr Pettigrew,' McGillivray said severely, emphasising the Mister as though the boy didn't really deserve the title, 'would that be an accurate account of the incident?'

'Er . . . yes . . . I suppose so.' Douglas was obviously embarrassed. 'I just went wild when Jim Dunne said that about May – Mrs White. I told you before, I was besotted with her at the time, and I just lashed out.'

The inspector held up his hand. 'Oh no, Mister Petti-grew, you didn't just lash out. That would have been the normal reaction, I agree, but you attempted to strangle this other lad. Not the usual method of showing displea-sure, if I may say.'

'I don't know what came over me, honest I don't. I've never done anything like that before, or since.'

'Are you absolutely sure of that?'

'Of course I'm sure.' Douglas was beginning to sound

139

slightly rattled. 'I only wanted to stop him saying anything else about May and I went for his throat.'

'Quite.' McGillivray's eyes bored into the young man's. 'And Miss Souter had also said some terrible things about your paramour. Are you sure you didn't end up trying to kill her, too, striking it lucky this time?' If he had hoped to goad the boy into admitting that he had, he was disappointed.

'I did feel like killing her,' Douglas said, honestly. 'But only for a few minutes. I'd never have done anything to hurt her, really, the same as I wouldn't really have strangled Jim Dunne. I only wanted to frighten him.'

'Which I've no doubt you succeeded in doing.' McGillivray leaned back in the rickety chair with his hands together.

After squirming uncomfortably for a few moments, Douglas said, 'If you're finished with me, I'd better get back to work. I know it's no excuse, but I was ashamed of what I did to Jim Dunne. I realised, afterwards, he was only speaking the truth, and I should have been grateful. I apologised to him the next day, you know, and we're still good pals.'

Callum McGillivray smiled. 'Good. I'm sorry we had to ask about it, but when we hear of somebody with a short fuse, we naturally have to investigate.'

'I suppose so. Is that all?'

'Did you ever have any medical or pharmaceutical training yourself, lad? Your father must have wanted you to learn the business?' The inspector looked searchingly at the boy.

'Who, me?' Douglas laughed derisively. 'I was a big round zero at school, and I left as soon as I was sixteen. My dad was a bit disappointed, but I always wanted to be a mechanic, so when George Dow offered me an apprenticeship, Dad didn't stop me.'

McGillivray changed his tactics. 'Can you account for your movements during last Wednesday night?'

'Eh?' The youth's expression showed no fear. 'I thought it was Thursday the old woman was poisoned. Or was it done the night before?'

'Just answer the question, please.'

'You surely don't suspect me of . . . ?' He stopped when he saw the stern expression on the inspector's face. 'OK. Wednesday? I was playing snooker in the church hall. They've got a table in the back for the Youth Club.'

'Can you prove that?'

Douglas raised his eyes to the roof, then sighed. 'Four of us were playing in pairs, and they'll all tell you I was there. Do you want their names, the other three?'

The inspector nodded. 'And their addresses, if you don't mind. We'll have to verify your statement. My sergeant will make a note of them.'

'OK.' Douglas said again. 'Well, Jim Dunne was one. You know, the one I nearly strangled a few weeks ago, according to you.' He gave a lopsided grin and reeled off the rest of the details, while Moore valiantly scribbled them down.

McGillivray gave a tight smile. 'Thank you. I think that will be all for now.'

The boy looked very relieved, and he shot out of the poky office as if someone had attached a lit firework to the backside of his trousers.

'Do you want me to check up on his alibi now?' Moore asked as they went out.

'No, we'd better go to Thornkirk first. You can do it when we get back. Hello, here's Black. What's he looking so upset about, I wonder?'

'Thank goodness I caught you,' the local sergeant said as soon as he opened his car door. 'There's been an attempt on Mrs Grant's life. Apparently, she'd been in agony since very early this morning with stomach pains, but she wouldn't let her sister call the doctor until about half past six. Randall thought it was food poisoning, and had her rushed to Thornkirk Hospital. They've just phoned to tell me they found traces of arsenic in the sample they tested after they made her sick. Her sister's there with her now.'

'Back to the Starline!' McGillivray wished that they hadn't come to the garage on foot. 'I'd meant to see the nephews next, but this takes priority.'

The local sergeant having given them a lift back to the Starline, it took less than five minutes for the two detectives to settle into the Vauxhall and head off, Moore tearing along the road to Thornkirk as if testing how fast the old car could actually go, and not one word of caution from his superior on keeping to the speed limit. The DCI had other things on his mind.

'Damn and blast!' McGillivray thumped his left hand with his right fist. 'I was afraid something like this would happen.'

'Has Mrs Skinner tried to silence her sister, do you think?' David Moore sounded his horn and passed a small Fiat doing fifty.

'I never jump to conclusions, but it seems more than likely. Mrs Grant was dangerously near breaking point, poor lady.'

Little else was said on the twenty-mile journey. The sergeant had to concentrate on driving at high speed, and the inspector was in a cold sweat at several near misses. When they arrived at the hospital, he asked to be dropped at the main door before Moore parked the car, and hurried to the information desk. 'Mrs Violet Grant?'

The receptionist checked and said, 'Still in Emergency, and she's not being allowed any visitors meantime.'

McGillivray was halfway along the corridor. 'Police,' he called over his shoulder.

Grace Skinner was sitting on a bench in the waiting area, whitefaced and dabbing her eyes, and she looked up mournfully when the inspector approached her.

'How is she, Mrs Skinner?'

'They didn't have to pump out her stomach, and she seems to be a little better, but there was arsenic in the test they made of her vomit.'

McGillivray looked uneasy. 'I have to ask you some questions, I'm afraid. Do you feel up to it just now, or would you rather wait until you're home?'

143

'I'd like to get it over as quickly as possible, if you don't mind.' She gave her eyes a quick scrub with her damp handkerchief and turned towards him.

He held up his hands. 'Just a minute, please. I'll find out if there's anywhere more private we can talk, somewhere out of the traffic.' He dodged a porter with a trolley and knocked on a door marked 'Private', where the sister told him he could use her office.

He showed Grace in. When they were seated, he took out a notebook and said, 'You haven't been affected at all?'

The woman's erect back gave way, and she slumped in the chair. Her coat was buttoned squint, her hair hadn't been combed, in complete contrast to her normal spruce appearance.

'I'm sorry, Mrs Skinner. Perhaps we'd better wait until you get over this.'

She sat up a little. 'I want to find out who did it as much as you do, Inspector, and no, I was not affected. I wish it *had* been me – I've a much stronger constitution than Violet.' She gulped and blinked her eyes. 'We often eat different things, she has a sweeter tooth than me, and I was trying to think, out there, what we did eat last night.'

'That was very sensible of you.'

'I remember I had cheese and biscuits afterwards, but . . . wait. Violet had made a steak and kidney pudding. That's right. Enough for two days, because we prefer not to have to cook on Sundays. We usually have our main

144

meal at half past six, and just have a snack at lunchtime, an apple, or a cup of soup, or something like that.'

'Did you have anything along with the steak and kidney pudding last night? Something that your sister took and you didn't?'

Grace Skinner thought for a moment. 'It's dreadful to have such a bad memory, but I can't seem to recall . . . Cabbage! Cabbage and boiled potatoes. Both of us had that.'

'Any sweet?'

'No, I stopped her making desserts. I felt I was putting on a bit of weight.'

McGillivray eyed the scraggy woman and wondered what had given her that idea.

'As I told you, I'd crackers and cheese with my coffee. Violet had . . . oh, yes, two of the pancakes she'd made earlier, spread with a little butter and some raspberry jam. Thickly spread, I might add, because I warned her it was very fattening. She didn't care, though.'

It crossed the inspector's mind that food must be the one area where Violet Grant had taken her own way. 'So the pancakes and jam were the only things she ate that you didn't?'

'As far as I remember, yes, and I'm almost sure.'

'Excuse me again, Mrs Skinner.'

He returned to the room in a very short time. 'I meant to get my sergeant to phone Sergeant Black to have the pancakes and jam collected from your house for analysis, but he reminded me that your door would be locked.'

She shook her head wearily. 'You know, inspector, I don't believe it is. I was in such a state when we left.' She felt her coat pockets. 'No, the key must still be in the inside of the door. I haven't even got my handbag with me.'

Having passed this information on to Moore, McGillivray seated himself again. 'There was nothing else your sister may have eaten, that you can think of?'

She shook her head. 'No, I'm sure she'd nothing else. We both had a cup of cocoa before we went to bed, which Violet made herself, but nothing to eat, and it was about half past two when she first complained about the pains.'

'Now we come to the most unpleasant bit.' The inspector stopped to call 'Come in' in answer to a tap at the door, and a young nurse carried in a tray.

'Excuse me, but Sister thought you might like a cup of tea.' She set her burden down on a small table.

'Thank you, Nurse, and thank Sister, too.' He offered the distraught woman sugar and milk, both of which she refused.

She took a sip of the piping hot black liquid. 'Oh, I was needing that. A cup of tea is really the only thing that can revive you. Now, you were saying, Inspector?'

'I was going to ask who'd been visiting your house over the past week or so?'

'We don't have many visitors. My daughter and her family live in Cornwall, and they only come once a year. They've three small children, so they usually bring their caravan with them, because we don't have enough room for all five of thm.'

'That would be the caravan that Miss Souter complained about?'

'That's right. Violet has no children, and we've no other relatives left alive, and no really close friends. It's enough that we've got each other. Mrs Valentine, the minister's wife, sometimes calls, though she hasn't been since just before the Sale of Work, and the minister pays a visit occsionally . . . and I nearly forgot, Mrs Wakeford popped in yesterday morning to see if you'd asked us the same questions as you'd asked her.'

McGillivray allowed no sign of his elation at this to show on his face. 'Mrs Wakeford, eh? How does she pop in?'

'She generally comes to the front door, but this time she came in through the kitchen. She'd come over the gardens, I suppose, since Janet Souter wasn't there to complain.'

'Where were you and your sister when Mrs Wakeford came in?'

'We were both in the living room. I was hoovering and Violet was dusting. We got quite a fright when Mabel opened the door.'

'Ah.' The inspector scribbled something down, hoping he'd be able to read it later, then underlined a few words twice before laying down his ballpoint.

The change in Grace Skinner's expression told him that she had just realised where all the questions were leading.

'Oh, you don't think that Mabel . . . ? Oh, no. I've known her ever since I came to Tollerton, nearly thirty years ago. I've been a widow for a very long time, and when Violet's husband died, eleven years ago, she moved in with me. We both love the village and our little cottage. No, no, no. It couldn't have been Mabel that tried to poison poor Violet.'

McGillivray closed his notebook and drummed his fingers on its hard cover. 'I'm sorry, Mrs Skinner, but by your own evidence Mrs Wakeford is the only person who had been in your house lately, apart from your sister and yourself.'

The agitated woman was still shaking her head at this, when the door opened and a smallish man in a white coat came in, his round face smiling benevolently. 'I'm Doctor Fields, Mrs Skinner, and I'm pleased to tell you that your sister's recovering nicely. In fact, you may go and see her for a few minutes.'

'Thank God!' Grace hurried out.

Fields looked at McGillivray. 'She was never in any real danger, though she's not very strong anyway. After we gave her an emetic and she got everything up, she soon rallied round.

'It was arsenic, I believe?'

'Just the faintest trace. She was lucky.'

'You don't know how lucky.' McGillivray looked grave. 'It was meant to kill her.'

'Oh.' The doctor seemed rather taken aback. 'I thought she'd been careless with some sort of . . . weedkiller, or something like that. Well, if somebody did try to poison her, they didn't use enough to do much damage, but it's your problem now.'

'Yes,' McGillivray said ruefully as he stood up. 'Thank you very much, Doctor.'

The two men left the room together, and met Grace Skinner coming out of the emergency ward looking very relieved.

'Violet says she feels much better now. Thank you, Doctor, and all your staff.'

'It's what we're here for.' Doctor Fields smiled and walked away.

The inspector's brain was in top gear. Was this woman really innocent, or was she the one who had tried to kill Violet Grant? She'd seemed so worried and was looking much happier now, but was it all genuine? Or was Mabel Wakeford the guilty party? Had she believed that Mrs Grant knew of her past secrets from Janet Souter, and made this attempt to silence her, too?

But both these women were unlikely killers, and how could either of them have obtained the arsenic? Unless . . . had one of them helped herself to a little from Miss Souter's shed before the old lady swapped it for flour?

'May we give you a lift home, Mrs Skinner?' He had just remembered that she had come to the hospital in the ambulance with her sister.

'No, thank you. I want to be here at visiting time. They're keeping her in until tomorrow, for observation.'

'It's probably better.'

149

'I'll have to find out where the ladies' room is. I've just realised I must look a frightful mess.'

'Have you any money, Mrs Skinner? You said you forgot to take your handbag with you.'

'Oh, dear, that's right. Could you please lend me enough for my bus fare home? What a terrible predicament to be in.'

'It's quite understandable.' McGillivray had taken a few crumpled notes from his hip pocket and held out two grubby ten pound notes. 'You'd better have this. You'll need something to eat, and things to take in to your sister.'

'You're very considerate, Inspector. I'll pay you back as soon as I can.' She folded the notes more carefully and placed them in her pocket before she went down the corridor.

McGillivray walked back to the waiting area, where his sergeant had been sitting patiently. 'Come on, you can't sit there all day.'

'No, sir. Which of the two nephews do you want to . . . ?'

'Good God! This damned business made me forget what we were supposed to be doing in Thornkirk, and it's not often I'm put out of my stride. Right, Ronald Baker first.'

As they pulled up outside 36 Newton Avenue, a smart modern villa on the outskirts of the town, David Moore noticed the net curtains move a fraction, and the door was opened almost immediately after he rang the bell.

The stout, middle-aged woman looked at them questioningly. 'Yes?' Her voice was breathless.

'Mrs Ronald Baker? I'm Detective Chief Inspector McGillivray and this is Detective Sergeant Moore. We are investigating the murder of Miss Janet Souter. Your husband's aunt, I believe?'

'Murder? Oh, God!' Flora's hands, and eyes, fluttered madly, but she led them into a large airy room, with picture windows along one wall, and a feeling about it of not being in regular use, although it was comfortably warm.

'Sit down. I'll get Ronald.'

Her fluffy slippers sank into the deep shaggy pile of the biege carpet, and, a moment later, she returned with a tall man, greying at the temples, who motioned smilingly to them to remain seated.

'Flora tells me Aunt Janet was murdered?' Ronald sounded suitably awestruck. 'We were very upset about her death when we thought it was just heart failure, but this is a real shocker. Are you anywhere near finding out who did it?'

'We're making progress, Mr Baker.' Callum McGillivray wished that he was as confident as he was making out. 'We have a number of suspects, but we're trying to narrow the field.'

'I take it I'm a suspect?' There was an edge to Ronald's voice. 'The next of kin usually are, aren't they? Especially when they expect to inherit a large sum of money. But I can assure you that I did not poison my aunt.'

The inspector decided that the 'real shocker' hadn't been severe enough to make the man lose his composure, and noted that he had already mentioned poison. 'We have to investigate every avenue, Mr Baker. You obviously knew about the arsenic your aunt kept in her garden shed?'

Flora's hands clenched convulsively at this, and Moore made up his mind to watch her closely.

'Er . . . yes, we did.' Ronald was hesitant at first. 'She told us she'd been given some, and when Flora said it could kill her if she wasn't careful, she said that should please me.'

'That was a nasty thing to say, wasn't it?'

'She *was* nasty, and mean, and spiteful.' Ronald sounded very bitter, and McGillivray was surprised by his vehemence.

'Ronald, you shouldn't be saying things like that to the inspector.' Flora was nervous and worried. 'He'll think you wanted to kill her yourself.'

Her husband laughed. 'Rubbish! I'm just telling him the truth. That's what you want, isn't it?' He smiled disarmingly at McGillivray, who felt the cheerfulness was much too forced.

'That's right, sir. We're trying to get at the truth. Now, we've been led to believe your engineering business is in some financial difficulty at present. Would that be the case?'

Observing Flora, Moore saw that she had become even more nervous and jumpy, and was twisting her wedding ring round and round her finger, her eyes resting anxiously on her husband.

'I don't know where you got your information, Inspector, but you're almost right. Things have been a bit sticky for a time, but there's no great problem.' Ronald's rigid back showed that he was not entirely at ease, and his fingers kept pulling at his cashmere sweater.

'I was told that you urgently required some capital to fulfil a contract you were negotiating.'

'There was no immediate urgency.' The man slackened his tie. 'I asked my aunt and she refused to lend it to me, but I could have found it from somewhere, I'm sure. I won't have to, now, of course, because Aunt Janet's money will be divided equally between my cousin and myself.'

Callum McGillivray eyed him quizically. 'Her death was extremely well timed, then, wouldn't you say, sir?'

'Look here! That's as good as saying I killed her.' Ronald was belligerent now.

'I merely passed a remark, Mr Baker, I'm not suggesting anything. You must admit, though, the facts could be interpreted as pointing your way.'

'Oh, Ronald.' Flora stood up in great agitation. 'I told you they . . .'

'Be quiet, Flora! There's absolutely no evidence that I could be guilty, as you very well know, Inspector. My wife and I had not been to see my aunt since the Saturday before she died, fully five days, so you see I couldn't have poisoned her.'

Flora, quite oblivious to the sergeant's scrutiny, had reseated herself on the edge of her chair, consternation and apprehension oozing from every pore of her worried face.

'As long as that, eh?' mused McGillivray, extricating himself from the deep confines of the upholstered cushions on which he'd been ensconced. 'Well, we won't bother you any more, meantime, Mr Baker, although we may have to talk to you again.'

It was a rather subdued Ronald who showed them out.

'Interesting. Very interesting,' the inspector remarked, as he settled himself in the Vauxhall. 'He seemed so sure of himself, but he was really as nervous as hell, and the wife's on absolute tenterhooks.'

'Yes, sir. Her nervousness was more than normal under the circumstances, I'd say.' Moore indicated to turn right at the crossroads and swung round smoothly.

The house at 147 Kingswood Drive turned out to be an old terraced one in the centre of Thornkirk, and Stephen Drummond himself answered the door. Facially, he quite resembled his cousin, but there the likeness ended. His hair was completely grey, and his stretched jersey hung loosely on him, as though it were several sizes too big.

When McGillivray introduced himself and his sergeant, they were taken into a small, cluttered room, where the high narrow window was darkened by the houses at the other side of the street, and even the bright-orange scatter cushions on the worn three-piece suite failed to brighten the dinginess.

'Sit down, Inspector,' Stephen murmured, 'and I'll fetch my wife.'

'No need, Mr Drummond. It's you we want to talk to.'

Ignoring this, Stephen opened the door and shouted, as if appealing for a lifeline, 'Barbara, it's two detectives.'

Almost at once, his wife came in, her hair drawn back in an untidy chignon, a purple sweater over trousers of the same garish colour. She sat down on a high seat beside her husband's armchair.

Moral support, thought McGillivray, who had correctly sized up the situation as the dominant wife syndrome. 'We are investigating the murder of Janet Souter, Mr Drummond. When did you last see your aunt?'

'On the Sunday before she died, four days before.' It was Barbara Drummond who answered, because Stephen appeared to have been struck dumb at the mention of murder. 'She was murdered, was she? How awful.'

McGillivray nodded. 'I've been told that you and your cousin visited her every weekend, Mr Drummond.' He said the man's name pointedly, and was gratified to see the woman bridle at the rebuff.

'Ronald and Flora went every Saturday, and we went on Sundays.' Stephen spoke nervously, and his wife laid her hand on his shoulder reassuringly.

'If you're trying to suggest that we had anything to do with it, neither Stephen nor I poisoned her,' she said bluntly.

'Then you knew about the bag of arsenic she had, Mr Drummond?'

'Y-yes, I did know. She didn't make any secret of it. Just asking for trouble, I thought.' Stephen shifted his legs, no sign of a crease in his shapeless flannels.

The thought that Aunt Janet's arsenic could kill her had crossed his mind, McGillivray was glad to hear. 'We have been exploring various avenues, and we found that your shop had been on the verge of bankruptcy about a year or so back.'

'Yes. Yes, it was, but I was lucky enough to receive a small inheritance from an uncle who died in Canada about that time.' Stephen's knuckles showed white against the dark cover of his chair, and he swallowed repeatedly.

The inspector's smile was deceptive. 'Was he a brother of your mother's, this uncle in Canada?'

Stephen looked miserable. 'Yes,' he whispered.

Barbara removed her hand from his shoulder. 'No, he wasn't. There were only three sisters in that family. Stephen's mother, Ronald Baker's mother, and Janet Souter. The uncle in Canada was his father's brother. You'll have to excuse my husband, Inspector. Finding out that his aunt was murdered has really upset him.'

'I'm sorry.' Stephen's apology was made in a low, flat voice. 'I *am* very shocked, and yes, he was my father's brother.' His eyes slid away suddenly.

'That's quite all right, Mr Drummond. Shock plays funny tricks on the best of us.' McGillivray soothed the man, while Moore marvelled at his superior's duplicity. 'So your father's brother left you some money? How much was it, exactly?'

'It was twenty thousand pounds. Enough to see me over my difficulties.'

'Very fortunate, I would say, and just at the right time, but we can find no trace of this uncle, be he your father's brother or your mother's brother.' The inspector decided to bluff a little. 'In fact, this uncle didn't exist, did he, Mr Drummond?'

'Oh, here!' Barbara cut in quickly. 'I think you're overstepping your authority, badgering my husband like this.'

'It's no use, Barbara,' Stephen patted her knee. 'I couldn't brazen it out, anyway. You're quite correct, Inspector, that was a lie. Aunt Janet lent me the money after I practically went down on my bended knees to her. She was a hard woman, with no compassion in her soul.' He took out his handkerchief and wiped his brow.

'Stephen! Watch what you're saying.' Barbara was alarmed by his look of hopelessness.

He shook his head. 'It doesn't matter any more. Aunt Janet was charging me twenty-five per cent interest on that money, Inspector, which meant I'd be paying nearly double the amount I'd borrowed, by the time I'd finished.'

'That was a bit over the top.'

'I offered her ten pounds the last time we were down, but she said it wasn't enough and laughed in my face. I couldn't repay her and I didn't know what to do.' Stephen buried his face in his hands.

Barbara shook her head in sympathy. 'Don't worry,

dear. It's all over now. She's dead, and you won't have to worry about money any more.' She turned to the Chief Inspector. 'My husband was at a very low ebb, as you can see, but he didn't poison his aunt. We weren't even there at the time.'

'No, Mrs Drummond,' McGillivray agreed, seriously, 'you weren't even there. Come on, Moore. It's time we left.'

They saw themselves out, and the younger man could scarcely contain himself until they were once again in their car. 'You came away just when he was ready to confess that he'd done it,' he accused.

'I don't think he did do it, lad. In fact, I'm nearly certain he'd nothing to do with his aunt's death. He may have thought about poisoning her, but that's not what we're after.'

'Maybe *he* didn't kill her, but I'm sure Mrs Drummond knows something about it.'

'I'm going to let it simmer for a while, Moore. We've turned on the heat, and the Stephen Drummonds and the Ronald Bakers will just have to stew a bit longer. Whatever the truth is, it'll come out eventually, once they're worked up enough.'

'Yes, I suppose so. I was thinking, though, it's peculiar, but several of the suspects have been on the verge of admitting something when you've upped and left them.'

'You've noticed that, have you?' McGillivray laughed. '*There's* a clever young detective sergeant.'

'Don't be sarcastic, sir. But Mrs Wakeford was first.

She'd have told you something else, if you'd carried on questioning her, and Mrs Grant said Douglas Pettigrew wasn't the murderer, as if she knew who was.'

Moore snatched a quick glance at his boss, who was smiling and nodding. Encouraged, he went on, 'Mrs Ronald Baker – her husband had to stop her before she came out with something he didn't want her to say, and, lastly, Stephen Drummond practically admitted to the murder, and you didn't pursue it.'

'Quite right, lad. I don't understand why, but, as you say, all those people have almost admitted to poisoning the old lady, or to knowing something about it.'

'One of them must have killed her, though.'

'You reckon? The really peculiar thing is that they all mentioned the confounded arsenic, yet there was no sign of it in her, nor in any of her foodstuffs. Unfortunately, poor Mrs Grant *did* have a trace of it, but whether her attempted murder was connected with Janet Souter's death, or was a different crime altogether, I can't tell yet. So the insulin side will have to wait till I unravel the arsenic business first.'

David Moore fished for his seat belt and buckled it on. 'Back to Tollerton now, sir?'

'After a bit of lunch, I think. I'm quite peckish.'

They found a Chinese restaurant on their way out of the town, and it was wearing on for three o'clock when they started their return journey.

'Quite an interesting morning, wouldn't you say?' The inspector's face wore a satisfied look as he leaned back.

159

'Every one of them was nervous and worried, though.'
Moore crashed the gears and winced. 'Makes you wonder
if any of them's guilty, or if they acted like that because
we're detectives. I suppose it must be quite daunting,
really, to speak to a 'tec for the first time.'

'That's a reaction you should've got used to by now,
lad. Most folk seem to go on the defensive, whether
they've anything to hide or not. It's human nature, I
suppose, but you begin to be able to tell the innocent from
the guilty after a while. Not that I'm having much success
with that at the moment.'

McGillivray reflected sadly that trying to solve a murder
was like throwing a stone into a millpond. The ripples
spread out in ever-widening circles. There was this ille-
gitmate child of Mrs Wakeford's, if that story was true.
He, or she, probably had nothing to do with this case, but
would have to be sought out and involved, just to be sure.
If the person concerned lived in Tollerton, and Miss
Souter had found out . . .

He'd have to visit this ninety-year-old and find out if she
knew anything more about it. Old people could often
recall events from their younger days much more clearly
than happenings over the past few years, or even what
they'd eaten for lunch.

The child would be over forty now, but whether male or
female was yet to be established, and he could think of no
one connected with the case so far who would fit as far as
age was concerned. Except . . . Barbara Drummond, he
realised with a start. But perhaps she was older than that, it

was difficult to tell. The same with May White, of course. She could be anywhere between thirty and forty-five; depending on what she wore and how she was made up.

His thoughts were interrupted when Moore braked suddenly as a tractor emerged from behind a thick hedge straight in front of them.

'Silly bugger!' the sergeant shouted, pulling out to overtake and narrowly missing a lorry travelling in the opposite direction.

'Keep your head, lad.' McGillivray smiled crookedly. 'A dead detective never solved a murder.'

The younger man's outraged face turned a deeper shade of red. 'It's all right for you, you haven't a nervous bone in your body, but I thought we'd had it.'

His superior shook his head. 'You'll get used to scares when you've been a bit longer on the job. But cheer up, lad, I've been lumbered with a lot worse than you in my time. Now, just keep your mind on the road and always expect the unexpected.'

Chapter Eleven

Sunday 27th November, afternoon

There was no sign of John Black when the two detectives entered the police station, but PC Derek Paul uncurled smartly when they walked in.

'The sergeant won't be long, Inspector. He's gone to sort out an accident just south of the village, but it's not serious.'

McGillivray smiled. 'Thank you, Constable. Tell him we'll come back later.'

Outside again, he turned to Moore. 'Stick the car in the Starline carpark then go and check with Douglas Pettigrew's pals about his alibi. I'm going to have a word with that old Mrs Gray at the foot of Ashgrove Lane, to see if she can tell me any more about Mabel Wakeford's past. I'll see you back at the station, or, if you take too long, I might be at the hotel giving my feet a rest after my hike.'

David Moore went into the car, and the inspector carried on walking up the High Street. He hoped that the old woman he was on his way to see could tell him where the child had been born, or have a guess at it. He must find a starting point, and his enquiries must be discreet.

When he arrived at the foot of the Lane, he looked at the name on the first door he came to, and was delighted to find that it was the one he was after. Right next door to the slinky May.

He noticed that the woodwork on the outside of this house needed a coat of paint – bits of it were cracking and flaking off – and the terylene net curtains, once white or cream, were a shade of dark grey, just screaming for a wash.

He rang the bell, waited, then rang again. After a while, he heard slow, shuffling footsteps, and the sound of the latch being taken off. 'Mrs Gray? I'm Detective Chief Inspector McGillivray, Grampian Police. Could I have a few words with you, please?'

The hunched figure studied him for a moment. Her sparse white hair was cut straight across and owed nothing to any hairdresser's art. The gnarled hand on top of the walking stick was blue veined and marked with brown pigmentation, but her eyes were alert behind the thick glasses.

'I suppose you'd better come in, then, and not have the whole street listening to what we're saying.' She preceded him, with an effort, into her living room and gestured to him to sit down.

Pushing an enormous, unwilling black cat off the in-dicated chair, McGillivray waited until Mrs Gray had lowered herself slowly onto her seat and hung her stick over the arm.

163

She pulled down her voluminous skirt and looked at him shrewdly. 'It'll be about that Janet Souter getting herself murdered, I suppose.' One side of her mouth curled up. 'Mind you, I wasn't surprised about it. She'd aye to go one better than other folk, even when she was young.' She moved herself into a more comfortable position.

McGillivray thought the old woman must be joking, but she seemed quite serious, and carried on.

'She was the oldest of that family, but she was aye a bit spoiled. She was the only one of the three of them that went to the Academy at Thornkirk, and it was just because she kicked up a fuss about it. Her father spoiled her rotten, you see. Both her sisters are dead now. Marjory was the quietest, and Alice was aye short of breath, I remember. Asthma, I think it was.'

Nobody could say that Mrs Gray was short of breath, the inspector thought with amusement, and it would probably be best to let her ramble on for a while.

'Janet tried to lord it over the rest of us that only went to the village school, but I was four years older than her and I didn't stand any lip. She was a bonnie lassie, no shortage of lads, but the one she was sweet on was killed in the war. The Second World War. That set her back a bit, and she had what they'd call a nervous breakdown now, but she got over it.'

The old lady stopped speaking, and ran her tongue over her lips. 'This speaking's thirsty work. Would you be good enough to make a pot of tea?'

After McGillivray took through the two chipped cups, she said nothing for a few minutes, and he wondered if he should prod her memory. People her age often forgot the thread of what they were saying if they were interrupted for any reason. He decided to wait until she finished her tea.

He took the opportunity to look around the small room, noting the crocheted squares covering the seats of the chairs; probably to hide torn or worn parts. The whole room was reminiscent of his grandmother's home. The old-fashioned dresser taking up one wall was chock-full of dainty ornaments that looked really old and were probably worth a fortune these days, though they'd likely been bought for next to nothing. The drop-leaf table in the centre of the room was shrouded in a tapestry, and a beautifully sewn cross-stitch valance was fixed to the high mantelshelf. It appeared that Mrs Gray had been a competent needlewoman before arthritis had twisted her fingers. The steel fender round the fire was in dire need of burnishing, and the mats on the linoleum floor would be the better of a good clean. The black doorknobs on the two doors were sticking out at rakish angles and would need replacing quite soon. The rag rug at the hearth, though, had probably been hooked by the man of the house and had been made to last a lifetime.

It was very clear that no relatives, male or female, ever visited the poor old soul. At this point in his reflections, McGillivray felt her eyes on him and gave an embarrassed cough.

'Have you seen enough, then?' she asked, though there was no hint of accusation in the words.

'I'm sorry, Mrs Gray,' McGillivray mumbled. 'It wasn't nosiness, honestly. I was reminded of my granny's kitchen, right down to the cleeked rug at the fireside. Brought back happy memories for me.'

The old lady beamed at him. 'I'm glad.' Satisfied, she carried on where she had left off. 'Janet must've had a good brain on her, though, for about a year after that, she went to Edinburgh as a typist. She worked herself up to being a company secretary, whatever that is, but it's supposed to be pretty high up.'

She held out her empty cup. 'Any tea left in the pot?'

McGillivray poured her another, and sat down again to wait. Janet Souter's life story wasn't what he was really after, but he might as well let her finish it before asking about Mrs Wakeford.

After a couple of noisy slurps, she resumed her tale. 'We heard she'd been left a lot of money when her boss died, though I couldn't tell you if there had been any hanky panky going on between them or no. Anyway, it was enough to let her come back here and buy that cottage. Her mother and father used to live down the High Street, but their house was sold when Albert Souter died, about two years after his wife. Pneumonia, if I mind right.

'They hadn't got much of a price for it in those days, and it had to be divided among the three daughters. Janet never worked after she came back, though she wasn't much over fifty. Some folk have all the luck. Me, I got married when I was eighteen and had to graft hard all my blessed days. When my Sam died, I'd to bring up two young bairns on my own, and it was an even harder struggle . . . no family allowances or suchlike then. I'd have been in clover if I'd got a few shillings from the Government.'

She was obviously working round to reminiscing about her own life, so McGillivray thought he'd better start channelling her memories in the right direction. 'You know Mrs Wakeford quite well, too, I suppose?'

'Oh, aye. I've known Mabel Dewar since she was born. Her mother was never married, but that's nothing against Mabel. She was a real quiet lassie, though there was a bit of a scandal about her when she was still in her teens, I think, and her mother sent her away. She'd been scared for what folk would say about mother and daughter both having fatherless bairns, but I think only a few of us guessed Mabel was in the family way.

'A fisherman out on the herringboats, it was. You know what it's like when young couples get kept apart. Mabel wasn't the only girl to be caught, mind. There's a lot of bastards round here, though some of them don't know it.'

He laughed along with her, but wondered if he should stop her from wandering off the topic again.

'Young wives, you know, with their men away fighting. When the tom cat's away . . . There was Millie McDougall, now, she'd two the time her Bill was in the Far East, and Netta Wilson . . .'

Enough was enough, so McGillivray interrupted her

flow at last. 'So Mabel Dewar, Mrs Wakeford, was sent away to have the baby? Have you any idea where?' He tried not to sound anxious, in case she dried up.

Mrs Gray idly stroked the purring cat, which had jumped up on her knee when she laid down her teacup. 'We were never told, of course, but her mother's sister had a house in Thornkirk, so I wouldn't be surprised if it had been there, for they were a close-knit family, the Dewars. She came back empty handed, though, so the bairn must've been adopted, or something.'

The cat's head stretched up sensually, so she tickled it under the chin. 'Mabel went in for nursing not long after, and landed on her feet a while after that. Near the end of the war she met this army major in a hospital somewhere, and they got wed when she'd have been about twenty or twenty-one. He was a lot older than her, but a nice enough man for all that.'

She paused until her pet turned round on her lap, and waited until it settled down again. 'He'd plenty money, but he moved in with Mabel and her mother, the same cottage as she's in now. Mary Dewar wasted away with consumption, though, and the Major had a heart attack and died . . . oh, maybe five years after her. He was out of the army long afore that, of course, and Mabel got all his money, so there's nothing hanging over her financially.'

Mrs Gray leaned back, musing. 'I feel sorry for her, though, for she lost her first lad, then her bairn, then her mother, then her man. Aye, money's not everything when you're left on your own, and I ken what loneliness is, for both my sons are in New Zealand. Mind you, Mabel hasn't even got that, has she?' Her eyes grew sorrowful behind the thick lenses.

Callum McGillivray sat forward. 'Can you remember Mabel's aunt's name, by any chance – her mother's sister? We want to trace the child.'

The old woman's cackle was not malicious. 'Oh ho! So you're going to stir up a hornet's nest, are you? Well, Mabel'll not be very happy about that, for she's kept it a secret these forty years past.'

'It'll be done very discreetly,' he said hastily. 'There won't be any need for Mrs Wakeford, or anybody else, ever to know anything about it.'

'Aye, maybe it's just as well. Sleeping dogs are better left. Let me think. Mabel's mother was Mary Dewar, and her sister's name was . . . um . . . oh, it's slipped my memory. Faces I can mind on, but names . . . That's the worst of being old.'

McGillivray stood up. 'Not to worry. Thank you for talking to me, and for the tea, and if you do happen to remember that name, please let me know. Don't bother to see me out, I'll manage fine.'

He was closing the front door, when he heard the old lady shouting, 'Inspector!'

'It just came back to me,' she told him when he went in. 'It was Elsie. That's right, Elsie Dewar, and she married the doctor's son, Eric Peters. Of course, he's dead long ago, Doctor Peters, I mean. Eric went in for medicine as well, trained in Aberdeen, then got a practice in Thornkirk. He'd be Doctor Peters and all, come to think of it, and he'd be retired long afore this . . . if he's still alive.'

'That's just what I was needing. Thank you very much, Mrs Gray, you've been a great help.' He shook her hand warmly.

A definite look of consternation appeared in Mabel Wakeford's eyes when she saw the tall figure on her doorstep, but she took him inside.

McGillivray leaned against the sink. 'Earlier today, I was at Thornkirk Hospital, where Mrs Violet Grant was taken after she'd been poisoned.'

Her hand flew to her throat in horror. 'Poisoned? I heard the ambulance this morning and saw them taking her away, but I didn't know she'd been . . . poisoned. Who could have done that?' Her face was white and her hands were trembling.

'The same person who murdered Janet Souter, I presume.' He was positive she knew something about it.

'Oh no! It wasn't . . . I mean . . .' She was panic-stricken now. 'Everybody hated Janet Souter, but Violet was such a kind, gentle person.'

'She may have known something the guilty person was afraid she might reveal, or she may have known who the guilty person was.'

'No, no. She didn't know anything.' Mrs Wakeford gathered herself together with an effort. 'She isn't dead, is she?'

'Mercifully, no.' He felt rather sorry for her, although

everything pointed to her being guilty of both crimes. 'You called at their house after we left yesterday morning?'

'Just to find out if you'd asked them the same questions as you asked me.'

'Did you see a jar of raspberry jam and some pancakes in their kitchen? You did go through the kitchen?'

'Rasp . . . berry . . . jam?' The words were drawn out, and she thumped on to a chair as if her legs had given way. 'Is that what poisoned her?'

'Either the jam or the pancakes, we believe. Did you notice them, Mrs Wakeford?'

'I didn't notice anything. I just went straight through.'

'Are you certain of that?'

She looked at him frankly. 'Yes, I went straight through, and I didn't see any pancakes or jam. If I had . . .' She stopped and her eyes dropped.

'If you had . . . ?'

'I wouldn't have thought anything about it,' she said, lamely.

He was disappointed. He'd hoped he could catch her out, but her nerve was stronger than he'd believed. She did know something about the jam, though. That was quite evident. He pulled himself away from the sink. 'That's all, then. Thank you, Mrs Wakeford.'

As McGillivray closed the door, he wondered if he should have carried on questioning the woman. She'd clearly been absolutely petrified with fear, but he hadn't been able to force himself to lean more heavily on her. Walking back along the High Street, his brain was working furiously. He was almost sure that Mrs Wakeford hadn't been responsible for the attempt on Mrs Grant's life – her shock and panic at hearing about it had not been simulated – but would she have confessed to the murder of Janet Souter if he'd put the heat on?

There was still this business of the child she'd had, but he wanted to wait until he found definite proof it existed, before he faced her with that. That must have been her motive, to keep the birth a secret, if she was the murderer.

Sergeant Black, returned from the accident, accompanied him into the incident room when he arrived at the police station. 'Have you turned anything else up, Inspector?'

'A lot of supposition, but no certainties.' McGillivray grimaced. 'Mrs Grant was never in any danger, though, and she's recovering. Did you get the pancakes and jam off to be tested?'

'Yes, and I told Constable Paul to let Thornkirk know we wanted the results as soon as possible. They'll likely phone them through.'

'Good. We saw the nephews after we left the hospital, and Flora Baker knows something, or thinks she knows something, about Janet Souter's death, and her husband practically had to gag her. Barbara Drummond was hard put to it to stop her husband from coming out with something, too. But it's funny, Ronald Baker and Barbara Drummond both mentioned the arsenic.'

'Oh-oh!' Black's mouth remained in a circle and his eyes widened. 'I'm sure they weren't told anything, just that the old lady had been found dead.'

172

McGillivray chuckled grimly. 'And being in Thornkirk, they couldn't have picked up any gossip, so Miss Souter's story about them trying to poison her must have been true. It looks like a bally conspiracy. But a group of people arranging for her death? That's bloody ridiculous – it only happens in books – but it's even more bloody ridiculous to think that several individuals were trying to kill her, unknown to each other.'

John Black shook his head. 'No, it couldn't be anything like that, and it wasn't the arsenic that killed her, that's another thing.'

'God! Something fishy's definitely been going on, and the arsenic's tied in somewhere. I went to see old Mrs Gray when we came back. She's a great character, and we'd a long chat – well, she did most of the speaking – and she gave me the name of Mrs Wakeford's aunt. The old lady thinks that's where Mabel went to have the baby. She's a Mrs Eric Peters, in Thornkirk.'

Before he could say anything else, Black had lifted the telephone directory and was leafing through the pages. 'Peters . . . Alexander . . . Bertram . . . mmm . . . Ah, here it is. Eric, 126 Mayfield Avenue. Doctor Peters, would that be right?'

'That's it, great. I'll go to see her tomorrow, but right now I'm going to the Starline to have a lie down for a while.'

He had been resting for only fifteen minutes, when David Moore knocked at the door and came in, his face red from hurrying, but wearing a satisfied look.

'They all verified that Douglas Pettigrew was playing snooker with them until the church hall was locked up at ten, then they'd all gone to the pub opposite the garage and stayed there till eleven.'

McGillivray looked interested. 'So his alibi's only good till eleven?'

The young sergeant unbuttoned his jacket and sat down. 'No, I went and checked with his mother, and she vouches that he went home about five past eleven and went to bed. She's sure he never left the house again.' His face changed and he gave an exasperated sigh. 'I'm whacked. I've walked the length of the High Street, and up and down several side streets. Two of them were at somebody else's house, so I'd to make double journeys.'

'A policeman's lot is not a happy one, tra, la, la,' the inspector chanted from the bed. 'Another suspect ruled out.' He tousled his hair with his right hand while his left covered an enormous yawn. 'Hercule Poirot had it easy, Moore. His little grey cells kept him informed, but mine have shrivelled up and died of old age.'

'You're not old, sir. Forty-five? The prime of life.'

'Some days I feel as old as Methuselah.' He grinned. 'Or at least as old as my friend Mrs Gray.'

'Oh, yes. How did you get on with her? Was she able to tell you anything more?'

'Yes, lad, she was. She gave me Mrs Wakeford's aunt's name, so we'll go to see her tomorrow.' McGillivray pulled his suspect list out of his pocket. 'We'd

174

better go over this again, in the light of what we've heard today.'

'It's been quite fruitful. I was beginning to think we were getting nowhere fast.'

'My sentiments exactly.' He flattened out the creases in the paper. 'Mabel Wakeford. Knows something about that raspberry jam, I'm sure, but I don't think she poisoned Mrs Grant. Oh, I've just remembered. Mrs Gray told me Mabel had gone in for nursing after her baby was born, so she could have known that insulin could kill, and she'd have been able to use a hypodermic needle. She's still a prime suspect.'

'It couldn't have been her.'

'Look, lad, she was prime before, and this makes her even primer. Murderers come in all shapes and sizes. You can't put them in little pigeon holes.'

'I know, but . . . I hope it's not her.' Moore frowned.

'I think we could rule out Mrs Grant now, though I'm inclined to believe she knows – or thinks she knows – who the murderer is. Mrs Skinner's a different kettle of fish. Strong personality, good motive . . . She hasn't mentioned the killing of their dog. But again we come to the question of the hypo and the insulin.'

'She might be a diabetic herself. We don't know.'

'So she might, and she had an opportunity at any time. She tried to muzzle her sister when we were there, so maybe she tried to muzzle her for good.'

'I can't really picture her doing that, sir. She seems very fond of her sister.'

'She's still a suspect, whatever you think.' McGillivray paused long enough to light a cigarette. 'Mrs White. Could possibly kill if she was riled enough, but she's not grieving over young Pettigrew, and there's nothing else, as far as we know. No, the beautiful May's not very likely.'

He waited for a comment from his sergeant, but none was forthcoming, so he continued. 'Douglas Pettigrew's off the hook, anyway. Three pals and his mother all vouching that he told the truth? I can't argue with that.'

'It's narrowed things down a bit, though.'

'Ronald Baker. His wife was absolutely terrified, and I'm inclined towards believing the story Miss Souter supposedly told Mrs Wakeford. The old woman was fly and made a swap in case they tried to poison her. They wouldn't know it was flour in the bag, not arsenic like she told them, and probably think that's what did the trick.'

Moore nodded. 'They act guilty because they think they're guilty? The same could apply to the Drummonds, then.'

'Likely, though he looks too ineffectual to try anything.'

Moore suddenly looked thoughtful. 'I've been puzzling over what Miss Souter meant when she told Mrs Wakeford she hoped her nephews would try to poison her but she didn't think they'd the nerve. Would she have been testing them out to see if they did have any initiative?'

McGillivray banged his fist on the bedpost. 'By George, lad. I think you've hit the nail on the head. She'd meant to cut them out of her will if they didn't measure up. We'll never know for sure, of course, but I think we'll leave the two nephews as possibles.'

'That just leaves us with four, doesn't it? Mrs Wakeford, Mrs Skinner, Ronald Baker and Stephen Drummond.'

The inspector ran his fingers over his stubbly chin. 'Eeny, meeny, miny, mo, which one made Miss Souter go?' He sat up suddenly. 'I think we should pay Randall a quick visit.'

The doctor, who lived above his surgery, directly across from the police station, ushered the two men in. 'What can I do for you, Inspector?'

'I'd like a list of your diabetic patients.'

'Ah, I wondered when you'd come round to that, and I've written them all down already. Just the usual old folk, and only six of them. There was a seventh, but she died a day or two before Miss Souter was murdered.'

'Are Mrs Wakeford and the two sisters at Honeysuckle Cottages amongst them?'

'No, none of them. My God, you don't suspect any of them?'

'Everyone who came in regular contact with the old woman is under suspicion at the moment.'

'That lets me out, then, for I haven't seen her for years. But I'd better let you know about my diabetics. There's a pair of old widows in the High Street, both wearing on for seventy, and both confined to the house. There's Sam Daniels in Victoria Street. He was a scaffie before he retired. Street orderly now, of course. Wally Liddell,

177

the ex-school-janitor, and his wife, Polly. And, last but not least, Mrs Gray, a ninety-year-old who lives down Ashgrove Lane.'

'She's out,' McGillivray said. 'She's crippled with arthritis.'

'And the others are all frail and doddery,' the doctor put in.

The inspector bared his teeth in exasperation. 'Yes, well. Maybe none of them could have had anything to do with the murder, but their families . . . or friends?'

James Randall held his head to one side to consider, then he said, decisively, 'None of them would have had any reason to do away with Janet Souter. She didn't mix with them at all, not that I'm aware of. You see, there's a kind of pecking order in a place like this, and she's near the top while they'd be bringing up the rear.'

'A bit of snobbery?' McGillivray raised his bushy eyebrows.

'You could say that, though the villagers accept it as being quite natural.'

The inspector rose slowly to his feet. 'I apologise if we've kept you from your meal, Doctor, and we'll have to get a move on if we're not going to be late for ours.'

'Sorry I haven't been able to help you, but I wish you luck in your quest.'

'Thanks. Luck is what I desperately need right now.'

Chapter Twelve

Sunday 27th November, evening

Over coffee, David Moore asked, 'Are we going into the bar again tonight, sir? We could maybe winkle something else out of the regulars.' His face was hopeful.

McGillivray helped himself to another cup, and added sugar before he answered. 'No, Sergeant, I don't think it would work a second time, but I've been considering calling on the minister. I know he hasn't been here that long, but he or his wife could have picked up a few odds and ends that might come in useful.'

The manse stood back from the High Street, in the glebe next to the church, and a neat woman, in her forties probably, opened the door to them. Mrs Valentine showed them into a large, rather old-fashioned room, the dark mahogany furniture probably having come with the house. The fire in the rather large fireplace was certainly not enough to heat the huge room, but a striking, well-built man with piercing dark eyes was sitting at a table some distance away from it. Papers and what appeared to be reference books were strewn across it, so presumably he had been writing his sermon for the following week.

He rose to greet them and came towards them, smiling, when his wife told him who the callers were. 'Good evening, Chief Inspector. What can I do for you? I don't for one minute imagine that you've come calling socially. Sit down by the fire there, it's a cold night and this is a very draughty old house I'm afraid.'

His wife laughed. 'Draughty and inconvenient, but it's home.'

'Thank you.' McGillivray took over one of the large armchairs, while his sergeant sat on the piano stool to allow Mrs Valentine to have the other comfortable seat.

The Reverend Adam Valentine moved towards the big sideboard. 'Would you care for a glass of sherry, Inspector? We were about to have one ourselves. I don't really approve of strong drink but a little sherry never harmed anyone, and I need it on a Sunday night after two services.'

'That's very kind of you.'

The minister turned to David Moore. 'Sergeant?'

'Yes, thank you.' If it was all right for the inspector, he reasoned, it was all right for a sergeant, and he would be glad of something to heat him up.

Callum McGillivray settled back. 'This is very pleasant indeed.' He raised his glass. 'Cheers to you and your good lady.' Taking one sip, he became more serious. 'I thought perhaps you could give us your opinion of some of the people involved in our case. We've uncovered a few pieces of scandal, as is usual in any small community.'

Mrs Valentine grinned. 'That's true. You can't cut your toenails without the whole village knowing.'

180

'Don't be facetious, Muriel.' The minister looked rueful. 'It does seem that nothing anyone does goes unnoticed but I doubt if I can help you much. We've only been here for five years, and my wife knows the ladies in Honeysuckle Cottages better than I do.'

'I don't know very much about any of them, either, but I do know Miss Souter could be a very disagreeable woman.'

Her husband looked at her disapprovingly, but said nothing.

'Did you have any trouble with her yourself?' McGillivray leaned forward.

'Nothing drastic, just niggly things mostly. But I was very annoyed at her a week or so back, when I was collecting things for our Sale of Work. She usually donates quite freely, but she was really awkward that day and said it wasn't convenient because she had the chiropodist there. It wouldn't have taken her a minute to give me whatever she had, that's what annoyed me.'

'I'm not surprised.' The inspector smiled sympathetically.

'It was raining heavily, and I'd been going round for quite a while, so I didn't bother going back. Her house is at the other end of the High Street from ours, and it would have been another long trail. I'm not a very good Christian, I'm afraid.'

'You're only human, Mrs Valentine, like the rest of us.'

'Thank you, but it's no excuse for me being so childish. You see, I didn't want to give her the satisfaction of having me traipse up there twice in one day.'

181

'Do you know of anyone who had real cause to be angry with her? Someone she'd snubbed, or been spiteful to, or anything like that?'

She frowned in concentration. 'There's Douglas Pettigrew, but you'll know about him?'

McGillivray nodded in encouragement.

'And that madam, May White. She's one of Adam's failures, isn't she, dear?' She glanced at her husband and laughed.

He smiled wryly. 'Yes, Inspector. I've tried several times to make Mrs White see the error of her ways, and advised her to be faithful to her husband.' He fiddled with his glass, obviously debating on whether to say more, then he laughed. 'She even tried to flirt with me, so I can fully understand why men lose their heads over her.' He spread out his hands.

'Yes,' McGillivray agreed. 'I said, after we saw her, that she was a man-eater. But can you recall anyone else who might have got on the wrong side of Miss Souter?'

After a minute's deliberation, Mrs Valentine said, 'Not that I can think of, offhand, but I've never met a soul with a good word for her.'

'You shouldn't be saying that, Muriel, though I'm inclined to agree with you.' The minister drained his glass. 'I've never met such a consistently provoking woman before. She was absolutely impossible, at times.'

'You weren't surprised to learn she'd been murdered?'

'Not really. The surprise was that it hadn't been done

long before.' The man absented-mindedly rose and re-filled his glass.

The inspector addressed himself to Mrs Valentine again. 'From what I've heard about her in the past two days, I'm quite surprised about that myself, but how did you get on with the ladies in the other two cottages?'

'They were a pleasure to talk to, Inspector, very obliging and helpful. A complete contrast to Janet Souter.'

'Hmmm. I'm afraid we have reason to suspect two of these very nice ladies.'

'What?' Both the minister and his wife looked staggered by this information.

'Surely not,' Adam Valentine said at last. 'They're so gentle, all three of them. Could I ask which two are . . . ?'

'I shouldn't be saying anything without proof, but, in strict confidence, Mrs Wakeford and Mrs Skinner.'

'But . . . my wife and I thought . . . what about the two nephews? They were the obvious suspects to us.'

'That would seem natural, but there are many different factors involved. We are keeping them in mind.'

Adam Valentine shuffled the papers in front of him. 'This makes one think, Inspector.'

'We've been told that Miss Souter had unearthed some scandal about Mrs Wakeford, which that lady might not have wanted to become public knowledge.' McGillivray looked grave.

'If it was the fact that she was illegitimate, everyone knew anyway. Janet Souter had already broadcast that.' Mrs Valentine spoke angrily.

'I'm afraid there's more to it than that, but I'm not at liberty to tell you.' The inspector took his cigarettes from his pocket, then looked enquiringly at her.

She smiled. 'I don't mind if you smoke. Neither of us indulge, but we're not against people who do. We all have our little vices – mine's chocolate. But what about Mrs Skinner? What reason would she have had to kill Janet Souter?'

'The arsenic that the old lady laid out in her garden to get rid of rats killed their dog, and I believe Mrs Skinner thinks it was deliberate.'

'My God!' Adam Valentine let out the expletive without realising it. 'That really was despicable, if it's true. No wonder you think Mrs Skinner's got a motive.'

An uncomfortable silence fell.

At last, McGillivray stood up and laid his sherry glass on the high mantelshelf. 'I'm sorry to have disturbed you in the middle of your work.'

'Not at all, Inspector.' The minister rose and opened the door. 'I'm only sorry that we haven't been able to help.'

'It's those two poor women I'm sorry for,' his wife said sadly. 'Whichever of them is guilty, if either of them is, she deserves a medal for ridding the world of that obnoxious old . . .'

'Muriel!' admonished her husband.

'I entirely agree with you,' laughed McGillivray, 'but the law won't regard it in that light.'

'By the way, Inspector,' Adam Valentine said, when he

184

was showing them out, 'her funeral is set for tomorrow afternoon at three. Everything's been cleared, and I will be officiating.'

'Ah! Then we'll have them all here at the same time. Good.' McGillivray bade the minister goodnight, and Moore thanked him for the sherry.

The two detectives walked along the High Street in silence until they had almost reached their hotel, then the inspector said, 'How about a wee snifter before we pack it in for the night?'

'Great.'

Unfortunately for the sergeant, who had been hoping for some fresh revelations from the locals, the bar was practically empty, and only a young man appeared to be serving.

McGillivray leaned his elbow on the counter. 'What's happened to Joe tonight?'

'It's his night off.' The stand-in served them, then went to the other end of the bar to speak to a young girl, probably his girlfriend, and their conversation was far removed from the murder of Janet Souter.

'Sunday night in Scotland!' McGillivray sounded disgruntled.

Chapter Thirteen

The wind still whistled past McGillivray's window, although it seemed to be quite clear and frosty when he looked out. He washed, shaved and dressed, quickly, then went down to breakfast.

David Moore was already sitting at their table, looking, as usual, like an advertisement for 'What the bright young executive will be wearing this season'.

When the waitress brought their coffee, she said, 'There's a phone call for you, Inspector.' She moved the sugar bowl to make room for the hot water jug and followed him out.

A smile lit up the inspector's crooked face when he returned. 'That was Black saying he'd had a call from the public analyst. The raspberry jam contained traces of arsenic, but the pancakes weren't contaminated.'

'So it's the jam we'll have to concentrate on?'

'Looks like it, but first we're going after the missing bastard, as my friend Mrs Gray so charmingly put it. He, or she, could hold the key to this whole business.'

186

'You think he, or she, could be guilty?' Moore looked puzzled.

'Could be.'

'But why? What reason would they have to murder Miss Souter?'

McGillivray spread a slice of toast before saying, 'There's nowt so queer as folk. There could be a thousand and one reasons, lad.'

'Give me one, then.'

'Well, you're a stickler, that's one good thing about you.' The inspector took a bite of the toast and went to work with his knife and fork on the heaped plate of bacon, eggs, tomatoes, mushrooms and black pudding. 'I love the full English breakfast – it sets you up for the day, doesn't it?'

'Don't try to change the subject. Give me one reason, that's all I ask . . . sir.'

'OK then. He, or she, may have learned that Janet was broadcasting about his birth mother's own illegitimacy and wanted to stop the truth going any farther. He, or she, could have a good position in life and is afraid it might be sabotaged by the old gossip.'

'What would be the point of killing her after the news was out? It's probably circulating round Tollerton like wildfire by this time.'

'God, lad, you can't let go, can you? I can't read the human mind, but maybe they were afraid that she would go on to spill the beans about his, or her, birth.'

'Aye, well, then.' Moore looked somewhat sheepish for not having thought of it. 'I suppose that could be it.'

'I don't know if that's it or not, Moore. I'm just as much in the dark as you, but we won't get anywhere unless we ruffle some feathers here and there, and this chappie, or chappess, is as good a place to start as any. Now, will you stop criticising and let me get on with my breakfast? Then we can get going.'

At 126 Mayfield Avenue, Thornkirk, Mrs Eric Peters, now over eighty, looked rather startled when the inspector told her who they were, then she said, 'You'd better come in, though I can't think what brings you here.'

McGillivray smiled disarmingly, he hoped. 'We've come to ask some questions about your niece, Mrs Mabel Wakeford, née Dewar.'

'Mabel? Nothing's happened to her, has it? We were just saying we hadn't seen her for a good while.'

'Nothing's wrong, but I believe she came to you for a few months when she was young?" He spoke gently, watching for the small, white-haired woman's reaction.

'Yes, she did. Just for a holiday, you understand.' Mrs Peters displayed no hesitation or awkwardness.

McGillivray thought it best to be blunt. No pussyfooting around. Time was marching – no, galloping – on. 'I have reason to believe that while your niece was here she gave birth to an illegitimate child.'

The old lady laughed. 'You've done your homework, haven't you? I thought nobody was supposed to know about that.'

'Nothing's sacred in a small village, and some people

have long memories. I want to find out what happened to that baby.'

She waved her hand airily. 'Her mother made her have it adopted straight away. I don't think Mabel even saw it.'

'How was the adoption carried out? A society?'

'My husband arranged it through his solicitor.'

'May we talk to your husband?' Callum McGillivray crossed his fingers and prayed that the old man would still be alive.

'Certainly, but he's upstairs in bed with a bad cold.'

At first sight of her, the inspector had thought she was quite frail, but she climbed the stairs without holding on to the handrail. Her husband, however, looked as if he were at death's door, his pale skin having a yellowish-grey tinge to it.

'Here's two detectives asking about Mabel's baby, dear,' the old lady said brightly. She turned to McGillivray and whispered, 'I hope you get something from him, his memory's not what it was.'

Her husband looked up at them with rheumy eyes. 'Mabel's baby? But that was long ago. It must be . . .'

'About forty years,' the inspector said, helpfully.

Dr Peters nodded. 'That's right. It must be forty years now. She was so ashamed . . . the father was a fisherman. I think he was lost at sea . . . but a couple of young patients of mine were desperate for a baby, so it was very convenient. They adopted it legally, you know.' His face suddenly screwed up, but the sneeze, when it came, was quite pathetic.

His wife handed him a tissue from a box on the bedside table. He blew his nose with a flourish and dropped the paper into a bin on the floor. 'So nice of you to call, but I'm feeling much better today.' He smiled vacantly.

'He suffers from hardening of the arteries, you know,' whispered Mrs Peters, and McGillivray's heart sank. Surely they weren't going to be thwarted at this stage?

'About Mabel's baby, dear.' She patted the skeletal hand. 'Can you remember that young couple's name?'

'Young couple? What young couple?'

'The ones who adopted Mabel's baby, dear. The inspector wants to find them.'

The old eyes cleared for a moment. 'Oh, yes. They couldn't have any of their own. Such a nice couple. They were delighted with Mabel's baby.' His voice became querulous. 'Is it about time for my elevenses, Elsie? I'm thirsty.'

'Yes, dear. I'll go and put the kettle on. Tell the inspector what their name was, won't you?' The woman left the room, and her husband lay back against the pillows with his eyes closed.

David Moore could see that the inspector was frustrated, so he bent down and spoke close to the old man's ear. 'Excuse me, Doctor Peters, but can you tell me the name of the people who adopted Mabel Dewar's child?' He kept his voice low, but firm, not actually expecting an answer.

He was as surprised as McGillivray, therefore, when the man opened his eyes and said, in a clear, strong voice, 'It's

190

no use asking me that, for I can't tell you. It's a secret between Matthew Dean and me.'

He was obviously back in the past, so Moore said, gently, 'Was it a boy or a girl, Doctor Peters?'

'A lovely seven-pound girl.' He closed his eyes again.

The sergeant straightened up and looked at McGillivray, who gave him the thumbs-up sign. 'Thank you very much, sir.' Moore didn't think the old man heard him, but it made no difference.

When they went downstairs, Mrs Peters came out of her kitchen with the teapot in her hand. 'Oh, you're leaving? I was making some tea for you. I'm sorry if you've had a wasted journey. His memory comes and goes.'

McGillivray beamed at her. 'It's all right, ma'am. We got enough information to enable us to carry on. Matthew Dean would have been your husband's solicitor?'

'Fancy him remembering that. I was trying to think of his name myself, but it wouldn't come to me. I'm afraid he died a few years ago. I remember Eric reading the death notice out of the papers. I've been trying to think who took over from him when he retired. I should know . . . Oh, yes. Martin Spencer.'

'That's Miss Souter's solicitor,' remarked Moore.

'By the Lord Harry, you're only right.' McGillivray looked ecstatic. I thought I'd heard the name before, but I couldn't place it. Well done, lad. You've earned your stripes today.'

'I'm glad you got what you wanted, but don't you have time for some tea?'

'No, thank you very much, Mrs Peters, but we have to carry on with our work.'

She stood at the outside door and watched them walking down the path, but, once inside the Vauxhall, McGillivray pulled out the sheet of paper which the constable had given him when they'd arrived in Tollerton on Saturday. 'Martin Spencer, 21 George Square,' he read out. 'Right, Moore, forward to George Square. We may as well strike while the iron's hot.'

They had only a short distance to go, and when they enquired if the solicitor could see them, the receptionist told them that Mr Spencer was engaged with a client.

'We'll wait till he's free.' McGillivray walked over to the row of blue vinyl-covered chairs and sat down.

In a few minutes, a stout gentleman emerged from one of the doors, followed by a rather fawning man in a neat, dark suit.

The fat man said, 'Thank you for all your help, Mr Spencer,' and McGillivray stood up.

'Excuse me, Mr Spencer,' he began, 'may we have a few words with you?'

Rather icily, the solicitor asked, 'Have you an appointment?'

'No, but I won't keep you long. I'm Detective Chief Inspector McGillivray, Grampian CID, and DS Moore and myself are investigating the murder of Miss Janet Souter of Tollerton. One of your clients, I believe?'

'I can only spare you a few minutes, because I've an

192

appointment at the other side of town in half an hour. You'd better come into my office.'

The office was far more opulent than the waiting room. A cheery fire burned at the right-hand side of the room. Spencer's chair was covered in lovely brown hide, as were the smaller chairs for his clients, and although these had no arms, they were still really comfortable, as McGillivray and Moore discovered when they sat down.

'I'll be as brief as I can,' the inspector said. 'We're trying to trace an adoption undertaken by Matthew Dean about forty years ago, through a Doctor Eric Peters. Would the records still be kept?'

'Oh, yes, they'll be in the archives, but it would take us some time to dig them out.'

'I'd be obliged if you'd do it, just the same, Mr Spencer. We know the natural mother, but we're trying to find the adoptive parents.'

'Leave it in my hands, Inspector.' The solicitor got up and moved to the door. 'I'll put someone on it right away and let you know as soon as I can.'

They left him instructing one of his clerks to find the information they required.

On their return journey to Tollerton, McGillivray observed, 'It's the funeral afternoon.'

David Moore wondered what was so significant about it, but smiled, 'That's right, sir.'

'I was hoping to do a touch of the Agatha Christies, you know, and get them all back to Honeysuckle Cottages to spring the name of the murderer on them – and arrest the guilty party – but I haven't a bloody clue yet.'

'Never mind, sir. We're getting there. Something's bound to give, shortly.'

McGillivray's mouth twisted. 'As far as I can see, lad, my sanity's going to be the first thing to give.'

Chapter Fourteen

Monday 28th November, afternoon

It was a very small funeral. Only Ronald Baker and Flora, Stephen and Barbara Drummond, the Reverend and Mrs Valentine, Martin Spencer, Sergeant Black and the two detectives attended. It was very clear that Janet Souter had not been popular in the village.

McGillivray was surprised that Mabel Wakeford hadn't put in an appearance. Had she a guilty conscience? The absence of Grace Skinner could be excused, her sister being newly home from hospital. They wouldn't feel very charitable towards the dead woman, anyway, on account of their dog, and perhaps it was Mrs Skinner who had the guilty conscience.

The service was quickly over, with no lengthy eulogy in praise of the deceased. In fact, there was only one good thing that Adam Valentine could find to say about her. 'Miss Souter was a regular churchgoer who hardly ever missed a Sunday, and she responded to every appeal put out.'

John Black tried not to smile as he recalled the young constable's remark on the evening the murder was

195

discovered, about her trying to buy her way into heaven, and held his head down in case anyone had noticed his flicker of amusement. Fortunately, the minister began his final prayer at that moment, so no one was any the wiser.

When the funeral service was over, McGillivray saw that Ronald Baker was deep in conversation with the solicitor – finding out about the will, probably – but eventually the few mourners dispersed.

Back at the police station, the inspector sat down at the table in the incident room, and accepted with gratitude the cup of coffee PC Paul brought through. Then he and Moore got down to the business of making up their report of events over the past two days.

While the young sergeant typed it out officially, Callum McGillivray fruitlessly searched for inspiration to help him solve the case. He could see no light at the end of the tunnel, however, and was glad when Moore said, 'That's it finished.'

'I noticed the two nephews and their wives didn't make for home when everything was finished,' he remarked, idly.

His sergeant smiled. 'Hot-footing it up to Janet Souter's house, I'd imagine, to fight over her belongings.'

McGillivray chortled. 'Oh to be a fly on the wall. I can just picture the bickering that's going on there right now. I'd better go and see what's happening. Heated arguments often reveal secrets unintentionally.'

The telephone rang, and he picked up the receiver, still

laughing. 'McGillivray . . . Yes? . . . What? . . . You're there now? We'll be with you as soon as we can.'

He turned to Moore. 'Things are moving now, with a vengeance. That was Spencer. His wife's in hospital and the doctors say it's arsenic poisoning, the same as Mrs Grant.'

'Good God! Why on earth would anybody want to poison Spencer's wife?'

The inspector, on his way to the door, stopped to tell John Black about this latest development, so Moore went past him to start up the car.

'There's more twists in this case than a bloody spiral staircase,' McGillivray muttered as he settled into the passenger seat.

Martin Spencer was pacing the corridor outside the emergency ward when they arrived at the hospital. 'Oh, Chief Inspector, this is really terrible. I got home from the funeral to find Irene in agony, so I called an ambulance, and the doctor told me later that it was arsenic poisoning. If I'd gone back to the office instead of going straight home, she could have been dead by now.'

His anguish made McGillivray say gently, 'I'm very sorry about your wife's trouble, Mr Spencer, but what made you phone me? Why not the Thornkirk Police?'

'It was another poisoning. It must be connected with the other two, so I want to find out who's responsible. Miss Souter died, but her next-door neighbour recovered and I hope Irene does too.'

'I certainly hope she does too, and I'm doing my best to

find out who's responsible. I'll have to find out if your wife has eaten anything which you didn't have, and work from there. Can you remember about that?'

'We'd exactly the same for breakfast and lunch. I normally have a quick snack at the café round the corner from my office at lunchtime, but I went home today because I'd forgotten to take my black tie with me, for the funeral. Mid-morning would have been the only time Irene could have had anything different.'

'When you're allowed to see her, ask her what she had. It's very important. We'll wait here with you.'

The solicitor sat down on the wooden bench and leaned forward with his hands between his knees. 'I can't think what anybody had against Irene, and she didn't know a soul in Tollerton.'

'She'd never met Miss Souter, or her nephews?'

'Never. She'd no part in my work at all, and I'd never met the nephews myself until this afternoon.' The approach of a doctor made him jump to his feet. 'How is she?'

'Your wife's going to be fine. You may see her for a minute, but remember she's still very weak.'

The two men disappeared into the ward, and McGillivray looked quizzically at Moore. 'How did he know Mrs Grant had been poisoned?'

'I suppose Ronald Baker could have told him that Janet Souter had been poisoned, and the doctor here might have told him about Mrs Grant.'

'That's probably right.' The inspector screwed up his

198

face in concentrated deliberation. 'This arsenic's a real bugger.'

When the solicitor came back, he said, 'The only thing she ate was a piece of sponge cake she baked herself a few days ago.'

McGillivray frowned. 'Curiouser and curiouser. I'll need a sample of it, for testing, I'm afraid. Do you need a lift home?'

'Thanks, I was wondering which bus I'd have to take. I came in the ambulance with my wife, you see.'

When the car drew up outside his house, he said, 'If you're coming in to get a bit of that sponge, you may as well have a bite of dinner. I'd be glad of the company.'

It was wearing on for eight o'clock, and the two detectives had eaten nothing since lunchtime, so this was a welcome invitation and McGillivray accepted gratefully.

An appetising aroma of roast lamb met them when the front door was opened, and Spencer led them into a room gleaming with chromium and pine.

'We usually dine about seven or half past, because I'm often quite late in finishing, so the meat shouldn't be too dried up. Irene's a great believer in long, slow cooking. I hope you don't mind eating in the kitchen?'

McGillivray smiled. 'As long as it's food, I don't mind where I eat.'

The solicitor carved the lamb with the touch of an expert, and dished it up along with the roast potatoes, sliced green beans, carrots and peas that had also been cooking in the oven. 'I'm sorry I can't make mint sauce, but . . .'

'Don't worry about that. This looks fit for a king.' The inspector lifted his knife and fork eagerly. 'Mmmm,' he said, with his first mouthful, 'it *is* fit for a king.'

Enjoying the delicious repast, they ate in silence, then Spencer stood up. 'I'll take you through to the sitting room, gentlemen, it's more comfortable for you to sit there while I organise some coffee.'

The large, beautifully furnished room he showed them into was already warm, and he motioned to them to be seated, then went back to the kitchen to attend to his duty as a host.

David Moore sat down, then hoisted himself further back, and was delighted when he discovered it was a reclining chair. Lying back, he stuck his legs out in front of him. 'This is the life, eh, Inspector?'

'Oh, yes,' agreed McGillivray similarly angled. 'I could get used to this.'

The solicitor returned, beaming. 'That's the percolator filled and gurgling, so we'll have our coffee shortly. Would you like a drink while we're waiting?'

The inspector would indeed have enjoyed a tipple after such a satisfying meal, but he thought it wiser to decline. 'It's very kind of you, but we'll just have the coffee, thanks.'

'Just as you please. Sit there and I'll bring through the sponge that Irene made.'

When the plastic cake box was placed in his lap,

McGillivray lifted the lid. A good-sized wedge had been cut from the tempting round of sponge, oozing with cream and jam. He halted as he was replacing the cover. 'Just a mo! That's home-made raspberry jam, isn't it? Did your wife make her own jam?'

Spencer looked bewildered. 'No. We hardly ever use jam, and she said it wasn't worth the effort. I got a jar from Miss Souter when I was there, last Monday, to be exact, and Irene baked the sponge to use some of it up.'

David Moore saw that the Inspector's bushy eyebrows were quivering. This was a definite tie up with Violet Grant's pancakes and jam.

McGillivray said, 'I'll take the jam, too, if you please.'

'Certainly. Do you think that's where the poison is?'

'In Mrs Grant's case it turned out to be in raspberry jam, but I don't know yet if her jar came from Miss Souter.'

'It must be the work of a maniac. Janet Souter would never have given away the jam if she'd known there was arsenic in it.' Martin Spencer went back to the kitchen and returned in a moment with a half-used jar. 'Here you are, Inspector, and I hope to God you catch the murderer quickly.'

'So do I,' the inspector said in heartfelt tones. 'Just for the record, can you tell me why you went to see Janet Souter last Monday?'

'She wrote asking me to call as she wanted to make out a new will.'

'Aha!' McGillivray jerked up suddenly and his feet fell to

201

the floor as the footrest disappeared under the chair. 'Did she cut her nephews out?'

'No. When I went there, she told me she had changed her mind again and was leaving her nephews as her beneficiaries after all.'

Before they left Thornkirk, McGillivray made Moore take him to the police station, where he left the cake tin and the jar of jam to be tested. 'I want the result pronto, if not sooner,' he told the sergeant on the desk.

It was after nine thirty when they drew up at Tollerton police station, and Constable Paul told them that Sergeant Black had gone off duty at nine. 'But he lives next door, if you want to see him.'

'Thanks. We may as well pop in for ten minutes or so.'

Between sips of Glenfiddich, with very little water added, McGillivray recounted the details of their visit to Thornkirk, while John Black listened with interest.

David Moore paid little attention to the conversation as he was rather discomfitted by Black's appearance. The local sergeant was sitting in front of a roaring fire with checked bedroom slippers on his feet, and his uniform jacket had been replaced by an old red pullover. His grey hair was tousled and falling over his eyes, and his face was as red as his jersey, probably as a result of having had several drinks before the detectives arrived. He looked very different from the official, slightly officious, Tollerton police sergeant.

Moore shifted his gaze, met the amused eyes of Mrs Black and coloured, realising that she knew what had been going through his mind. He looked away in confusion, and concentrated on what was being said by the other two men.

Callum McGillivray was speaking. 'You know, this case is like a flaming maze. We think we're on the home stretch, then another path opens up or comes to a dead end. It's this business of the two actual poisonings that's the devil of it. I'm beginning to doubt if they've anything to do with the murder at all, but I can't figure either of them out.'

Black shook his head in sympathy. 'I'm glad it's not up to me to unravel it, that's all I can say.'

Chapter Fifteen

Tuesday 29th November, morning

'Oh! It's you, Inspector.' Violet Grant looked startled. 'What . . . ? You'd better come in.'

McGillivray smiled, and motioned to David Moore to follow him. 'Thank you. I hope you're quite recovered now?'

Violet gave a tremulous smile before she walked ahead of them. 'It's the inspector again.' She hovered beside her sister, leaving her to deal with the unexpected visitors.

Grace Skinner remained seated at the kitchen table. 'Good morning. To what do we owe the pleasure of your company at this early hour?'

The calculated flippancy was not lost on McGillivray. It was a common enough reaction when guilty people tried to cover up their nervousness, but also sometimes with innocent people unfortunately. 'Good morning, Mrs Skinner. I'm sorry to interrupt your breakfast, but I won't bother you long.'

'It's quite all right, and, before I forget, I must pay you back the money you lent me.' She turned round and lifted an envelope from a shelf on the kitchen cabinet. 'It was very thoughtful of you. Thank you.'

Highly embarrassed, he placed it in his breast pocket. 'Thanks. Now, will you please tell me where you obtained the raspberry jam that Mrs Grant used on her pancakes?'

'That's easily answered. Janet Souter handed it to me over the fence the day after we found our beloved Benjie's dead body in her garden. She said it was to compensate us for our loss. She hadn't realised that the poison she laid out to kill the rats would kill our dog as well. She had the gall to say she was sorry. Old hypocrite! She meant to do it.'

She had told him the truth about the dog's death at last, but the inspector let it pass without comment. 'Why didn't you tell us before that the jam came from her?'

'I don't know. I never thought about it, I was so worried about Violet.'

'It may interest you to know that the arsenic was contained in the jam.'

'Good gracious!' Violet clutched at the edge of the table. 'Do you mean she was trying to kill us as well as Benjie?'

'We're not sure of that, Mrs Grant. Someone else may be responsible for adding the stuff to the jam, with the intention of killing Miss Souter herself. The thing is, she also gave a jar to her solicitor, whose wife has been affected in exactly the same way as you.'

'What does it mean, Grace?' Violet appealed to her sister.

'I'm sure I don't know. Do you, Inspector?'

'Not yet, ma'am, but we're doing our best to find out.'

Violet Grant slumped into her chair. 'You didn't put it in the jam as well as the flour, did you, Grace?' She stared accusingly at the other woman. 'You should have told me. I'd have known not to use it.'

'Oh, Violet.' There was no trace of reproach as Grace laid her hand over her sister's.

The rather touching tableau gave McGillivray no satisfaction, and after a few minutes, he coughed discreetly.

Grace looked up at him, hopelessly. 'I may as well confess, Inspector. I killed Janet Souter. She was an evil woman and deserved to die after what she did to poor Benjie. We went round to her house on the Friday night when she was out, and I took some of the arsenic from her shed and put it in the flour bin, where I thought it wouldn't be seen.'

'Did you add some to the raspberry jam, too?' McGillivray asked, gently.

'No. I didn't even see any jam there. I was concentrating on the one thing I had to do. I knew where she kept her flour, because I once had to borrow a cupful though I never asked for anything again. She was really quite sarcastic at that time, and said I should be more organised. What happens now? Will you arrest me?'

'Oh, Grace, it was my fault as much as yours,' Violet sobbed, but her sister's look silenced her.

'Nonsense! I was the one who suggested it and carried it out. Violet had no part in it, Inspector.'

David Moore's face was a study in perplexity. 'But sir . . . the flour . . . you know . . . Inspector, you can't . . . it wasn't . . .'

A hint of a smile lurked at the corners of McGillivray's mouth. 'What my sergeant is trying to say, although not very coherently, is that the flour, along with all Miss Souter's other foodstuffs, was completely free from any contamination.'

'What?' Grace Skinner's chin dropped in amazement. 'But I tell you, I did . . .'

'I understand you had provocation and were under a great deal of stress, but I swear to you that you did *not* kill Janet Souter. There were no traces of arsenic in the contents of her stomach, nor in her bloodstream.'

'But I've been living with the terrible guilt ever since that Friday – it's only just over a week, but it feels like eternity.'

'Clear it from your conscience, dear lady, and think twice in future before you try dispensing justice. The plastic bag in full view in her shed contained ordinary flour, and we think she made the substitution herself. She told Mrs Wakeford that her nephews were trying to poison her but they'd be disappointed, so she must have laid out the flour for them to use. We found the arsenic later – hidden under her barrow.'

Looking intently at the haggard woman sitting white-faced in front of him, McGillivray added, 'She must have made the swop before Ronald Baker was due on the Saturday, so you'd only put more flour in her bin.

Now, Mrs Skinner, I'm going to forget we've had this conversation, and I'd advise you to put the whole thing out of your mind.'

Her eyes filled with tears, but as he turned to leave, she said, 'Inspector, you said she wasn't poisoned, so can you tell me how she was killed? It must have been murder, otherwise you wouldn't be investigating her death.'

He didn't look round. 'I'm sorry, I can't tell you that. Good morning to you both.'

David Moore glanced at Violet, who was weeping silently into her handkerchief, then smiled to Grace and followed the inspector out, happy that Mrs Skinner was no longer a suspect.

'There's no need to report any of that,' remarked McGillivray, gruffly. 'And if you're thinking of saying anything, don't.'

'No, sir.' Moore could view his superior in a different light now. He was just a big softie.

Halfway down the path, McGillivray halted. 'It might be worth paying another call on Mrs Wakeford when we're here. We've broken down one of our prime suspects, and we may as well try for a second.'

Mabel Wakeford's greeting was quite bright. 'I hope you don't mind talking in the kitchen, Inspector. I'm just finishing my breakfast, as you can see.'

'Not at all. It's very cosy in here.'

'That's because the cooker's been on. May I offer you both a cup of tea?'

'That would be very acceptable, thank you.'

As she poured tea into the two extra cups she set out, she looked at McGillivray, waiting for him to state his business.

'We're making enquiries regarding jars of raspberry jam,' he obliged.

'R . . . raspberry j . . . jam?' she echoed faintly, her face blanching.

'It appears that Miss Souter had presented a jar to one or two people, and we wondered if you were also a recipient?'

'No, no. Please, Inspector, who did she give them to?'

'Mrs Grant, for one.'

The blood rushed from her face. 'Oh, no! It was the jam after all, was it?'

'I'm very much afraid so, and . . .'

'Who else?' she interrupted, her eyes staring wildly.

'Her solicitor, and his wife had also to be taken to hospital.'

'Oh, dear God, what have I done?' Mabel dabbed her eyes with her serviette. 'I didn't mean to hurt anybody else, just Janet.'

'What had she done to you that you wished to hurt her?' The inspector had a good idea of the answer to his question, but he wanted to hear it from her own lips.

Her blue eyes lost their wildness. 'I may as well tell you. She was so two-faced, pretending to be friendly, but waiting for a chance to stab you in the back. She'd found out, or remembered, that I was . . . that my mother . . . that . . .'

209

'That you were an illegitimate child, Mrs Wakeford?'

'Oh! You knew about that?'

'I've known for some time, and it's really nothing to be ashamed of. Many famous people were born out of wedlock.'

She shuddered at the word. 'I couldn't bear to think of people sniggering at me.'

'Only people like Janet Souter would snigger, but there was more to it than that, wasn't there?'

'What do you mean?' Her eyes refused to meet his.

'There was another reason for you wanting to silence her. Something even more private.'

'I suppose you know about that, too.' She straightened her shoulders. 'Yes, I was afraid she'd find out about my own illegitimate child, and I couldn't have that circulating round the village. I wouldn't have been able to hold my head up.'

She took a sip of her tea and laid the cup in the saucer carefully. 'She'd been going on about how she hoped her nephews would try to poison her with the arsenic in her shed, that's what put the idea into my head. When I saw her going out one morning, I went round to her house. There were three jars of raspberry jam sitting on her draining board, and I thought, raspberry jam's got such a strong flavour she wouldn't taste the stuff if I put it in there.'

She paused for a moment, reliving the horror of what she'd done. 'I got the bag from her shed, and took the covers off the jars. She always uses circles cut from red gingham to make them more attractive. Then I added half a teaspoonful to each jar.'

The irreverent thought crossed David Moore's mind that it was almost as if she were giving them a new recipe. Rasp and Arsenic Jam. He tried to stifle the laugh which welled up in him and it came out as a spluttering cough, making the inspector kick his shins under the table. With a great effort, he kept listening to what the woman was saying.

'I stirred it in well, to be sure it was mixed thoroughly.'

At that, the sergeant whipped his handkerchief out of his pocket and held it over his mouth, trying to make his mirth sound like a choking fit. 'I'm sorry,' he gasped, after a moment. 'Tea went down the wrong way.'

Clearly annoyed by this untimely, and unseemly, interruption, McGillivray glowered at him. The look was enough to quell Moore's giggles.

Mabel Wakeford had scarcely noticed the young man's confusion. 'Then I replaced the covers and washed her spoon, before I put it in her dustbin just to be on the safe side. I returned the arsenic to her shed, of course.'

She looked imploringly at the inspector. 'I must have been mad. Later on, I was appalled at what I'd done, but she'd come back by that time, and there was no way I could do anything about it. I didn't have the least idea that she'd give the jars away, that's really awful. But she must have used the third jar herself, or she wouldn't be dead, would she?'

McGillivray leaned forward and said quietly, 'I don't

think she did. She hadn't ingested any of the arsenic. Now, when did all this take place?'

'It was nearly two weeks before she died, and I've been through absolute hell since then.'

'Was that before the church Sale of Work? It strikes me the jam and cakes had been laid out to give to Mrs Valentine.'

'That's right. Mrs Valentine had been round collecting later on that same day, now that you speak about it.'

Without thinking, McGillivray helped himself to a piece of toast, and stretched across for the marmalade. 'Now, we've . . .'

'Inspector.' Mabel's anxious voice interrupted him. 'How could Janet Souter have given the jars of jam away, when she gave them to Mrs Valentine?'

'That good lady apparently arrived at an inconvenient time, so the old lady refused to get them for her.'

'She could be very nasty, but what a thing to do to the minister's wife, she's such a pleasant young woman.'

Taking a bite of toast, McGillivray chewed and swallowed. 'As I was about to say, we've accounted for two of the jars, but you said there were three. I wonder where the other one went? It wasn't amongst the stuff that was taken away to be tested.'

'I hope to God you trace it before . . .' She paused, her eyes tortured. 'What'll happen to me now? Will I be charged with murder? I deserve to be, because I meant to do it, but only to stop her vicious tongue.'

'Do you know what happened to your child?'

212

The abrupt question startled her. 'No, I never saw it. I don't even know if it was a boy or a girl. I shouldn't have let my mother persuade me to have it adopted. Even if I'd kept it, the shame I'd have gone through wouldn't have been nearly as bad as the disgrace this is going to bring me.' Her voice broke and she dabbed her eyes again.

Wiping his mouth with the back of his hand, McGillivray looked at her compassionately. 'You didn't commit murder, Mrs Wakeford, whatever your intention, although two innocent ladies have had to endure discomfort because of you. However, until we find the missing jar of jam, I'm going to leave things as they are.'

'Thank you, and I hope you find it quickly. I don't know what came over me, and I know I'll have to pay for my sins.'

'One thing more. When the body was found, why did you cast suspicion on Miss Souter's two nephews? It would have been more sensible if you'd held your tongue and accepted Randall's verdict of a heart attack as a godsend.'

Her shoulders lifted briefly. 'I really can't tell you why. I suppose I felt so guilty about what I'd done, I subconsciously wanted to be found out and punished. But Miss Souter did say that about Ronald and Stephen trying to poison her, and that they'd be disappointed. I presumed they'd be in the clear.'

The inspector stood up. 'Things would have been very much worse for you, if you'd succeeded in your purpose.' His voice was reproving. 'Be thankful you didn't.'

David Moore glanced back as he closed the door. The woman was staring into space, twisting her serviette round and round her fingers, and his heart went out to her in her misery.

'I can understand why that poor lady tried to shut the old harpy up,' McGillivray remarked. 'The thing is, she didn't accomplish it. Who did?'

He stopped with his hand on the gate. 'We'll have to find that jam, before somebody else falls foul of the stuff.' He walked towards the car, then halted again. 'Who else would have called on the old woman between the time she laid out these things for the minister's wife and the day she was found dead? That's over two weeks – there must have been somebody.'

'Sir, she told Mrs Valentine that the chiropodist was in her house when she called. Would she have given it to him?'

The inspector looked more cheerful. 'Could be, though she fully expected Mrs V. to go back for her donation. I tell you what. You go back to the station, lad, find out the chiropodist's phone number, if Black's got it, and ring him up and ask.'

'Yes, sir.' Moore idly wondered what McGillivray intended to do in the meantime.

'Another thing that's just come to me. If Mrs Wakeford added half a teaspoon of arsenic to each jar, it would have been pretty lethal, I'd have thought, yet two women were only slightly affected. Go and have a word with the retired glass worker about what he actually gave to Miss Souter.'

Moore looked puzzled. 'D'you think he'd diluted it?'

'He might have done, to make it less deadly before he gave it to a woman of her age.' McGillivray's eyes twinkled suddenly. 'Can you remember all that with your limited intelligence?'

Moore ignored the wisecrack. 'Contact the chiropodist, then the retired glass-worker. Anything else, sir?'

'Yes, make a report of all we've done since the funeral. I'm going down to see Mrs White.'

A cheeky grin appeared on the sergeant's face. 'Have you succumbed to the delectable May's charms, sir?'

'Not on your life! I'm a confirmed bachelor, lad.'

'They're often first to fall, especially to women like her.'

'Ach shit!' said McGillivray companionably.

Moore set off down the High Street chuckling. At the police station, his telephone call to the chiropodist drew a blank, so he walked, rather sadly, to the address Sergeant Black had given him for the retired glass-worker.

Davie Livingstone looked up from his newspaper when his tiny wife showed in the visitor. Quite stout, almost completely bald, his red face was cheery and welcoming.

'I'm Detective Sergeant Moore,' the young man began, but got no further.

'Speak o' the devil. I was just sayin' to the wife, nae ten minutes ago, "It's funny the 'tecs havena been to see me." An' she says to me, she says, "You'd better go an' have a word wi' them." An' here you are.'

Moore's eyes widened. 'Yes?'

'It's this business o' Janet Souter bein' murdered. They

215

tell me a'body thinks it was the arsenic I gave her that killed her, but it couldna've been.'

'No?'

'No.' Davie folded his paper methodically, then stretched over to lay it on the table.

The sergeant watched him rather impatiently, but when the man took his pipe off the mantelpiece and began to fill it, slowly and deliberately, Moore could wait no longer. 'Why could it not have been the arsenic?'

Davie looked up from his absorbing task. 'It's like this. After I tell't her I'd give her some, I got to thinkin'. I'd warned her to be careful, but she was a really auld woman and could easy've got muddled. So I puzzled my brains how to tone it down a bit, then I minded about the powder the wife uses when she's had a bath.'

'Talcum powder?'

'That's the stuff. She's got a sensitive skin, so she says, and she buys the kind that's nae scented, in a thing like a bowl. Well, I mixed the powder four tablespoons wi' one tablespoon o' arsenic in a polythene bag, afore I took it up to Janet Souter. So you see, Sergeant, unless somebody shovelled the whole bloomin' lot doon her throat, that stuff couldna've killed her. Mind you, if she'd forgot to wash her hands, or let some on her food by mistake, she'd have got a real bad bellyache.'

Davie stopped, then said, 'What was it you wanted to see me about, though?'

Moore couldn't tell him that Janet Souter hadn't been poisoned at all, so he did some quick thinking. 'We just wanted to confirm that it was you who gave her the arsenic. Thank you for telling me about the talcum powder, and we'll bear it in mind.'

'You dae that, and I hope you discover what poison did kill her, for it wasna the arsenic I gave her.'

There was one thing more that Moore felt obliged to say. 'Mr Livingstone, you know, of course, that it's against the law to keep . . .'

'I ken that fine, laddie, but there's nae much left now, and it's well locked awa'. You'll nae report me?'

'I should, but . . . just be careful. And don't give any more of it away.'

'There's nae enough left to be dishin' it out, in ony case.'

Moore returned to the station to make up his report of their activities since the funeral.

As Callum McGillivray locked the car door, the window of Mrs Gray's house opened and the old lady shouted, 'Can you come in a minute, Inspector? There's something I want to tell you.'

By the time he sat down in her living room, she'd forgotten that she'd asked him in, and started reminiscing about the old days again. He quite enjoyed her anecdotes about her own past, and the pasts of several others in the village, because her dry wit appealed to his sense of humour, but time was passing.

He jumped in when she stopped for breath at the end of a long and involved story. 'You said you'd something to tell me?'

She found it difficult to drag her mind back. 'Did I? Oh, aye, of course.' She launched into another long, involved account which boiled down to the fact that she'd seen a man she thought she should know leaving May White's house late on the night of the murder.

McGillivray had had experience of very old ladies before, and knew the lies they could concoct if they took an ill-will against someone. 'Why do you think this man you can't identify had anything to do with the murder? We've no reason to suspect him of anything other than seeing Mrs White. We can't go accusing any Tom, Dick or Harry, you know.'

'I know that, but the more I think about it, the surer I am. He came out of her back door and over the paling into my garden, then over the other paling into the field. Then he went out of my sight.'

'You'd say he didn't want to be seen?'

'Oh, he did not want to be seen, skulking about like a thief, he was. I just about broke my neck trying to watch him, and it was near midnight and me in my nightie.'

McGillivray stifled a laugh at the picture of this arthritic old woman in her nightdress craning her neck to watch the man who'd been visiting May White so late at night.

She caught the amusement in his eyes and gave a throaty chuckle. 'Aye, it's a good thing nobody could see me.'

'But it was dark?' Her thick glasses meant that her eyesight must be pretty poor.

'There was a full moon, Inspector. I couldn't see his

218

face but there was a kind of swagger about the way he walked that reminded me of somebody, but I'm dashed if I can remember who.' She shook her head in anger at her shortcomings. 'I was making a cup of tea before I went to my bed, or I wouldn't have seen him at all.'

'I really can't do anything, Mrs Gray, until you can give me a name.'

'As soon as it comes to me, I'll get somebody to tell you.'

'Good, I'd be really grateful. It could be our first real lead. Now, I'll go next door and see what Mrs White has to say about it.'

'She'd swear black was white and have you believing it, but she likes to blaw about her conquests so you'll maybe be lucky. She's not that bad as a neighbour, mind, for she often does errands for me, but I'm warning you, watch yourself or you'll be a goner.'

McGillivray laughed uproariously. 'I can look after myself. I've met her kind before, and I've never been lost yet.'

A few minutes elapsed after he rang the bell on the next door before it was opened, fractionally. May White held it wider when she saw who it was, and he was shocked to see her enveloped only in a large bath towel.

'Come in, Inspector. I was just having a bath.'

It crossed his mind that she'd seen him going into Mrs Gray's, and had done this on purpose in case he called on her, too, but he sat down on an upright chair. His eyes were drawn to her long, slender legs, on show for as far as was possible, and the deep cleavage which stopped short of revealing her breasts completely, but he averted them hastily.

Her light, musical laugh emphasised her femininity, if anything more was needed to do so. 'Does this bother you, Inspector?' She indicated the towel. 'Would you prefer me to put something on?'

She grinned at his nod. 'Shan't be a tick. Would you like a drink?'

'No, thank you.'

The long sheer negligee she was wearing when she returned showed every part of her as though she were naked, and she lay back provocatively on the settee.

McGillivray's temperature rose by several degrees. This was even worse than the towel. If this was how she received her gentlemen callers, no wonder they fell.

The femme fatale swivelled round to lift a packet of cigarettes from the cocktail cabinet behind her, then stood up and came towards him. 'Will you do the needful and kindle me, Inspector?' It was said with stressed double entendre as she pointed to the lighter lying on the coffee table at his other side.

When he held the flame up for her, she bent over with her breasts brushing his hand, rousing him in spite of himself, so he quickly crossed his legs on the pretext of replacing the lighter. 'You have quite a number of male visitors, I believe, Mrs White?'

She laughed again, knowing how she'd affected him. 'I have to pass the long winter evenings somehow. You wouldn't like to think of poor little me being lonely, would you?' She fluttered her long eyelashes.

'It's got nothing to do with me,' he said as coldly as he could with the blood pounding in his ears. 'If you give me names, in confidence, we'll try to eliminate each one.' He actually hoped she could deny the stories he'd heard about her.

But her eyes were dancing with . . . pride? 'God knows what any of them have to do with Janet Souter's murder, but I don't mind telling you. I've had most of the men around here, and quite a lot of the boys. It's great fun teaching a young lad all the intricacies, you know.' She stroked her thigh lazily.

A strong revulsion swept over him. She was anybody's, after all. Just a whore. Calming, he listened to her rattling off a list of names, most of which he hadn't heard before, although a few caused him to raise a mental eyebrow. It suddenly occurred to him that she could be shielding someone, so he quietly mentioned two reputable men that she had missed.

Her eyes held his for an instant, then she laughed. 'Of course, them, too. You men are all the same, aren't you?' She rose and moved towards him, but he jumped up and sidestepped away from her.

'Thank you very much, Mrs White. That's all I wanted to know.' He strode to the door.

'Inspector,' she called after him, and he turned to see the folds of chiffony nylon lying at her feet.

221

Looking at the typewritten sheets he'd just completed, David Moore reflected that, although he and the inspector had solved some of the problems with which the case was riddled, the original murder, and its perpetrator, was still a mystery, as was the whereabouts of the last jar of jam.

A whodunnit writer would probably call this story 'The Case of the Missing Raspberry Jam', he thought, and realised that it would pass the time to think up more titles. He took out another sheet of paper and began to write.

No.1. The Case of the Missing Raspberry Jam.

No.2. The Mystery of the Diluted Arsenic.

No.3. The Revenge of the Dog Lovers.

No.4. The Bashful Bastard.

He chuckled. Alliteration was more clever, and more fun. He was finding this quite enjoyable.

No.5. The Paperboy's Puzzle.

No.6. The Milkman Misses the Murder.

No.7.

He stopped in the middle of working out one for the postman. How could he have forgotten? There were three other people who had called regularly at Janet Souter's cottage. She could have given one of them the third jar.

He ran through to the front office excitedly. 'Can you give me the addresses for the postman, the milkman and young Willie Arthur?'

PC Paul, although surprised by the sudden order, looked up the telephone directory and read them out while Moore scribbled them down then ran out without a word of thanks.

The sergeant's first call was on the milkman.

'Jam?' Bill Smith looked puzzled. 'Janet Souter never gave me nothing, nae even at Christmas. No, that's nae true. She once presented me wi' a Christmas pud one of her nephews' wives had given her. She said it was an insult, for she aye made her own. My family enjoyed it, though.' He let out a loud laugh. 'Why were you asking about jam?'

'It's a long story, and probably nothing to do with the murder. Thanks just the same.' Moore ran off again.

The postman, Ned French, was just as unhelpful. 'No, I never got anything from her. She never gave anything away, as far as I know. Tight as a duck's arse, she was. But she did used to give me the edge of her tongue if I was late with the post.' He laughed hilariously at the old chestnut.

'Thanks.' David Moore hurried to the last address in Garden Street, which went off the High Street halfway between the police station and the garage.

'Willie's not home from school yet,' Mrs Arthur informed him. 'He shouldn't be long, they get out at ten past twelve.'

Moore looked at his watch. Going off twenty past. 'How long does he take to walk home?'

'It should only be five minutes, but you know boys. He'll be kicking a ball round the playground, I suppose, or making up to the girls. Can I help at all?'

'Did Miss Souter give Willie a jar of jam recently?'

'Old Miss Souter? Her that's been poisoned? You'll be one of the detectives from Edinburgh?'

He smiled. 'That's right.'

'Willie never took home any jam, nor never mentioned any. I don't think she ever gave him anything. Not that he told me.'

'Thanks, Mrs Arthur.' The young sergeant turned sadly away from the door, his bright idea having come to nothing, and was about to go back on to the High Street when he saw young Willie coming from the bottom of the hill. He was kicking a stone in front of him, and Moore went to meet him, in the faint hope that he might have passed the jam to someone other than his mother if he had received it.

'Hello, Willie. Can I have a word with you?'

'Hi, Sarge. Sure, fire ahead.' Willie's final kick sent the stone soaring into a nearby garden.

'Did old Miss Souter give you a jar of jam a week or so back?'

'Huh! Not her! Not a blooming thing. She wouldn't have given you the dirt from under her fingernails.'

Moore laughed. 'So I believe.'

'Why are you asking about jam, Sarge? That's a funny kind of question, isn't it? Was that where the poison was?'

'It's just that there's a jar of jam we can't account for,' Moore said, cagily. 'Miss Souter had laid them out to give to the minister's wife for the Sale of Work, but she didn't give them to her after all. They weren't in her house when it was searched, and we've managed to trace two, but there's one still missing.'

'Who'd pinch a measly jar of jam?' Willie looked sceptical. 'Hey! Wait a minute. You reminded me, speaking about the minister's wife, I did see Mr Valentine up at that end of the High Street one day, carrying a jar of red jam. That's right. It wasn't in a bag or anything. He maybe got it from Miss Souter.'

'Willie, I think you might have hit the jackpot.'

'Huh?'

'I mean, thank you very much. I don't suppose you noticed anything about the jar?'

'Are there different kinds of jars? I never knew that. It was just an ordinary glass jar with a lid on it. No, it wasn't a lid. It was something red and white checked, with a frill.'

'Yes!' David Moore executed a little dance, much to the boy's amazement, then dug into his pocket and extracted a two-pound coin from the handful of loose change. 'Here you are, Willie, and don't spend it all in one shop.' He hurried away, leaving the boy looking at the coin in his hand.

'Blimey, I'm a ruddy copper's nark.' Willie had picked up quite a lot from reading Sexton Blake since Sergeant Black had taken him into his confidence.

David Moore ran up on to the High Street and along to the manse. 'Excuse me, Mrs Valentine,' he said, breathlessly, when she answered the door. 'Did your husband get the gift of a jar of jam from Janet Souter a few days before she died?'

'Why, yes, Sergeant. At least, he didn't tell me it was from her. He just laid it down in the kitchen one morning, the same as he does with all the other little things his

225

parishioners sometimes give him. I knew it was from her, because of the red gingham cover. It was probably one of the things she'd meant to give me for the Sale of Work, and that had been her way of rubbing in the fact that I didn't go back to collect them.'

'That's right. It was originally intended for the Sale. Have you used it yet?'

'Not yet. Why? Do you want to see it?' She took him into the kitchen and lifted it off a shelf where it was sitting in the midst of several other jars of different kinds of preserves.

'I'll have to take this with me, I'm afraid.'

'A vital clue? How exciting.' Mrs Valentine laughed, not taking her own words seriously.

'Thank you, and good morning – or is it good afternoon?'

Moore headed straight back to the police station, where the inspector was waiting for him with a frowning countenance.

'Where have you been gallivanting off to, Moore, and what's this stupid list?' He held up the paper with the book titles. 'I see you've finished the report, but did you find out if the chiropodist had the jam?'

'Yes, sir, I did, and no, he hadn't. But look!' The young sergeant opened the paper bag which Mrs Valentine had given him to carry the jam, and produced the jar with a flourish. 'Voilà!'

The bushy eyebrows quivered. 'Somebody local, was it? Who? Come on, lad, stop mucking about.'

'Well, sir, after I typed out the report, I'd really nothing to do, so I got to thinking up titles that a whodunnit writer might give to our case.' He looked apologetic for a minute, then remembered that he'd no real cause to be sorry about it, because it was what had led him to the recovery of the jam.

'When I came to the milkman, I remembered that Bill Smith, Ned French and Willie Arthur had all been regular callers at Miss Souter's house. So I went to check if any of them had the jam.'

'Which of them, Moore? You're dragging this out on purpose.'

'None of them.' The young man smiled tantalisingly.

'For God's sake, then how did you . . . ?'

'I'm coming to it. Willie recalled seeing Mr Valentine carrying a jar of jam one day, so I went to the manse to check.'

McGillivray grunted. 'What did the minister have to say?'

'I didn't see him, just his wife, and she thought it was a bit of a joke.'

'Probably just as well.'

'So, you see, my list helped me to find the jar.' David Moore grinned broadly and waited for a verbal pat on the back.

The inspector's eyes twinkled mischievously. 'I'm indebted to your childish mentality, then.'

Moore screwed up his face and stuck out his tongue.

'What about the poison provider? Ha! You're not the

only one that can be alliterative. But, with all your creativity, did you remember to go to see him?'

'Yes, I went before that, sir, and he *did* add something to the arsenic, in case Miss Souter got muddled and wasn't very careful with it. Unperfumed talc, would you believe?'

'Moore, I'd believe anything in this bloody case.'

'And he said what he gave her couldn't have killed her if it had got into food, though it would have given her a real bad bellyache, as he put it. Just like Mrs Grant and Mrs Spencer.'

McGillivray grunted with satisfaction. 'That explains why they weren't worse. Thank God he'd the sense to tone it down a bit, but he shouldn't have the bloody stuff at all.'

'I told him that. He's only got a small amount left, and he says it's safely locked away. I don't think he'll dish out any more.' Moore suddenly remembered what the other man had been doing. 'How did you get on with the beautiful May?'

'You wouldn't believe me if I told you, lad.' McGillivray's slight blush whetted the young man's curiosity.

'Go on, sir, tell me the gory details. Did she try to . . . ?'

'She did, my boy, but it's not for innocent ears like yours.'

'For Pete's sake, Inspector, what happened?'

'First, she came to the door with just a bath towel on.'

'Wow! You saw quite a lot of her, I suppose?'

McGillivray laughed. 'Oh yes, quite a lot. Then she offered to put something on.'

'What a shame, spoiling your view like that.'

'I got a better view, lad. She'd put on a see-through robe, or whatever they call those titillating garments.' He could laugh about it now.

'A negligee, probably.'

'Whatever, I could see every curve of her, and she made the most of it. You know, I feel sorry for all the men she boasted about. They never stood a chance.'

'What about you, sir? Weren't you even tempted?'

McGillivray ran his fingers through his hair. He'd certainly been tempted, confirmed bachelor though he was, and if she hadn't bragged so much about the men she'd seduced, he could easily have become involved, too. But her boasting had disgusted him.

He looked at Moore's eager expression and sighed heavily. 'Yes, Sergeant, I must admit I was tempted, but I had my job to do, and I couldn't let myself be ensnared by a cheap whore who'd laid every Tom, Dick and Harry in Tollerton.'

David Moore was astounded. McGillivray must have come pretty close to being ensnared before he was calling her that. 'So you managed to get out still a virgin?'

The inspector let out a loud guffaw. 'Who said I was a virgin when I went in? But seriously, she knows all the wiles. Even when I was leaving, without having done what she openly wanted, she dropped the bloody negligee altogether.'

'Oh, I wish you'd sent me there instead. I'd have enjoyed all that.'

'I've no doubt.' McGillivray was at his most sarcastic. 'And you'd likely never have been seen again. She eats young lads like you for breakfast.'

At that moment, Derek Paul knocked and popped his head round the door. 'That was Thornkirk on the phone. The lab's just notified them that the jam from Spencer's house also contained a very small amount of arsenic.'

McGillivray smiled. 'Fine, and here's another jar to keep them going.'

The constable took it from him, smiling wryly. As he was closing the door he added, 'Oh, and the hospital phoned. Mrs Spencer is recovering nicely.'

The inspector lit a cigarette. 'You know, I thought the arsenic was a red herring laid by the killer, but I'm not so sure now. It might just be an unfortunate coincidence that the murdered woman had been given the stuff, and had told everybody.'

Moore considered this. 'At least you've found out that there was no attempt on the lives of the other two ladies,' he said, helpfully. 'So there's only one crime to solve.'

McGillivray snorted. 'And we're no nearer solving that than we were when we started, are we? There's still the matter of Mrs Wakeford's statement about Ronald and Stephen trying to poison their aunt. We haven't got to the bottom of that yet.'

'Does it matter, seeing it wasn't arsenic that killed her?'

'Yes, dammit! It does matter. I hate loose ends, even if they've nothing to do with the case.' McGillivray drummed his fingers on the table, and stared at a mark on the formica. In any case, one of the arsenic users could have had a second attempt.'

Moore sat in sympathetic silence and tried furiously to think of some suitable suggestion. It seemed that every time they thought they'd found a lead, it came to a dead end. 'We don't have to worry about anybody else being poisoned, though, now that we've accounted for the three jars of jam.'

There was a brief pause before the inspector heaved a weary sigh and pushed back his chair. 'I suppose we have placed a few more pieces in the jigsaw today, but it's a slow, slow business. We'd better give our brains a rest for a while, and concentrate on stoking up the inner man. I function better on a full belly.'

Chapter Sixteen

Tuesday 29th November, afternoon

'We'd better have another look at our list, I think. Things have changed somewhat since we went over it last.'

Inspector McGillivray spread the paper out on the table in the incident room. He and Moore had finished their lunch, and were ready to plan their next line of investigation.

'Mabel Wakeford,' he began. 'We know she added arsenic to the three jars, but I don't think she carried out the actual murder. She was too upset about the consequences of her act, and she honestly seemed to believe Janet Souter had been poisoned.' He rubbed his chin. 'She's unlikely.'

Highly bloody unlikely, thought the sergeant, but kept his opinion to himself.

'Grace Skinner. It's the same with her, really. She meant to kill the old woman, and thought she had till we told her different. And there's no evidence of her attempt because she must have used the substitute bag.'

'She'll be unlikely, too, though?'

'Yes, unless she's a better liar than we think. Mrs White

now. She may be easy – she *is* easy – but I don't believe she worried about anyone knowing what she was up to, not even Janet Souter. In fact, she boasts about it, and the whole place knows . . . except her husband, probably. Another unlikely.'

David Moore rubbed his hands together in glee. 'That's narrowing them down. Who's left?'

'Douglas Pettigrew's out, anyway, but Ronald Baker . . . His motive's all too obvious so he's still a possible suspect. Which brings us to his cousin, Stephen Drummond. I don't think he's guilty, but his wife poses a problem.'

McGillivray scratched his head. 'She's got the nerve, I fancy, and could have bumped off the old auntie to let Stephen get his inheritance. His jitters could have been because he knew she'd done it, though I can't see what opportunity she had. But she's a very strong possible. What d'you think, Moore?'

'I'm inclined to agree with you, and she could be Mrs Wakeford's child, which might have something to do with it.'

'Right. I think we'll go back to Thornkirk this afternoon and have another word with Ronald and Stephen. It should be quite interesting without their wives being there, and I'm going to put on the pressure a bit. We seemed to be on a lucky streak this morning, so I hope it holds.'

Ribco, Ronald Ian Baker's small engineering firm, seemed busy enough, and he greeted the two detectives

233

quite pleasantly when they were shown into his office. He gestured to them to take a seat, and they sat on what were obviously chairs for his prospective clients.

'More questions, Inspector?'

'I'm afraid so. We have reason to believe that you planned to murder your aunt.'

Ronald gasped, and the colour drained slowly from his face. Even David Moore was surprised at the suddenness of McGillivray's shock tactics, but he watched the man very closely.

'I . . . I wasn't even there at the time,' Ronald said, desperately.

McGillivray continued to look at him, saying nothing, but hoping that Ronald didn't have an iron nerve.

He didn't. He collapsed against the back of his chair. 'I don't know how you got on to me. I thought it was safe enough, because I would be miles away when the arsenic killed her.'

Moore glanced, with disappointment, at the inspector, who, although he said, 'Tell me about it, Mr Baker', was also thinking that this was surely another dead end.

Ronald took a deep breath. 'My Aunt Janet was a vile woman, as you've probably discovered. She toyed with Stephen and me like a cat toys with mice, and held her money over our heads.'

He took a handkerchief out and wiped his brow. 'I'd asked her for the loan of some cash – you were right about the firm being in difficulties – and she refused. Then she told us about the arsenic and the idea just drifted into my

234

head. I thought it was foolproof. She was the one who had got it, and I wouldn't be anywhere near when she used it.'

'Where did you put it?' McGillivray's voice was low.

'In her flour bin, of course. Isn't that where you found it? You likely sent all her food to be tested, I'd forgotten about that, when I was making my plan.'

The colour was gradually coming back into his cheeks as he poured out his story. 'I've been living in dread this past week, but I'm glad you found out. I couldn't have gone on much longer.'

'Yes, guilt is more gruelling than any other emotion.'

'I'm ready to come with you.' Ronald stood up. 'I'll get my coat. But – am I allowed to phone my wife to let her know what's happening?'

'Just a minute, Mr Baker. What would you say if I told you that no arsenic was found in your aunt's flour bin?'

Ronald gasped again, and sat down with a thump. 'What do you mean? There must have been. I shook in a fair amount and left it lying on top without mixing it. It might not have worked if it had been stirred in properly.'

'It was only the flour bin you touched?'

The man seemed quite perplexed by the question. 'Oh yes. I was scared that my aunt would come through to the kitchen and catch me red-handed – um, white-handed.' He smiled a little at his pathetic attempt at a joke, then went on, 'I'd told Flora to keep her talking, you see, but I can't depend on my wife for anything, so I did it as quickly as I could and put the polythene bag back in the shed.'

McGillivray placed his fingertips together. 'I see. You didn't go back to her house on the Wednesday night?'

'No, why should I? It was just a case of waiting. Flora and I were on edge from the Saturday until the Thursday evening when the local police notified us that she'd been found dead.'

'And you thought you were responsible for her death?'

'Naturally. I *was* responsible.'

'As I said already, no traces of arsenic were found in her system.'

'I can't understand it. Didn't she have any arsenic, then? Was it all a lie? I knew she took Stephen and me for fools, but, God Almighty, that's really wicked.'

'Yes, she was given arsenic, but, for some reason, she meant to get you to try to poison her, so she hid it away. There was only flour in the bag you used, Mr Baker.'

Ronald opened his desk drawer and took out a half bottle of whisky. 'Do you mind, Inspector? This has all come as a terrible shock.'

He took a good swig from the bottle, and sat thinking, while McGillivray turned and shrugged his shoulders at his sergeant.

'You are quite innocent of murder, if what you say is true,' he said quietly.

Ronald placed both his elbows on the desk and dropped his head on his hands. He stayed like that for some time before he lifted his face to look at the detectives again. 'Oh, God, it's like a last minute reprieve from the death chamber, I can tell you. I thought I was a goner when you came in first.'

236

'Just answer me one question, please. Can you account for your movements on the Wednesday night?'

'The night before she was found? The night she was murdered, you mean? Let me see. That was the night we had the Cruickshanks in. I remember, because Flora and I were both so tensed up it was a relief to have somebody else there. We had quite a drinking session. They did not go until after one in the morning and they'd to take a taxi because neither of them was fit to drive. They left their car here and came back for it the next day. You can check with Tom Cruickshank, if you like.'

'Yes, I'm afraid I'll have to. Would you mind giving me his address?'

'Phone him from here, Inspector. It's 546621.'

The man who answered McGillivray's call laughed at the memory of their convivial evening, but confirmed that he and his wife hadn't left the Bakers' house until after one.

'And Ronald was absolutely pissed by that time, too,' he added. 'We left Flora about to put him to bed, though she was almost as bad herself.'

McGillivray laid down the phone. 'Oh well, that seems to be that. He corroborated everything you said.' He thought it unlikely that Ronald Baker had forewarned his friend.

'Before you go, Inspector, would you mind telling me how my aunt died if it wasn't the arsenic?'

'I'm sorry, sir. I can't divulge that information.'

'Have you any idea as to who did it?'

'We are whittling down the suspects.'

'You mean . . . there's more than one? Who on earth could have . . . ?'

McGillivray glanced at his sergeant, who sprang up to open the door. Ronald was unscrewing the cap of his bottle again when they went out.

Both Stephen Drummond and his young assistant were serving when they entered his shop, and he gave a start when he saw them.

When Stephen's customer went out, the inspector said, 'May we have a private word with you, Mr Drummond?'

In the back shop, McGillivray took the direct attack again. 'We have reason to believe that you planned to murder your aunt.'

The reaction this time was different. Stephen looked him straight in the eye and said, 'I don't know who told you that.'

'Is it true?'

'Is it a crime to think about murder?'

'Not unless you actually do something about it.'

Stephen smiled. 'Then I can tell you the truth, Inspector. I'd often wished that my aunt was dead, then that day, when she told us about the arsenic, I thought it was a heaven-sent opportunity to dispose of her. I came home and decided to put some in her flour bin the following Sunday, that being where it would be least likely to be noticed.

'When I got the chance, the next week, I lifted the lid, but the flour was almost at the top, so I looked in the sugar

238

bin. That looked just as powdery as the flour – Barbara said she always used caster – and I thought it would do as well in there.'

'So you put it in the sugar instead of the flour?'

Slowly, Stephen shook his head. 'As my wife keeps telling me, I'm useless. When it came to the crunch, I couldn't do it.'

'So you didn't really attempt to poison her, after all?' McGillivray believed the man's story. It was too ridiculous to be fiction.

'No, I didn't, so I was very surprised when the two policemen came on the Thursday night to tell us Aunt Janet had been found dead. I thought it must have been from natural causes till you came asking questions.'

'Unfortunately, it wasn't from natural causes, Mr Drummond. She *was* murdered.'

'But who?' The man was clearly at a loss, and stood with his brow furrowed. 'Would it have been Ronald? She'd likely told him about the arsenic as well, and he was trying to get money from her, I know.'

'Your aunt didn't die of arsenic poisoning.'

Stephen's face reflected the turmoil in his brain. 'Well, I can't think of a soul other than Ronald and myself who'd have benefited from her death. Er . . . Excuse me, Inspector, can you tell me how she *was* killed?'

'I'm not at liberty to say anything more, I'm afraid.'

Stephen sat down weakly. 'I honestly thought she'd had a well-timed heart attack. I won't pretend to be sorry she's dead, as I was never very fond of her, but . . . murder!'

239

'You planned to murder her yourself,' McGillivray reminded him.

'It didn't feel like murder, you know. More like doing a service to mankind in general, and myself in particular. But I didn't do it.' He looked rather regretful.

Making one last token gesture, McGillivray said, 'What were your movements on the night she was murdered?'

'Thursday? No, that was the day she was found. Did she die the previous night? Well, last Wednesday, Barbara and I had a very quiet evening at home. To be frank, she was giving me hell because there was no word of Janet's death, and I was terrified she'd find out I'd funked it. We passed a very unpleasant evening, and we couldn't even afford any whisky to cheer us up.'

His woebegone expression made McGillivray smile. 'You were together the whole evening?'

'Unfortunately, yes, and the whole night.' He pulled a wry face.

'That's all, then, Mr Drummond. We'll let you get back to your customers.'

The inspector sighed when they went back to the car. 'That was another wild goose chase.'

Moore revved up the engine and let out the clutch. 'It explains why Mr and Mrs Drummond were both so nervous last time we spoke to them. She thought he'd done it, and he was scared she'd find out he hadn't.' He blew the horn as a little Datsun overtook and drew close in front of them. 'Look at that stupid blighter. That kind of

240

thing makes me mad.' He shot a quick look at his superior. 'It's back to Tollerton now, is it?'

'Aye, nothing else for it. But we've written off our two main suspects. Or, at least, who everybody thinks were the two main suspects.' McGillivray's voice was gloomy. 'As Gilbert and Sullivan said, "A policeman's lot is not a happy one." Ha, bloody ha! We'll have to start on Mrs White's conquests, after all, my last hope.'

'Oh, she did give you something, did she? I forgot to ask about that.'

'She named some of her regular callers.'

'I bet you were surprised at some of them, eh, Inspector?'

'Yes, I was, and not much surprises me these days. But Douglas Pettigrew's father was one. No wonder he was so upset when he learned his son was another of her customers. Oh, what a tangled web some men weave.'

'Do you suspect the chemist now?'

'I don't know,' admitted McGillivray. 'He might have been scared in case May spilled the beans about him to his son, but I can't see why that would make him bump off Janet Souter.'

'He could have been worried in case she'd tell his wife if she'd seen him coming from May's house, too.' Moore sounded eager.

'You've got something there, lad, and the needle and insulin would have been at his hand. Speaking of that, the other name I dragged out of Mrs White was the doctor, would you believe, and he's another one with the means

241

to kill her at hand and the know-how to use them. It was the blasted arsenic that set me off on the wrong track, and it looks like it had nothing to do with the case at all. He should have been one of the first suspects. Funny how your brain gets fogged up and just works in one direction.'

'You solved all the problems about the arsenic, though,' the young man consoled. 'That took a bit of doing, sir.'

'Aye.' McGillivray put his hands behind his head and stared at the roof. 'I've got the feeling Mrs White's definitely connected somewhere, and somebody silenced the old woman because they were scared they'd be found out taking up with her.'

David Moore was agog to know which of the other men in the village had been in the habit of going to May White's, and, after a minute, his curiosity got the better of him. 'Um . . . who else was involved with her, sir?'

'The butcher, the baker, the candlestick maker – that sort of thing. Most of the tradesmen and anybody of any consequence, even some of no consequence at all except to themselves, though she likely magnified their involvement.'

'So we've got a whole new list of suspects?' There was a downhearted tone in Moore's voice.

'I think not: I can't face that right now. I've just the two medically inclined gentlemen in mind at present, but if they prove false leads, I'll have to spread the net wider.'

When they arrived back in Tollerton, the inspector went into the police station in case there were any messages, while Moore parked the Vauxhall then sat in the Starline lounge to wait for him.

Excitement shone from McGillivray's eyes when he appeared ten minutes later, but he merely said, 'Upstairs.'

In his room, he kicked off his shoes and sat down on the bed. 'I've just found out something – the identity of Mrs Wakeford's child, at long last.'

His sergeant, who was in the middle of loosening his tie, halted with his hand at his neck. 'How? Who?'

'Your command of the English language amazes me at times, Moore. 'The "how" came about because Martin Spencer had left a message for me to phone him. One of his clerks had been trawling through the archives to find the name of the adoptive parents. They were a Mr and Mrs Patton of Thornkirk, both now deceased.'

'Don't tell me the trail ends there?' Moore looked very crestfallen. 'This person could be the murderer, if it's somebody with a position to keep up, and it wasn't one of the men who's been associating with May White.' He hesitated, then said, accusingly, 'But you said you'd found out the identity, so you haven't told me everything. Come on, out with it.'

The inspector smiled enigmatically. 'You're right, my young friend. The trail didn't end there, fortunately, or unfortunately, whichever way you look at it. It seems old Matthew Dean had written the child's baptismal name on the back of the adoption document, in pencil. Felicity.'

Moore's brow wrinkled. 'Felicity Patton? But there isn't a Felicity anything connected with our case, is there?'

McGillivray was enjoying keeping him on tenterhooks. It made up for being kept waiting to hear who had the last

243

jar of jam. He put his fingertips together and gripped his mouth for a moment. 'Have patience, lad. There's more. Also on the back of the document, Matthew Dean had pencilled, at a later date, "Felicity Muriel Patton, married Adam Valentine, 23.7.86." Now do you understand my reluctance to involve her?'

The sergeant gave a low whistle. 'The minister's wife! Wow! He calls her Muriel, her middle name. I wonder why?'

The inspector took out his cigarettes and tried his lighter hopefully. 'Blast! I should have bought some stuff to fill this.' He dug in his pocket for matches. 'There could be any number of reasons why she uses her middle name. Her adoptive parents might have started it; she might hate the name Felicity; she could have feared it was her natural mother who'd called her that and avoided using it.'

'In case the mother recognised it,' Moore put in, full of excitement. 'It's an unusual name.'

'Exactly, but none of these reasons are criminal. She's at liberty to call herself by her middle name if she wants to. The thing is, had Janet Souter found out the truth somehow, and . . . ?'

'Oh, sir, Mrs Valentine would never have killed her.'

'Probably not, so we're no further forward, after all.'

Moore, however, was thinking of something else. 'Mrs Wakeford and Mrs Valentine might be delighted to be brought together, sir. They're ideally suited as mother and daughter. Couldn't we . . . ?'

'No, no,' McGillivray said hastily. 'We can't interfere in

that kind of thing. Mrs Wakeford would possibly be delighted, but Mrs Valentine mightn't even know she was an adopted child. We can't muck up her life.'

He drew on his cigarette. 'Two things have begun to bother me, Moore. The chemist never mentioned to you that Miss Souter had spilt the beans to him about Douglas, did he?'

'That's right. We'll have to look into that. But what's the other thing that's bothering you, sir?'

The inspector dropped his ash into the glass ashtray. 'The other thing is – why didn't Adam Valentine tell us he'd seen the murdered woman that week?'

'You mean the day she gave him the jam? She could have called him in, or gone out herself, and just given it to him.'

'I'd like to jog his memory, just the same. She might've said something about somebody that would help us.'

'But he said he didn't know anything.' Moore went no further.

'I think we'll pay the chemist a visit after dinner, now we've discovered he's got a motive, and then put the frighteners on Randall. If we've no luck with either of them, we'll give the Reverend a quick call. We might just manage to squeeze some relevant information out of him, though he probably doesn't realise he knows anything.'

Chapter Seventeen

Tuesday 29th November, evening

At seven twenty, Douglas Pettigrew called for his re-instated sweetheart, Phyllis Barclay, and they stood outside her house for a few moments, discussing where to go.

Tollerton boasted no cinema, disco or any other place of entertainment, just a slightly grotty pub at one end of the High Street and the Starline Hotel in the middle, plus the Youth Club, which met only on Wednesdays in the Church Hall.

The lack of facilities was no hardship to young courting couples in the summer, as they usually took a walk beyond the village into the countryside, though the more passionate of them often ended up by going down Ashgrove Lane, and climbing the wall at the foot to cross the railway line. At the other side of the tracks, a fairly dense wood provided many exciting secluded spots where inhibitions could be overcome – or forgotten altogether.

But lying under the trees on a bed of dead leaves was not a pleasant prospect on this bitterly cold night, the second last in November, so Douglas and his girlfriend plumped for the Starline, which was warm and clean, if not very private.

Having bought a tomato juice for Phyllis and a half pint of lager for himself, he carried them across to the table in the corner and sat down very close to her. 'I'm glad we're back together again,' he murmured, taking her hand and squeezing it.

'So'm I.' Phyllis snuggled against him on the padded seat. 'I really missed you when you were . . .'

'Making a fool of myself,' he finished for her. 'I don't know what the hell got into me. It all, sort of, happened.'

A glutton for punishment, Phyllis wanted to hear how a – to her – middle-aged, married woman could have lured Douglas away from a girl his own age. 'How did it happen? What did she do?'

He took a sip of his lager. 'The first time, she stood watching me till I put a new fuse in one of her plugs, then she offered me a drink. I didn't want to let her know I'd never drunk spirits, so I took this large glass of whisky.'

'Did you get drunk?' That might excuse his behaviour.

'I don't think so. A bit happy, maybe, but I was scared out of my wits when she sat down beside me on the settee, so I moved away a bit. She laughed at that and I just stood up went home.'

'But you must have kept on going back?' she persisted.

He looked even more uncomfortable. 'Oh, you don't want to hear any more, Phyllis. I was just plain daft.'

Realising at last that it would probably be too painful to hear all the sordid details of his affair, Phyllis changed the subject. 'I wonder if the detectives have got any further with their investigiation? The sergeant came into the shop, you know, asking what Miss Wheeler knew about Janet Souter.'

'They suspected me of doing her in.' He could laugh about it now, but he'd had the wind up at all the questioning. Innocent men had been arrested before.

'You did threaten her on the street,' she reminded him. 'And a lot of people heard you.'

Phyllis wasn't actually one hundred per cent sure if she really believed he was innocent. That's what gave a touch of mystery and fascination to their dates now. 'Yes, I was the murderer's girlfriend,' she could say to the reporters after he was found guilty. She pulled herself up with a jerk when she realised what she was thinking – Douglas could never have done it.

'I know I said I'd sort her out,' he was saying, 'but I never really meant to do anything, especially not murder. But I'd a good alibi, so it's all over now, and that's enough about it. Did you see that new pop programme last night?'

The current favourite groups, their albums and singles, held their attention for the next hour, until Phyllis said, 'I told Mum I'd be home early tonight. I want to wash my hair, and I promised I'd give her a hand with the ironing – my own things, anyway. Don't bother coming home with me.'

Her house was just three doors along, but she was rather disappointed that Douglas didn't insist on accompanying her. She'd only herself to blame.

He couldn't help thinking about his visits to May, Phyllis had brought it fresh to his mind, and he remembered their first kiss. He'd kissed girls before, including Phyllis, but never anything like that, and he'd been completely lost.

Recalling their nights of passion, he felt an unwanted need of her surging up in him, and he rose to buy another lager to cool down. His train of thought refused to be broken, however, and he remembered how pleased he'd been, with her and himself, when they'd finished their lovemaking that last night, until she rolled over and laughed at him.

'You can't make love like a man, Dougie boy,' she'd taunted him. 'My men can be animals, and that's the way I like it.'

'Your men?' He'd been horrified at what she was inferring.

'Most of the men round here have been in this bed at one time or other. You name them, I've had them.'

He'd named two men he imagined to be unlikely and she'd laughed again. 'Yes, they've both been here. Ask them if you don't believe me, though I bet they're too scared of their wives to admit it. They weren't too bad, but there's one . . . Oh, boy! As a lover, he's absolutely marvellous.'

'Your husband, I suppose?' Jealousy of that lucky man often came to his mind.

'God, no. Not Gilbert. Lean over and I'll whisper his name in your ear.'

Masochism, and sheer curiosity, had made him obey, and he'd been shocked when she told him, although he hadn't fully believed her. He'd been sickened by her boasting, and had left as soon as he pulled on his clothes. He'd felt sapped, knowing that she'd been laughing at him all along.

That had been the night before old Nosey Parker Souter told his father about him, and he'd been secretly relieved to have the excuse not to go back to May's house.

He took a gulp of his lager and something else stirred in his mind. Something he'd thought nothing of at the time, but now it came back vividly and meaningfully. He'd seen the very man May had raved about coming out of Janet Souter's garden after midnight one night, stealthily and furtively – or was he just imagining that bit?

It was the night that he'd gone down to spy on May, to settle the seething unrest inside him, to know for sure that she had other men friends. He'd hung around the foot of the Lane for almost an hour, lurking in the shadows of the railway wall, but had seen nobody coming in or going out, and had given up his vigil about five past midnight, frozen to the marrow.

She was a liar as well as a tart, he'd thought angrily as he walked up the hill, and had laughed at himself for believing what she'd told him. She'd been wanting rid of him – that's what it had been. That was when he had made up his mind to go back to Phyllis Barclay again, if she'd have him.

He'd treated her badly, and he wouldn't blame her if she refused to have anything more to do with him, but he'd ask her. She was a decent girl, and he respected her for stopping him when she thought he was going too far. It wouldn't stop him from trying, though, if he got the chance. He smiled to himself.

When he was halfway between the bottom group of houses and Honeysuckle Cottages, he'd seen the man coming out of the middle gate, wearing the long coat he always wore in the winter. It was difficult to see his face at first, but when he turned into the High Street his profile had been unmistakable in the light from the street lamps.

That had been on the night he was playing snooker, Douglas remembered then; the night the inspector was interested in; the night that Janet Souter had been murdered.

The youth's blood ran cold. He'd better find McGillivray right away and let him know.

He jumped up quickly and went through the bar into the hotel itself and after enquiring at the desk for the inspector's room number, he took the stairs two at a time and knocked on the door. When he received no answer to his second knock, he raced down and out on to the street.

Thinking that Sergeant Black would know where to find the CID men, he ran along to the police station, where the local sergeant looked up in surprise when he burst in breathlessly.

'What's up, Douglas?'

'Where's the Chief Inspector?'

'He'll be at the Starline.'

'I've just come from there. I've got to find him, it's very important.'

John Black could see that the boy was in a state of extreme agitation. 'Is there anything I can do?'

'No, it's to do with the murder, and it's McGillivray I'll have to tell.'

Slightly offended, Black said, 'I've no idea where he is, if he isn't at the hotel. They're maybe not in the village at all. They often go to Thornkirk to interview suspects, though he usually tells me before he goes.'

Douglas shook his head. 'Their Vauxhall's sitting in the Starline carpark. I noticed it when I came past.'

'They must be around here somewhere, then, but I can't tell you where, because I don't know. I think you'd better tell me whatever it is that's got you so steamed up.'

It came pouring out. 'It was the night of the murder, you see, and I'd gone down to watch May White's house.'

He saw the sergeant giving him a peculiar look and tried to explain. 'I'd been a bloody idiot and I was glad to be finished with her, but I wanted to prove to myself that she'd been telling the truth about all the lovers she'd had. So I went and hid beside the railway wall and waited for nearly an hour, but nobody came near her. She'd told me, as well, about this special man, this best lover, and when I was halfway up the Lane to go home, I saw him coming out of old Miss Souter's gate. It would have been about ten past twelve, maybe just before.' He stopped for breath.

John Black, who'd been listening with only half an ear

to the boy's ramblings, suddenly straightened up and took notice. 'What night did you say that was?'

'Last Wednesday, the night before she was found. I didn't think anything about it at the time, but now – well, he must have just done her in and it wasn't arsenic.'

'How did you know it wasn't arsenic?' The sergeant's voice was sharp and suspicious; this information had been kept from the general public.

'The inspector asked me if I'd ever trained as a chemist, so I guessed she must've been killed with some other kind of poison. A bloody fiend, that's what he is.'

'Who was this man?'

Leaning across the counter, Douglas said the name quietly, then stood back, enjoying the expression on the other man's face, and knowing exactly how he felt.

'Douglas Pettigrew! You've been drinking! I can smell it on your breath.'

'I only had two halves of lager, that's all. I'm dead sober, and I tell you, that's who it was. I saw his face by the streetlight, so I'm positive.'

'And you say Mrs White told you he was the best . . . ? Oh no, I can't believe that. A man of the cloth? She must have been lying through her teeth.' Black's scandalised face was almost as red as the youth's now.

'She might well have been, Sergeant, I'm not denying that, but it *was* him I saw coming out of Janet Souter's gate that night. What'll we do?'

Rubbing his jaw, Black considered for a moment. 'Well, I don't know. It's Derek's night off, and I can't leave this place unattended. The inspector'll likely call in here before he goes back to the hotel. I think you'd be best to wait here for him.'

'It's the only thing I can do, I suppose.' Douglas shrugged and went over to sit on the bench. 'He's going to be bloody annoyed at me, anyway, for telling him a lie about Wednesday night. Well, not a lie, exactly, but not the whole truth.'

'You're speaking in riddles.'

'He asked me to account for my movements, and I told him I'd been playing snooker all evening. That was true enough, but we went into the pub for about an hour, I forgot about that when I was speaking to him. My mum told the young sergeant I was home by five past eleven and never went out again, which wasn't true, though she didn't know.'

'I hope the inspector can understand what you're at, Douglas, for I'm dashed if I can.'

'She didn't know I went out again. I told you, I wanted to spy on May, so I nipped out of my bedroom window on to the roof of my Dad's lean-to store. I've done it often enough before, and I always went back the same way. I didn't tell the inspector, because I didn't remember it was the same night.'

'How did you come to put two and two together?'

'I was in the Starline lounge bar with Phyllis and she was asking me about May, and after she went home I began going over things in my mind, and it just struck me. If he denies everything, McGillivray'll suspect me again, and I *was* in the Lane that night. My God! It'll be the finish of me, for I know who the inspector's going to believe.'

Douglas turned stricken eyes on the sergeant, who didn't know what to think, and was turning Douglas's incredible story over and over in his mind.

At last Black said, 'We'll have to wait till the inspector gets back, but stop worrying, Douglas. I'm sure the truth'll come out, whatever it is.'

When his wife took the two men into the room, Sydney Pettigrew raised his head in annoyance at the intrusion. He was watching the BBC news and objected to being disturbed, particularly by these two.

He recognised the young, well-dressed sergeant who'd come into the shop asking questions on the day they arrived, and he presumed the other one was the inspector. There was always something about policemen, even in plain clothes, that you couldn't mistake, apart from the size of their feet. They'd been harassing Douglas, but that was all sorted out now according to the boy, so why had they come here?

With barely concealed resignation, he rose and switched off his television set. 'Yes?'

'We won't take long, but we'd like to ask you a few questions, Mr Pettigrew. I suppose you know we're investigating the murder of Janet Souter?'

It was the older man who spoke, and Sydney thought that he didn't look much like a detective chief inspector – more like an uncouth farm labourer with his rough

255

clothes, or a boxer, with his broken nose. 'Yes, I know who you are. Moore and McGillivray, I believe. A fine-sounding double act, but your performance doesn't measure up too well. Have you run out of suspects, or are you casting about blindly for inspiration, on the off chance of striking it lucky?'

'Neither, sir.' McGillivray was careful to remain polite, but he hadn't cared for the man's sarcastic remarks, nor for him putting the sergeant's name first. 'We've to be as thorough in our search as we can. How well did you know the murdered lady?'

The chemist raised one shoulder. 'Fairly well, as a customer, and I've sampled her vile tongue for years, like all the other shopkeepers in Tollerton, as I told your sergeant.'

'Even in your line of work?'

'Oh yes. She complained about my prices every time she came in, and then there was the business about our Douglas and May Falconer, er, White, which I've no doubt you'll have sniffed out. She was very outspoken about that, although I was glad she told me. I soon put a stop to it.' His stern expression was that of a Victorian father.

The inspector coughed discreetly. 'That would have given your son a very good motive for killing her, of course.'

'It would look that way to your suspicious mind, but I think the boy had seen the error of his ways before that. He wasn't too upset about it.'

There had been enough shilly-shallying, McGillivray decided. 'Mrs White has been giving the names of the men who've been involved with her, and I must say she seems very popular. I expect there are quite a lot of married men shaking in their shoes right now, in case their liaisons with her come to light.'

He thought he could detect a slight, very slight, flash of alarm in the man's eyes, but it was quickly gone. Perhaps he'd been mistaken.

'She's well known to be a bit of a story-teller.'

'A liar, do you mean?'

The chemist shifted uncomfortably in his seat. 'A stronger word than I'd have used, Inspector, but I think she wanted people to think she was a *femme fatale*, and exaggerated a bit for effect.'

He glanced at his wife, who was listening to the questioning, and smiled to her. She smiled back. There was no anger or suspicion on her face, and their relationship appeared to be genuinely warm and loving.

Watching him watching the inspector, David Moore felt that Pettigrew wasn't in the least affected by the ominous silence with which McGillivray was trying to break his nerve.

Pettigrew lifted his pipe from the mantelpiece and took a box of matches from his pocket. 'D'you mind if I light up?'

McGillivray waved his hand dismissively, so the chemist struck a match and drew on the stem of his briar, his hands quite steady.

At last, the inspector spoke. He'd been debating on whether or not he should accost the man about his infidelity, and had decided against breaking up a seemingly happy marriage. 'You supply hypodermic syringes, I presume?'

Pettigrew appeared to be genuinely puzzled. 'Of course, just a few, to diabetics with a doctor's prescription. We've to be careful nowadays, in case of drug takers.'

'I see.' Callum McGillivray stood up, aware that his strategy hadn't paid off this time. 'Thank you.'

The chemist showed them out, more polite than he had hitherto been. 'I'm sorry I haven't been able to help you, Inspector. You know, I was rather annoyed when you came in, about you suspecting Douglas, and . . .'

'He's in the clear now. I'm sorry if you thought we were badgering him . . .'

'I realise you've your job to do. Murder's a terrible crime, and if there's anything you want to know, don't hesitate to ask me.'

Outside, McGillivray sighed. 'Either he deserves an Oscar, or he knows nothing. I believe he might have been involved with Mrs White at some time, but it's not our business, unless . . .'

'I'm sorry to interrupt you, Doctor,' McGillivray said when John Randall opened the door to them himself. 'We've a few questions to ask you.'

'Come in, come in. You're not interrupting anything. I was just reading the *Evening Citizen*. He ushered them into a large square room, obviously furnished in the twenties or thirties – and lovingly cared for since. Probably his childhood home, Moore guessed . . .

Indicating the tray of dirty dishes sitting on the table, he said, 'Don't mind me. I generally eat off a tray. My daily prepares a meal for me, I just carry it through, and, being a bachelor, I don't always bother to clear things away.'

'I'm the same myself,' the chief inspector admitted.

'Good. Now I don't feel so remiss. What can I do for you?'

McGillivray decided to take off the kid gloves this time. 'We believe that you were one of Mrs May White's callers?'

Randall's face turned a deep scarlet. 'Who told you that?'

'I'm glad you're not denying it. It came from the lady herself.'

The doctor was obviously thinking how to explain his behaviour, but decided to brazen it out. 'A year or two ago I was attending her for a bout of shingles, and . . . we . . . she persuaded me to be more than her physician.'

'Weren't you afraid you might be seen?'

'I suppose you mean Janet Souter. Now I see what you're after. No, I had no worries about being seen. I am a single man and it is nobody's business what I do.'

'Yes, you're quite right, Doctor, but you have a position to uphold . . . ?'

'I've never given a damn what other people think of me, Inspector, and I've no intention of apologising to you for that.'

'No, of course not, I'm sorry. It's just . . . we've . . . run out of suspects and . . .'

'You were going to put the blame on me? My God! You've got some nerve!'

'No, Doctor. You've got me all wrong.'

Randall suddenly exploded with laughter. 'Good God, man, I haven't enjoyed anything so much for a long time. To think you've got me down as a profligate! I only . . . dallied, shall I say, with the ravishing May once, and it left me feeling dirty and ashamed. I did not repeat the experience, though the next time she called me in, on some trivial pretext, it took all my willpower to refuse her. You don't know what she's like.'

McGillivray grinned ruefully. 'Ah, but I do know, Doctor. I'd the devil's own job to keep from . . . I'm sorry if I stepped out of line earlier, but you can surely understand . . .'

'Don't be sorry, McGillivray, I do understand. You have your job to do in the way you see fit, and I had a damned good laugh out of it.'

'It's good of you to take it like that, sir, and goodnight to you.'

Moore, who had said nothing since they entered the house, couldn't help smiling as Randall winked at him while they went out.

In the car again, McGillivray said, 'Don't say a word, lad. I know I handled that badly, so just learn from my gaffe.'

'Yes, sir. Where to now?'

'Where do you think?'

Muriel Valentine came to the door of the manse when McGillivray rang the bell. 'We'd like to speak to your husband, if you don't mind.'

'Adam's out on one of his calls, but he shouldn't be long. Please come in and wait.'

She was neatly, if not stylishly, dressed in a pleated skirt and woollen jumper, and her knitting was lying on the small table where she'd laid it before answering the door.

'Does your husband make many evening calls?'

'Quite a lot. Most families are all out working during the day, so he finds it easier to get them at home in the evenings.' She picked up her knitting and carried on with it.

McGillivray persisted. 'Is he ever out till the early hours?'

'There are times when he has to stay with relatives of a dying person, or with somebody who's in trouble. He's like a doctor, really, always on call.'

'Aren't you scared, being alone in this big house on the dark winter nights?'

'A bit nervous, sometimes, but some of the Guild ladies call occasionally to ask about things we've planned to raise money.'

The sound of a key in the lock heralded the return of the minister. 'Oh hello, Inspector,' he said cheerily, when he came in. 'And Sergeant. Were you waiting to see me? Just a minute till I hang up my coat.'

He disappeared into the hall and came back rubbing his

261

hands together. 'It doesn't get any warmer, does it? But we've Christmas to look forward to. What can I do for you?'

What a striking couple they made, Moore thought, fleetingly. She with her blonde, wavy hair, pink and white complexion and liquid blue eyes, and he with his dark good looks, piercing brown eyes and tall, muscular body.

'We're trying to trace anybody who came in contact with Miss Souter over, say, a week before she was killed,' the inspector was saying. 'They may have noticed, or heard her saying, something which could give us a lead, though they don't think it's important. We'll be able to sort the chaff from the grain. When did you see her last, sir?'

'Let me see.' Adam Valentine lifted his hand to his broad forehead, but, after thinking for a moment he said, 'No, I'm sorry. It was three weeks before her death that I paid her a visit, and I haven't seen her at all since then.'

'So you won't be able to help us?' McGillivray shrugged. 'Ah, well, it's all in the game. It's a pity, in a way, that there aren't more people like Miss Souter herself. She noticed everything that was going on, more than she was meant to sometimes, I imagine.' He chuckled softly.

'Yes, she did,' Mrs Valentine said. 'But she was a cruel, malicious gossip, and we're very glad that there aren't more like her in our village.' Her voice had risen slightly.

The inspector smiled. 'It's just as well everybody's made differently, but old Mrs Gray at the foot of Ashgrove Lane has been telling me quite a few things.'

'I wouldn't give too much credence to what Mrs Gray says,' remarked the minister. 'She's failing, you know.'

'She's still got all her faculties, Adam.' His wife sounded rather indignant.

'She was telling me what she saw from her window,' McGillivray went on. 'And Mrs White, next door to her, was doing a bit of boasting about her various lovers – likely greatly embroidered, of course, to impress a bit more. It must be a lonely life for her, with her husband away so much.'

As far as Moore could see, the minister's only reaction to this was a slight tightening of his jaw, but Mrs Valentine's laugh was full of scorn.

'Don't waste your sympathy on her, Inspector. She has lots of comforters. As I told you before, she's one of Adam's failures. You've tried to reform her several times, haven't you, dear?' Her tone was lightly sarcastic as she glanced at her husband.

'To little avail,' he replied sadly.

'I blame the men as much as her,' Mrs Valentine went on, hotly. 'Married men, most of them, and should know better. It's their poor wives I feel sorry for.'

'I suppose it's her husband's fault as much as anyone's,' observed McGillivray. 'He should stay at home with her.'

Valentine surprised them all by jumping up abruptly and making for the door, his face expressionless.

His wife frowned. 'Where are you going, Adam?'

'I've just remembered. I promised to call on Alice

263

Dawson tonight. Excuse me, Inspector, Sergeant.' He rushed out.

Mrs Valentine laid down her knitting. 'I don't know what's wrong with him these days, he's so forgetful. He *did* see Janet Souter recently, a few days before she died. She gave him a jar of jam. Remember, Sergeant, the one you took away for some reason.' Her fidgeting hands betrayed her anxiety.

'We'd reason to believe the jar had been contaminated with arsenic,' Moore murmured.

Her alarm was greater at this, and was made even more so when McGillivray leapt to his feet.

'Excuse me, ma'am, may I use your telephone?' His face was dark and grim.

'It's in the hall.'

He closed the door behind him, and dialled the police station, then waited impatiently until the receiver at the other end was lifted. 'Black? Will you . . . ? What?'

His eyes narrowed as he listened, then he said, crisply, 'No, Sergeant. He's not mistaken, and he's corroborated my suspicions. Take him in the car with you, collect your constable if he's not there, and pick me up at the manse. What . . . ? Lock the place up, you damned fool! I'll take full responsibility.'

He returned to the living room, where Muriel Valentine was sitting on the edge of her seat, her eyes troubled and her face ashen, the reason for all the activity having dawned on her.

'You think Adam's the murderer, don't you?' she

264

whispered. 'And that he's gone to silence May White as well?'

David Moore had also just fully come to terms with the situation, and his sympathy went out to her even as his adrenaline started flowing with excitement.

'Don't be afraid to tell me.' Her voice was stronger, quite calm now. 'I've suspected, deep down, that his interest in her didn't lie altogether in her soul.'

McGillivray took a seat near the door. 'It looks very black for him, Mrs Valentine. Do you have any relatives, or close friends, you could call on for support?'

Tears welled up in her eyes. 'I've no family left now. Both my parents are dead, and a minister's wife can't really make close friends in a small place like this without causing offence to others. I'll be quite all right.'

She was putting a brave face on it, but McGillivray knew the anguish she must be experiencing. 'I'll leave my sergeant with you,' he said, compassionately. 'He's quite a decent human being, in spite of his appearance.'

She summoned up a wan smile. 'I'm sure he is. Thank you.'

A car horn sounded outside, and McGillivray rose and went out without another word. Moore jumped up and followed him into the hall. 'Can I tell her about . . . ?' he whispered.

'It might be a comfort, lad, but maybe she's had enough shocks tonight. Play it by ear, though.' He strode out into the night.

The young sergeant went slowly back inside. 'Would you like me to make tea or coffee for you, Mrs Valentine?'

She got to her feet quickly. 'Please let me do it myself. It'll help to take my mind off . . .'

He held the door open for her. 'I'll come through with you.'

'I don't intend to do anything silly, you don't need to guard me.'

'Oh, no.' He was disappointed that she'd taken his offer the wrong way. 'I just meant to be company for you, and the kitchen's usually the most homely place in a house.'

'I'm sorry, I'm a bit on edge. I should have understood.' She busied herself filling the kettle, switching it on, laying out mugs, sugar and milk, while Moore sat down at the table.

'I've never felt really happy since we came here,' she said pensively. 'It wasn't the people. They made us very welcome, and we were soon part of their community, but Adam changed not long after we arrived. It was about the time he started telling me how worried he was about Mrs White and her behaviour, now that I come to think of it.'

Her preparations ready, she sat down to wait for the kettle to boil. 'I think his intentions were good to begin with, but she must have ensnared him and he visited her more and more often. Then he stopped telling me when he was going, and that's when I began to worry. If only I'd had somebody to . . . An outsider might have realised what was going on before it was too late.'

Pouring milk into the mugs, she carried on, almost as if she were speaking to herself. 'I suppose I was too tangled up with my own emotions at the time. My mother had just died, and I was devastated, though she wasn't my real mother. She told me about that when I was old enough to understand.'

Elated that she'd brought up the subject, David Moore felt sure that it wouldn't come as such a shock to her now, if he told her about Mrs Wakeford, and it might compensate her for the terrible ordeal she was about to face.

Her monologue continued. 'My mother and father – I'll always remember them as that – couldn't have any children, but their solicitor knew of a young, unmarried girl who was having a baby, so he arranged for them to adopt it. I've always felt sorry for that poor girl, having to give up her love-child like that, and I've often wondered what became of her.'

The sergeant had been trying to figure out a way of letting her know, and he admired her all the more for the concern she was showing for the mother she'd never known. 'Mrs Valentine,' he ventured at last, 'wouldn't you like to find out who your real mother was?'

She rose to make the tea, and her sudden silence disquieted him. Had he made a mistake? Perhaps he hadn't been sensitive enough, and should apologise, try to explain that he'd only said it out of kindness and to find someone to care for her, but the proper words wouldn't come.

Placing a cosy over the teapot, she resumed her seat.

'It's funny you should say that, Sergeant. I've been thinking about it ever since Mum died. It would be nice to have somebody of my own, especially now. I'm scared I won't be able to cope if . . .'

She gulped, and he hoped that she wasn't about to dissolve into tears. He'd never known how to deal with weeping women.

Fortunately for him, she carried on speaking. 'I don't know where to start looking, though, because the old solicitor, the only link I know, died a few years ago.'

Taking the plunge, Moore burst out, 'I know, but we traced her.' Seeing her mouth fall open, he rushed on. 'We'd unearthed this illegitimate child in the course of our investigations, you see, and we had to check it out.'

'Do you mean . . . ? My real mother . . . ? Is she someone here in Tollerton? Somebody I know?'

'Yes, Ma'am.'

'Not Janet Souter.' The horror of this possibility was quite unthinkable.

'No, no. It's . . . Mrs Wakeford.' He held his breath.

'Mrs Wakeford? But that would be marvellous, she's such a kind, gentle person, but . . . Are you sure of the facts?'

Her delighted smile, and her ensuing abstraction, told Moore that she was dreaming of a new relationship which could be about to open for her, so he rose and poured the tea. 'There's one thing you'll have to consider.' He looked apologetic.

The smile was still on her face as she said, 'What's that?'

'Would Mrs Wakeford want to be reminded of her indiscreet past? She's kept it hidden for a long time.'

He thought of Mabel Wakeford's desperate attempt to stop Janet Souter from spreading this very information – adding arsenic to the jam, to which Muriel Valentine herself had almost fallen a victim. That would have been the ultimate irony, but the poor woman had been driven to it. The minister's wife would fold up altogether if that came out.

'So you think I shouldn't approach her?' Mrs Valentine asked, after a pause.

'It's none of my business. If you feel strongly enough that you want to make yourself known to her, just go ahead and do it. She'd probably be pleased her daughter was a minister's wife.'

The mention of her husband brought the clouds back into her eyes. 'She wouldn't want to be related to a murderer's wife.'

Moore hastened to console her. 'It's just suspicion on the inspector's part. Your husband could be innocent.'

They both knew it was a false hope.

Chapter Eighteen

Endings

There were no doubts in McGillivray's mind that Adam Valentine had killed Janet Souter. Douglas Pettigrew's story, as relayed by John Black over the telephone, had been the final proof. Now, it was only a case of hoping he'd be in time to avert a second, and perhaps third, murder.

He was furious with himself for endangering old Mrs Gray's life, as well as Mrs White's, but he'd thought the minister would break down and give himself up, not boldly attempt to silence them under the very noses of the police.

When the inspector came out of the car, a short distance before Mrs Gray's house, he was in a quandary. Which one should he go to first? He took a gamble. 'Constable, you come with me, and Sergeant, you take young Pettigrew round to Mrs White's back door. He might try to escape that way, if he hears us at the front.'

Walking stealthily in front of Derek Paul, while John Black and Douglas Pettigrew went round the back of Mrs

White's house, he prayed that he hadn't made the wrong choice.

If he had – and the thought caused him to break out in a cold sweat – another old lady could be dead by the time he discovered his mistake. When he reached May's door, he paused to take a deep breath, then he turned the handle inch by inch, trusting that she hadn't locked it behind Valentine if he was in there. Luckily, the door gave and he edged it slowly open.

Tiptoeing into the narrow hallway, with the constable at his heels, McGillivray could hear the murmur of voices from the living room. Mrs White was still alive, but could he be sure it was the right man who was with her?

Indecisively, he took up his position at the inner door, and before he could do anything, May's voice rose in alarm.

'Adam, darling, you know I wouldn't kiss and tell. That inspector's been having you on.'

Satisfied that he'd found his prey, McGillivray held up a cautionary finger to the constable. 'Any minute now,' he mouthed.

The man's voice was droning on, but the woman's scream galvanised the inspector into action. He flung the door open and rushed across the room to pull Adam Valentine's hands away from her throat, while Derek Paul raced forward to prevent him escaping.

The minister put up no fight, however. He slumped down on the settee and covered his face with his hands. 'Oh, God! Oh, God!' he moaned.

McGillivray felt no pity, no exultation, only a great relief that he'd got there in time. 'Let the other two in,' he instructed Derek Paul, then, looking over at the woman who was cowering against the wall, her face a red-blotched grey, her hands at her neck, he asked, 'Are you all right?'

She nodded, and swallowed painfully. 'If you'd been any later . . .' Her voice was low and rasping.

'Yes,' he said, curtly. 'You were lucky.'

When Douglas Pettigrew appeared from the back door with John Black, he made a bee-line towards his former lover. 'You got what was coming to you,' he said, vindictively. Then, casting a glance at the pathetic creature on the settee, he laughed mirthlessly and added, 'He's not so bloody marvellous now, is he?'

After McGillivray made the formal arrest, Adam Valentine remained silent and motionless until John Black stepped forward, then he stood up. 'I'm ready to go with you, Sergeant.'

Turning to face the inspector, he said, 'Will you please make sure someone looks after my wife? This will be a dreadful shock to her, and I'm deeply ashamed. I don't know what possessed me to get entangled with . . .' His voice tailed away.

McGillivray knew. He knew only too well. 'My sergeant's with your wife meantime, and I'll make sure she's not left alone tonight.'

'Thank you.' The minister walked out behind John Black, with Derek Paul bringing up the rear.

Addressing Douglas Pettigrew, the inspector said, 'Will you be stopping here?'

'Not me! I've learned my lesson.' The young man hastily followed the others out.

Left alone with the still-recovering woman, McGillivray said, 'I hope you've learned your lesson, too, Mrs White. You were playing with fire and you were bloody nearly burned to a cinder.'

'I know.' It was a hoarse whisper. I thought it was great, leading all those men on, and making them unfaithful to their wives, but . . .'

'That gave you a thrill, did it?' McGillivray's sarcasm was all the greater because he knew how close he'd come to being another of her trophies.

'Yes, at the time. I suppose I was trying to pay Gilbert back for being away so much, but I was worse than a prostitute.'

'I'm glad you're seeing sense at last.'

'I'll never do it again. Oh! Gilbert won't have to know about . . . everything, will he?' Her eyes were less wild, and she looked forlorn and miserable.

McGillivray hardened his heart. 'He'll have to know, Mrs White.' Then he realised, with a sense of remorse, that she'd be quite alone when he left, and after what she'd been through . . . 'Have you a friend you could go to? Or what about your parents?'

Her eyes darkened. 'The women are all jealous, and Mum and Dad have hardly spoken to me since Sydney Pettigrew went and had that row with them.'

'You shouldn't be on your own, not tonight.'

After a moment's thought, she said, 'Mrs Gray next door might take me in. She never treats me like dirt, the way some of the other women do, and she can be very kind.'

The inspector smiled. 'She's quite a character, your Mrs Gray. She's the one who tipped me off about Adam Valentine, though I thought she was blethering at first, and didn't take her seriously.'

'I've nobody else till Gilbert gets home in about three weeks. He said he'd be back for Christmas.'

McGillivray, suddenly compassionate, thought that she likely wouldn't have her husband either when he learned what had been going on during his absences. Poor bitch! 'Get whatever you'll need for an overnight stay, and I'll take you next door.'

When Mrs Gray came to her door, he said, 'Can Mrs White stay here tonight, please?'

'She's very welcome. Just go through, May.' The old woman hobbled to the side to let the trembling young woman past, then she looked at the inspector. 'What's up?'

'I've arrested Valentine, but not before he attempted to strangle Mrs White. She's been through a terrible experience, so go easy on her.'

'You can trust me, Inspector. I've never wished her any ill, for she's her own worst enemy. I'll look after her as long as she needs me.'

'Thank you very much.' McGillivray held out his hand.

'Goodbye, Mrs Gray. I won't be seeing you again, but I've really enjoyed our little chats.'

'Me too.' She grinned, toothlessly.

When he reached the waiting car, he sat in front with John Black. Behind them, Derek Paul and Douglas Pettigrew were on each side of the minister, whose bowed head lifted at McGillivray's entrance.

'Janet Souter was threatening to tell my wife about my . . . adultery, Inspector. She'd seen me going up the Lane very early one morning, and guessed where I'd been.'

'She was good at that,' the youth muttered.

'She accused me last Tuesday, when she called me in to give me a jar of jam. She wouldn't listen to reason, so I went back on the Wednesday night to try to persuade her to change her mind, but it was useless. She said it wouldn't be long before the whole place knew about my infidelity, and taunted me so much I lost my head completely.'

'You must have gone there with the intention of murdering her, though,' McGillivray pointed out. 'You'd the syringe and insulin with you. Where did you obtain them?'

Adam Valentine sighed. 'I took them from a house where an old lady, a diabetic, had just died, and it was quite innocent on my part. Her daughter had just received a fresh supply of insulin, and I told her I'd return it to the chemist, to save her the bother. That was on the Monday night, but my mind was so occupied on the Tuesday with the worry of what Miss Souter meant to do, that I forgot

275

all about it. I was practically out of my mind with fear, remorse . . . self-pity.'

'Carry on,' murmured McGillivray.

'It was when I was arguing with her on the Wednesday night that it came to me I had the means of silencing her in my pocket. I didn't really intend to use them, but . . . a desperate man takes desperate measures.'

'How did you know insulin would kill her?'

The minister gave a dry laugh. 'I studied medicine for a time, before I went in for the ministry.' He was silent for a moment, then he said, 'I know there's no excuse for what I did, but it was so that Muriel wouldn't be hurt by hearing about what I'd done.'

Callum McGillivray couldn't help snorting coldly. 'She's going to be far more hurt at what you did tonight in addition to what you did before.'

Valentine's head went down again, and McGillivray turned to John Black. 'Right, let's get going, but take me to the manse before you go back to the station.'

As the sergeant switched on the engine, Valentine said, 'Will you please tell my wife how much I regret . . . everything?'

'I'll pass on your message, and I'll see that she's well cared for.'

'Thank you.' Adam Valentine leaned back.

David Moore and Mrs Valentine were still in the kitchen when the DCI went in. 'We've arrested him,' he told her, quietly. 'And we got there in time to save Mrs White.'

'Thank God!' Her hands fidgeted for a moment. 'Did he say anything?'

'He told me exactly what had happened, and he wants you to know that he regrets everything he did to hurt you.'

'It wasn't my Adam,' her voice was low and sad. 'That woman changed him completely.'

'She could put a spell on a man,' McGillivray agreed. He experienced an unexpected surge of pity for the minister, who had stood no chance against May White's wiles, and who had sacrificed his career, his marriage and his freedom because of her.

'Inspector,' Moore said, eagerly. 'I've told Mrs Valentine about her . . . about Mrs Wakeford, do you think . . . ?'

Looking at the miserable, defenceless woman, McGillivray changed his mind about not interfering. 'Pack some things, Mrs Valentine, and we'll take you up there, but I'd better go in and talk to her first.'

'I understand, and thank you.' She hurried out.

'What have I let myself in for?' he groaned, then, brisk once more, 'Bring the Vauxhall down here, Sergeant.'

When Mabel Wakeford answered his knock, the inspector first apologised for calling so late, then asked, 'May I come in?'

In the kitchen, she waited for him to state his reason for being there, finally prompting him. 'Yes?'

'Have you ever wondered what became of the child you gave away all those years ago?'

She was taken somewhat by surprise, but answered readily enough. 'Very often. If I hadn't agreed to the adoption, I wouldn't be on my own now. I do have an old aunt and uncle in Thornkirk, but it's not the same.' She stopped, puzzled.

'I thought you might like to know that we've traced her.'

'Her? A girl?' Her eyes lit up. 'Can you tell me who she is and where she lives?' There was a breathless expectancy in her voice.

He could think of no way to break it to her gently. 'It's Mrs Valentine.'

'The minister's wife? Oh, I couldn't wish for a better daughter . . . Does she know about me?'

He smiled. 'Yes, and she's as delighted as you are.'

Mabel stood up, full of excitement. 'I'll go to her this very minute.'

McGillivray's hand detained her. 'I'm afraid there's something else you ought to know, Mrs Wakeford.'

The two words he'd used to prefix his caution alarmed her, and she stared at him anxiously.

'Adam Valentine's been arrested for the murder of Janet Souter, and he was attempting to strangle Mrs White when we reached him.'

'Oh my goodness!' She sat down weakly. 'What a tragedy. Poor woman. But . . . she needs me more than ever, now.'

'She's waiting in the car outside. I'll bring her in.'

When Muriel Valentine walked through the door, she

278

stood uncertainly for a moment, then she took a step forward, and, in the next instant, their arms were around each other and tears streamed down both women's faces.

The inspector closed the door quietly behind him and walked to the car. 'They'll be alright, Moore,' he said, gruffly. 'Come on. Our work here's finished.'

Once inside, he observed, 'That Janet Souter must've been a real number-one bitch, to have four different people trying to do away with her, not to mention the Reverend, who made a proper job of it. It's unbelievable.'

'You're right there, sir.' Moore released the handbrake. 'But you nailed him in the end.'

Pulling out his seatbelt, McGillivray laughed modestly. 'Not without the help of my friend Mrs Gray, although Douglas Pettigrew could have put us on to him earlier, if he'd remembered a bit sooner.'

He relaxed against the back of the seat and sighed. 'You know, I couldn't believe it when the old lady told me she'd seen the minister sneaking away from the house next door, and even when Mrs White confirmed it, I thought she was kidding. It's funny how the mind refuses to credit anything it doesn't want to. I'm slipping, lad.'

'It's because he was a minister,' Moore sympathised. 'We don't want to believe bad things about ministers.'

'I've come across a few bad ministers in my time, and doctors, and any other profession you can think of, including 'tecs, but . . . I don't know. Valentine struck me as a decent sort, and I was obsessed with getting to the bottom of the arsenic racket.'

'And so you did, sir. Everything's explained now.'

'Aye, but I wasted a lot of valuable time on it, when it really had nothing to do with the case at all. Anyway, it's back to the Granite City tomorrow, so you can make out the final report there.'

This gave David Moore the opening he'd been needing to ask about something that had niggled at the back of his mind for some time. 'Inspector, what are you going to do about Mrs Wakeford and the raspberry jam?'

Callum McGillivray turned his head, and his mischievous eyes met his sergeant's briefly. 'What raspberry jam, lad?'

BIRLINN LTD (incorporating John Donald and Polygon) is one of Scotland's leading publishers with over four hundred titles in print. Should you wish to be put on our catalogue mailing list **contact**:

Catalogue Request
Birlinn Ltd
West Newington House
10 Newington Road
Edinburgh EH9 1QS
Scotland, UK

Tel: + 44 (0) 131 668 4371
Fax: + 44 (0) 131 668 4466
e-mail: info@birlinn.co.uk

Postage and packing is free within the UK. For overseas orders, postage and packing (airmail) will be charged at 30% of the total order value.

For more information, or to order online, visit our website at **www.birlinn.co.uk**

Birlinn Limited
IMPRINTS: JOHN DONALD · POLYGON